POSTED AS MISSING

by

Michael Walsh

Recent Fiction by Michael Walsh

Spilt Wine
Published 2017 – ISBN – 978-09940936-6-0

Missing
Published 2017 - ISBN - 978-0-9940936-3-9

Back In Action
Published 2017 - ISBN - 978-09940936-5-3

Unknown Diners
Published 2017 - ISBN - 978-0-9940936-4-6

Recent Non-Fiction by Michael Walsh

Sequitur – To Cape Horn in Comfort and Style
Published 2013 – ISBN – 978-09919556-0-2

Carefree on the European Canals
Published 2014 – ISBN – 978-09919556-4-0

Carefree Through 1001 French Locks
Published 2015 – ISBN – 978-09919556-7-1

Canal Cruising in France
Published 2015 – ISBN – 978-09919556-9-5

Posted as Missing

ISBN: 978-0-9940936-2-2

Published by Dark Ink Press, Canada

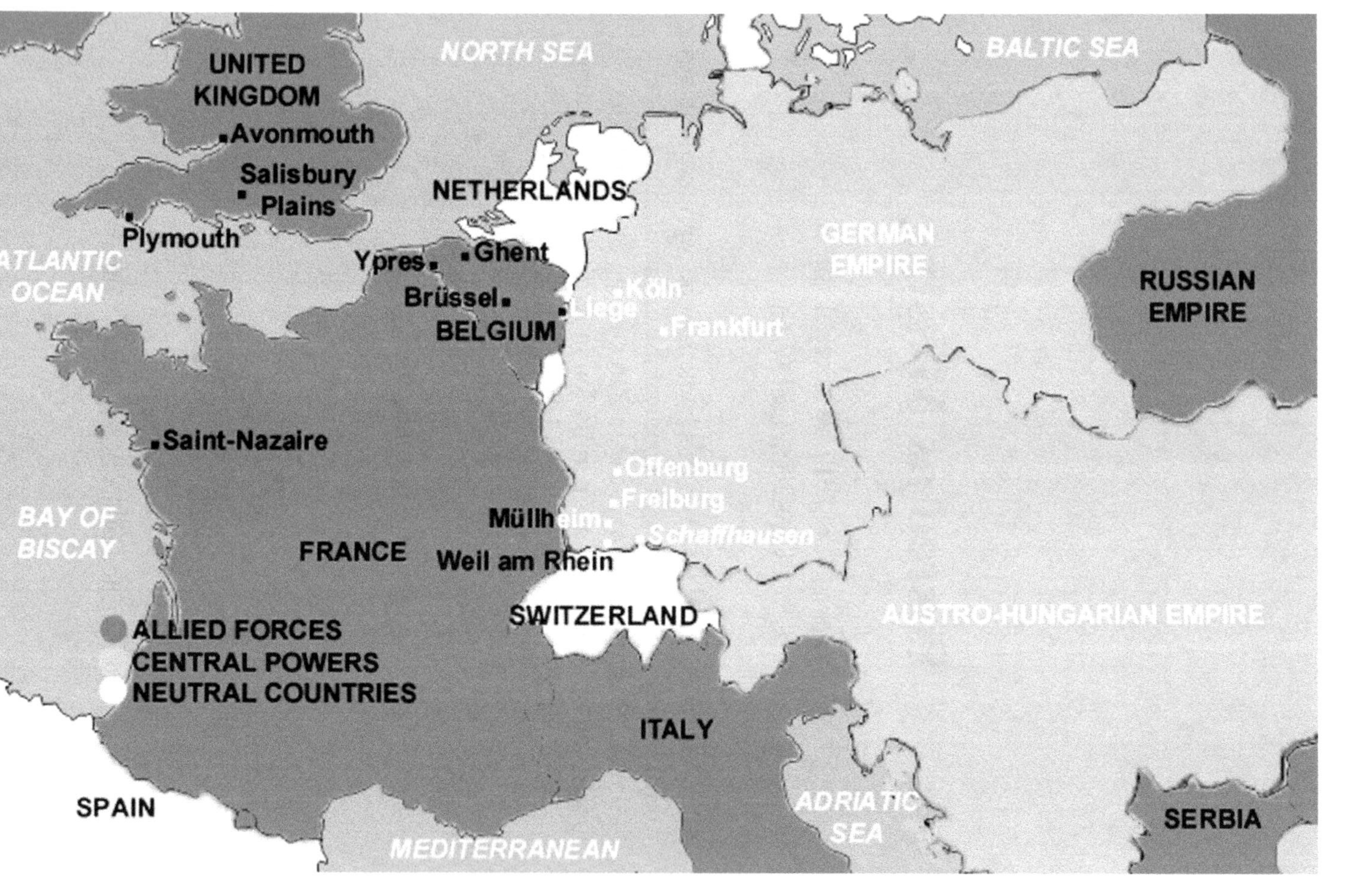

UNITED KINGDOM
Avonmouth
Salisbury Plains
Plymouth
NETHERLANDS
Ypres
Ghent
Brüssel
Köln
Liège
Frankfurt
BELGIUM
Saint-Nazaire
Offenburg
Freiburg
Schaffhausen
Müllheim
Weil am Rhein
FRANCE
SWITZERLAND
ITALY
SPAIN
SERBIA
GERMAN EMPIRE
RUSSIAN EMPIRE
AUSTRO-HUNGARIAN EMPIRE
NORTH SEA
BALTIC SEA
ATLANTIC OCEAN
BAY OF BISCAY
MEDITERRANEAN
ADRIATIC SEA
ALLIED FORCES
CENTRAL POWERS
NEUTRAL COUNTRIES

Author's Note

Although this is a piece of fiction, most of the geography and history in it are real. Many of the details and adventures in the Schwarzwald are based on my experiences, beginning half a century later while I was serving there with NATO.

Michael Walsh
Friesland
July 2017

Dedication

To the more than twenty million
dead and wounded in World War One
while defending us against aggression.

About the Cover

The envelope images are taken from my personal collection, and they inspired this story. I did some Photoshop manipulation to alter the soldier's name, initials and regimental number. He had been posted as missing, but after evading for a while, he was captured and spent the remainder of the war as a prisoner. My story paints what might have happened had his evasion been successful.

Historical Background

On the first day of August 1914, the German Empire declared war on France and Russia. Three days later, they invaded neutral Belgium. Their intention was to quickly sweep across that country and into France to encircle Paris and cause the French to surrender. With that accomplished, they would turn to concentrate on the Russians.

As the German armies swarmed into their country, the Belgians destroyed their own railway bridges and other transportation infrastructure, slowing the advance toward Paris and forcing it to stall as it outran supply lines. The stalled German positions became the Western Front, and this remained rather stable during more than four years of horrific trench warfare.

When Belgian neutrality was violated on the 4th of August, the British Empire declared war on Germany and the Austro-Hungarian Empire, bringing Canada and other Commonwealth nations into the conflict. After being recruited and mobilised and undergoing initial indoctrination, the Canadian troops were transported to England for further training. They arrived in France in February 1915, and within days, they were sent into the trenches to become accustomed. In mid-April, they were moved north to Flanders to take over large sections of the Front Line near Ypres.

The opening scene in this story is during the Second Battle of Ypres, which began on the 22nd of April when the Germans released chlorine toward our trenches as the first effective use of poisonous gas in warfare. The French fled from their positions, but the Canadians, despite heavy casualties, held on.

When the Germans advanced toward the broad gap left by the French, the Canadian 8th Battalion was ordered forward from reserve to push them back and retake the higher ground near Saint-Julien. The line moved back and forth for three days with fierce fighting and more gas, as the Canadians continued, unreinforced, bluffing being a larger force. By the 25th, their numbers were so diminished, their ruses were no longer credible.

The preceding paragraphs are fact. The fictional story opens in the late afternoon as David watches the casualties from recent skirmishes being carried down the slope toward Ypres. Among them are the last of his company's officers and NCOs.

◇◇◇

During this battle, John McCrae penned his poem, *In Flanders Fields*, marking the beginning of the poppy as our symbol of remembrance.

> *In Flanders fields the poppies blow*
> *Between the crosses, row on row,*
> *That mark our place; and in the sky*
> *The larks, still bravely singing, fly*
> *Scarce heard amid the guns below.*
>
> *We are the Dead. Short days ago*
> *We lived, felt dawn, saw sunset glow,*
> *Loved and were loved, and now we lie*
> *In Flanders fields.*
>
> *Take up our quarrel with the foe:*
> *To you from failing hands we throw*
> *The torch; be yours to hold it high.*
> *If ye break faith with us who die*
> *We shall not sleep, though poppies grow*
> *In Flanders fields.*

Chapter One

Ypres, Belgium — 25 April 1915

David knelt in the shallow shell hole as he watched the last of the stretchers disappear down the slope. He bowed his head, then replaced his cap before he spoke to the two soldiers beside him.

"Let's regroup. Make the four platoons into two, then protect ourselves and our position. You're the new Platoon Commanders."

"But we're only privates."

"Yes, and so am I. That's all we've left now. Somebody has to take charge." David pointed to the German trenches across the slopes to the east. "We're a bit higher than Fritz here, so their gas shouldn't reach us. But to be safe, have the men continue saving their piss."

"When's reinforcement coming?"

"Captain said tonight." David winced, then looked over his shoulder, down the slope toward Ypres, while he thought. "When the men have been organised, set them at deepening and connecting these craters."

He scanned his scribbled notes to find priorities. "Holmes, when the platoons are sorted, have a few men set up a latrine area. Nothing fancy, we won't be here long. Tompkins, cut me a squad to help the Engineers deploy the barbed wire. I'll show them where at dusk."

A quarter hour after sunset, David was with the squad twenty yards in front of their position when he heard the whistle of an incoming mortar.

<><><>

Black... Nothing but black.

Oh, God! I'm blind.

David closed his eyes and drifted at the edge of consciousness. His face felt like it had been ripped off, but the stench of spilt guts and scorched flesh showed his nose still worked.

He rolled onto his back, head throbbing with the effort. Then opening his eyes, he stared into the blackness. The sky slowly came into focus, and he blinked to clear his vision.

The Milky Way. The stars.

I'm alive. How much of me?

He began a digit check, feeling all twenty fingers and toes still attached and functioning. Then he tensed.

Fuck! Cold, wet crotch.

No! Please, no.

His probing relieved his mind and stirred smells of stale urine as he relaxed and began breathing again.

Twenty-one. So, now what?

He tried to remember where he was. Thoughts of the squad working with barbed wire drifted in, so he rolled his head side to side to examine his surroundings and saw scattered bodies. Then pausing his breathing, he listened.

Quiet.

Not a sound.

David rolled and rose onto his elbows to look around in the dim light and check on his comrades.

No movement. Unconscious. Maybe dead.

He scanned back and forth, finding it difficult to count the mangled and dismembered bodies, stopping as he struggled to quell a gag.

Six or eight of us. Some made it back. Maybe captured.

Down onto his back again, he fought his nausea and the pain.

Focus, David, focus. Ignore the pain. Which way back?

He opened his eyes and turned his head to again scan his horizon for movement. Satisfied there was none, he sat to check beyond the scattered bodies. In the middle distance, he saw shapes moving. Dark shapes silhouetted in the starlight.

Spiked helmets. Fritz. Wrong way.

He lay back and closed his eyes, wondering how many were still alive.

"Anyfuf...' His attempt to speak in a low voice was cut short by the pain in his mouth.

"Lo... Lo..." *Easier to say.* He listened.

"Lo... Lo." He listened again, then repeated the process.

Enough. Up onto his elbows again, he scanned for motion among the bodies and beyond.

The Germans are still there.

He looked for his hat without success, then with his rifle slung, he crawled from soldier to soldier.

Cold.

All of them.

After finding an unbloodied forage cap, he checked the enemy's position again. Then he rose to a low crouch and headed away from them, lurching and stumbling across the uneven terrain in the faint starlight. He tripped over a dead soldier and fell to his hands and knees. As he tried to calm his breathing, he peered into the gloom.

More than far enough now. Where are they?

He shook his head, feeling the pain increase as he rose to his knees.

Can't be! Wrong way?

Looking up at the Dipper then back at the spiked helmets, he nodded.

Bugger damn! Heading east. Fritz pushed the line past me. Now what?

He unslung his rifle and pulled back the bolt to load the chamber, finding it had jammed again. "Idiot," he mumbled, feeling the pain intensify as his mouth flapped loosely. He moved his hand to check but stopped.

Don't touch. Filthy hands.

Still curious, he ran his tongue through his gaping cheek and felt his face had been ripped to shreds. With rifle slung again, he crept farther from Fritz, then dipped into a shell hole for another look at his surroundings.

Lots of them over there. Appear to be searching for living among the dead.

David examined the bodies strewn around the crater, pleased to see most were in German uniforms. His pleasure was short-lived.

What a waste of young men. Ours. Theirs. What's it matter? He shook his head. *So where to from here? Don't even know where here is or what's —*

An approaching voice startled him. He plastered himself to the moist soil and held his breath as two German soldiers passed about ten yards away.

"... sogar leicht verwundet?

"Ja, keine Gefangenen mehr. Der Leutnant hat gesagt dass wir zu viele hätten. Schneide deren Kehlen. Der warme..."

David listened to the voices recede as he lay on the crater's slope, absorbing what he had heard. Too many wounded prisoners. Kill all the warm ones. Knowing surrender meant death, he examined his other options.

He could try to sneak back across to his side of the line. But with so many Germans in his way, he'd likely be shot, and if not, then be captured and have his throat slit. He considered clearing his rifle and charging their rear, taking some of them with him.

Bloody Hell! That's quitting. I'm not ready to quit.

David focused on the dead bodies again, and after checking the horizon for signs of movement, he crept out of the crater and into the increasing stench of spilt guts and rotting flesh to search for the least bloodied uniform, sending scavenging rats scurrying from his path. Unable to hold his gag, he dropped to his hands and knees as he puked, feeling the retch of his empty stomach and the sting of bile in his mouth wounds.

Easier to quit. He shook his head and looked up. *Have to keep going.*

After searching for a while, he paused at a dead soldier.

Shot in the head. Looks about my size.

He dragged the body into another shallow shell hole and sat still to listen and assess his surroundings. There was still a strong stench of shit, and he realised much of it was coming from his own trousers.

He undressed and used his shirt and water from his canteen to clean up from his unconscious fouling. Feeling fresher, he stripped the uniform from the dead soldier, his cold, trembling fingers making the buttons awkward. He was relieved to find unsoiled trousers.

Must have gone just before...

He held his gag as he looked away from the bullet hole.

Unfamiliar with the uniform, he fumbled as he dressed. With his own identity discs in one of his new boots, he finished by putting the cord of the soldier's tag around his neck and pocketing the wristwatch.

After emptying his old uniform, he put it against the steep side of the crater, dragged the corpse on top of it, and using his Ross rifle, he collapsed the earthen wall to bury them. With a careful look around, he flung the rifle into the darkness.

Piece of shit! Works better as a pickaxe.

He stepped up out of the crater and searched among the bodies for a Mauser, grabbed one and continued slowly onward.

Onward seems the only safe way. Need to see what my new name is.

He pulled out the metal tag to read it, finally realising the moon had gone and that he must have been unconscious several hours.

Have to play stunned. Good thing my mouth's buggered. Disguise my strange German accent... Must remember not to be too guttural.

He began running old conversations with Conrad through his mind to refresh his German vocabulary and grammar. His thoughts wandered through their expansive, rambling discussions in the mountains while they climbed and explored.

Such delightful times. Love his way of thinking. That camp below the rib on Bugaboo Spire —

"Halt! Identifiziere dich!" came a voice ahead through the dark, quite close.

Startled by the order, he froze, stopped breathing and peered into the dimness of the starlight, searching for the owner of the voice. Images flashed through his mind. Weapons pointed at him. A firing squad lined up and aiming.

Stupid idea. Should have headed back.

"Hallo," David replied with a mumbled and slurred voice, *"Mund tut so weh. Bitte, Sani."*

"Bei welchem Bataillon bist du?"

"Schwer zu reden, zu denken." He stepped closer to the sentry and motioned

to his face with a trembling hand, feeling relief when he saw the horror in the soldier's expression. Pleased his need had been recognised, and that the sentry had forgotten about identification, David nodded, grunted and played stunned for the remainder of the exchange.

As another soldier led him farther into enemy territory, he tried to spot landmarks, thinking they'd be useful. But it was too dark to see any detail as they followed a path across an open field.

After about a quarter mile, they arrived at a brick barn at the edge of a small hamlet. The soldier helped him down onto the cloth-covered hay along a dimly-lit side of the makeshift dressing station. The place was crowded with wounded soldiers, and he fit in well. He felt safe, so he lay back and closed his eyes as he used his tongue to analyse the source of the pain.

Bottom lip gone. Big chunk of cheek missing. Three teeth out. Maybe only two. Jaw feels broken. He shook his head. *Enough of this.*

He wondered how the rest of them fared when the Germans advanced. Surely the reinforcements had arrived by then.

Three goddamn days for the Frogs and the Brits to move their reserves forward. Bloody Hell! We mustered in less than an hour.

As David lay waiting, he looked at his options, thinking that once his wounds have been treated, he could surrender.

Stupid. Why give up now? I can find a way out of this.

His turn came, and after an examination, he was given an injection of Heroin. Then his wounds were cleaned and dressed by an orderly, who finished by adding several layers of gauze around his mouth and the back of his neck and another multiple wrap under his jaw and over the top of his head.

David communicated with hums and nods as a clerk wrote information from his identity tag onto a white paper card and hung it around his neck, telling him he'd be heading to the field hospital for stitches. After giving David a tin of Aspirin tablets for when the Heroin wore off, he had a soldier lead him outside to a troop truck two-thirds full with walking wounded.

A hint of dawn lit the horizon as David sat, and he finally realised he had been out for many hours.

We started the wire at dusk. Now it's dawn. I'm not tired. Was I unconscious the whole time? Did I sleep part of it? Probably a bit of both.

He was pleased how seriously wounded he must have appeared with the bandaging.

Great for my ruse, but I wonder how long the supply of gauze will hold out in the clinic. Seems wasteful. The medic used so much this helmet rides even higher now.

He glanced around at the soldiers, checking if he was being watched. Seeing the others all absorbed in their own misery, he removed the helmet to examine it, finding it odd. The souvenirs he'd seen had all been made of thick leather, and he thought Fritz must have run out of it kitting these kids for the trenches.

My God, they're so young.

After another quick scan of the soldiers, he put the tip of his little finger through the single bullet hole.

This must have been mercifully quick. He shuddered. *Blood's now dried.*

He pushed the thick felt tatters together from the inside to close the hole, then smoothed the nap on the outside.

That's better.

Closing his eyes and slowing his breathing to try to ease the pain, he assessed his situation.

It's working so far. Just blend in. Be part of the scene. Move with it as it evolves. An opportunity will emerge.

The truck soon filled, and the sun had lit the eastern sky when they started moving. He pulled out the stamped metal tag to learn his new name.

Strange, the clerk called this a hundemarke, a dog mark.

He read it.

No name, only a unit and a number. Shit!

Could play amnesia.

Chapter Two

Trail, British Columbia, Canada — 5 June 1915

"Gerald! — Gerald, oh my God! — GERALD!"

"What is it, Rose?" he shouted from the kitchen. "What's wrong?"

"David's letters have come back."

Gerald and Rosaline had been away in Edmonton since the end of April, helping their daughter through a difficult late pregnancy with their first grandchild. They had just returned home, and while Gerald had gone to light a fire in the kitchen stove, she was sorting through the pile of mail from the box.

"Wrong address again?" he asked as he walked into the dining room. "That's such a complicated address."

"No, he's missing — David is missing." She held out two letters to him with a trembling hand.

He scanned the envelopes, then gently took her hand as they merged in a silent hug. Silent but for her sobbing.

The letters had been addressed to their son:

> *Private D.M. Berry No. 23414*
> *No 2 Company*
> *7th Battalion*
> *2nd Brigade*
> *1st Canadian Contingent*
> *British Expeditionary Force*
> *Army PO London, Eng.*

The addresses had been marked out in blue pencilled lines and stamped:

Undeliverable For Reason Stated
Return to Sender

In small pencilled letters at the top of each envelope was:
Missing

The postmark on one was stamped: Annable BC, 29 April, the other was postmarked 3 May from Edmonton. On the backs of both letters were pasted stamps imprinted:

Officially Sealed
in the
Returned Letter Section
London Postal Service

There were smudged stamp imprints on each, dated 19 May in London and 3 June somewhere in BC.

"There are also two letters there from David," she finally said in a low, croaking voice, "and a brown envelope marked *On His Majesty's Service*."

They continued their hug but kept their thoughts private.

After a long silent pause, Gerald quietly spoke, "We should take a look at the official letter."

They sat at the dining table, he slit open the envelope and unfolded its contents, a single page of buff paper. A form letter, Army Form B. 104 - 83. The date was rubber-stamped 29 Apr 1915, and the blanks were filled in with a bold, black round hand:

(No.) *23414* (Rank) *Private* (Name) *Berry, DM*
(Regiment) *7th Battalion, 1st Can. Contingent*
was posted as "missing" on the *26 Apr 15*
at Saint-Julien, near Ypres

The form letter continued in stilted Army language: *The report that he is missing does not necessarily mean that he has been killed, as he may be a prisoner of war or temporarily separated from his regiment.*

Michael Walsh

Official reports that men are prisoners of war take some time to reach this country, and if he has been captured by the enemy it is probable that unofficial news will reach you first. In that case, I am to ask you to forward any letter you receive at once to this office, and it will be returned to you as soon as possible.

Should any further information be received it will be at once communicated to you.

"My God, what was he doing in Belgium? The last thing we had from him was the postcard the middle of February with the picture of Stonehenge. I thought he was still training on the Salisbury Plains. Maybe we've been too worried about Elizabeth's pregnancy."

"He's a tough one, Rose, he'll be just fine. Maybe when he's back, he can teach the Army to write normal English."

"My poor boy. My dear sweet little boy." She began to weep again.

"He'll be fine. Let's see what he had to say in his letters." He picked up the two envelopes and shuffled them to find the oldest postmark. "This one first, it's postmarked 12 April."

Dear Mamère and Dad;

I am well, but other than that, I can't say much. This is my third attempt at writing a letter to you from here. I've had two returned by the censors, with notes saying there was no need to even send them since they had cut out so much. I still have to learn what not to say.

I can't tell you where I am, how I got here or where I'm going. Much of this they won't even tell us until long after we've arrived. But I'm pretty sure I can say that I'm in Europe and that the weather is horrid. A lot of cold rain, long periods of steady rain. Not like the crisp winters and fluffy snow we have in the Kootenays.

I hope Elizabeth is over her illness and that her baby wasn't affected.

I got the valentine you sent, Mamère, and the box with all the cookies and fudge. I was very popular for a while.

Love from your faithful son.

"It's so strange stringing together correspondence like this," she said, "when it takes six or seven weeks between letter and response... Open the other letter."

He put his arm around her waist and she leaned her head on his shoulder as they read it together:

Hello from Flanders;

They tell me I can now say Flanders and Belgium. I guess it's because the Germans finally know we're here. We're outside of Ypres. Most of the fellows, except those of us who can speak French, call it 'Wipers', but whatever it's called, it is cold and wet. The weather can't decide to freeze and give us some nice snow, so it just continues with cold rain. Steady rain.

Your Easter greetings arrived and so did that huge stash of Bourbon creams and Garibaldis. Are you trying to get me attacked by friendly forces?

I am well, though I'd rather be up in the mountains than down here in the trenches. ~~Actually anywhere, even accounting~~ — no, strike that through — I'll stay here, rather than go back to studying accounting; I cannot imagine another life so lifeless as one spent cyphering.

Your loving son,

David

Gerald spoke quietly as he held his wife closer. "It seems we should have paid more attention to all those front page stories in the Edmonton Bulletin. I forget how many thousands were missing in the fighting around Ypres."

"They said it was so difficult to determine the categories of those who are missing, wounded, captured or..." She trailed off and sobbed.

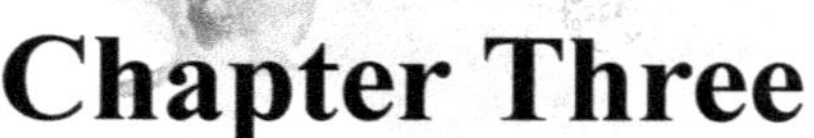

Chapter Three

Freiburg, Germany — 26 April 1915

Maria left the hospital with her books clutched tightly to her bodice and walked toward Bahnhof Platz, enjoying the sun on her cheek while deep in thought.

I must find out. So interesting. What would it be like?

Her mind wandered, and her body began tingling. She paused beside a low wall and turned to look over it into the park as she pressed her free hand to the front of her skirts to ease the growing sensations there. She shivered.

I truly must find out.

Smiling at her thoughts, she turned and continued to the gasthaus across from the train station. She sat at the large round table in the corner, reviewing her notes for nearly an hour before she rose and put on her serving apron as the first patrons arrived.

Passchendaele, Belgium — 26 April 1915

The truck full of wounded German soldiers creaked and groaned as it lurched and jarred through the deeply rutted field for a long while before it reached a road. Aware now he'd likely be shot as a spy if his identity were uncovered, David continued to run German phrases through his head, reliving climbing adventures with Conrad, remembering the corrections Conrad had made to his grammar and pronunciation. He recalled having to speak as if he needed to constantly clear his throat of phlegm.

He winced at the pain in his mouth as he smiled at remembering his first thoughts listening to the language spoken by the locals in Flanders. Their accent was very guttural, much like German, and he had joked that the Flemish speak Phlegm.

He wiggled his feet in the oversized boots to feel his identity disks and his gold. His father had insisted he carry the coins. "I hope you don't need these. Thirty dollars for emergency only," he remembered his father saying as he pressed them into his hand while they waited for the train.

I hope I don't need them either, he thought as he toed the two Fives and two Tens. *All dated 1914, glistening fresh from the bank. I'd like to keep them.*

Satisfied with his inventory, he turned to finding out who he is. He did a slow, systematic survey of the pockets in his still unfamiliar uniform, watching his neighbours in the truck to see if he was attracting any attention.

They all seem to be immersed in their own world, too concerned about their circumstance, their pain and their moaning and groaning, to pay any attention to me, to anything outside themselves.

He found a postcard in the left breast pocket of his tunic, took it out and looked at the picture, a meticulously rendered view up a mountain valley. Probably an enhanced aerial photograph. The names of the mountains and hills were labelled, as well as the towns, the villages and settlements. There were roads drawn in red and trails drawn in white. It was a beautifully done image. At the mouth of the valley, in the centre of the foreground, was a small town labelled Müllheim. In the background stood a tall peak named Belchen.

David turned the card over and read the address.

So I'm Josef Krings. He read the long note. *This has to be from his wife or girlfriend, the sentiments are too close and personal for anything else.*

She, Freda was the name she signed, wrote of their wonderful hiking, climbing and lovemaking through the Schwarzwald last summer, before the war turned everything strange.

He paused to adjust himself. *I'm getting lumpy from her writing. Glad to see that still works. So, I'm still a climber and still into futtering. I could adopt Müllheim as home, but I need to find out where it is.* He looked again at the drawing. *Freiburg to the left, Basel to the right, Müllheim in the centre, this should be easy to locate once I find a map.*

To ease the pain of his wounds, David began running pleasant memories through his mind, joyous memories of exploring and climbing in the mountains up the valley, the Selkirks, the Purcells, the Bugaboos, and straddling the Alberta border, the Rockies.

Dad always griped about my wasting my weekends and summers in the mountains. Wasting good time, he used to say, rather than setting myself up for the realities and the hardships of life. What good would accounting and business administration do me here?

With another look at the image, he slid the postcard into his breast pocket and continued to think of the mountains and of his climbs with Conrad.

When did we meet? That was in the Purcells, the summer before Dad sent me off to University School in Victoria... That was 1911. So wonderful to escape back into the mountains the next spring. It didn't take me long to clear my head. What a glorious three months I had. Mostly alone. So many great climbs.

His mind clouded as he thought of heading to Vancouver to start university in the autumn.

Let me skip that, move to more pleasant thoughts. The Bugaboos with Conrad the following spring. Those were exhilarating climbs, such solid granite, so many wonderful discussions. I love his way of thinking, of seeing things.

I felt so honoured when he asked me to work with him, to assist him guiding the Alpine Club climbing camps. Lake O'Hara, Spectacular! No other word for it. Then Robson Pass made the ruggedness of O'Hara seem gentle. Conrad led the first ascent of Mount Robson, the highest in the Rockies. I wonder what he's doing. Surely they haven't incarcerated him as an enemy.

David's mind clouded again, and he felt the pain in his face more intensely.

Back to more pleasant thoughts. Last summer again in the Bugaboos. Sometimes solo, but often with Conrad when he was free. Climbing and philosophising, refining his English and polishing my German as we explored. Such carefree times.

At the beginning of August, Canada went to war against Germany and the Austro-Hungarian Empire. David and Conrad missed the news; they were high in the mountains.

When they finally came down and heard about the war, Conrad wanted to do something, but he didn't know what he could. He had emigrated from Austria to escape the horrors of the Germanic aggression he had foreseen. David immediately volunteered and was issued a train ticket to travel across the country to become part of the Canadian Expeditionary Force, which was being assembled.

Within days of the declaration of war, a camp was begun at Valcartier, sixteen miles west of Quebec City. In the following weeks, the site was prepared by a huge team of engineers and workers. The recruits then poured in and were processed. In the first six weeks from the declaration, over forty thousand had volunteered from across Canada, far more than thought necessary, so the prime group of thirty thousand was assembled into a division and a half, equipped, trained and readied to head overseas. The remainder was put in reserve.

So quick. Down from the mountains in mid-August, enlisted as an infantry-man the other side of the country the beginning of September. They didn't even have uniforms for us for the first three weeks.

David had been assigned to the 7th Battalion, formed with some eleven hundred other recruits from British Columbia. While this new army did its preliminary military training, many other works were underway. Mills in Montreal had been commissioned to manufacture khaki cloth, tailors converted this into uniforms, greatcoats and cloaks. Weapons were hastily manufactured and issued to the new soldiers.

Battalions were juggled, shuffled and rearranged into regiments and brigades. Stores of all description were manufactured and accumulated. A fleet of transport ships was assembled. It was an immense undertaking in a very short time.

David looked around again at the other wounded soldiers in the truck.

I wonder what their stories are. Most of them are so young. That one over there with his arm off at the elbow, he doesn't look old enough to shave. He seems so scared — I daren't do anything, but I wish someone would comfort him. What a horror this is, what a waste of young men.

Chapter Four

As the truck of wounded German soldiers swayed along the uneven road, David watched several as they battled motion sickness. Three who had taken positions hanging over the tailgate reminded him of the Atlantic crossing and the seasick soldiers lining the rails.

To some the sea voyage was torture, but to me, it was such an enjoyable experience.

He continued running pleasant thoughts through his mind to avoid thinking of the pain.

Thirty-four transport ships, the largest army ever to have crossed the Atlantic, they told us. The people in Plymouth were so surprised to see us; they had no idea we were coming. Guess that's the purpose of censoring our letters and cards.

Again he scanned the crowd of wounded soldiers in the back of the truck, looking at all the different uniforms.

Seems they're like us, many different regiments and battalions, many different uniform styles. Wonder if there are any here from Josef's — from my battalion. They wouldn't recognise me, anyway. Of the eleven hundred in the British Columbia Regiment, how many do I recognise? We're all the same, an army of ants, especially now wounded and looking inward. If they're like us, their hospitals are too crowded to take any who can move on our own.

He thought of the long process of disembarking the tens of thousands of soldiers and then transporting them to camps on Salisbury Plain. His pain returned again acutely as he thought of the four dismal winter months, training in mud, cold and rain.

But the trip to Stonehenge and the ones to Bath and Bristol, he diverted his mind back to more pleasant times, *those were delightful breaks from the training, from the dripping tents and the crowded, fetid huts. They call me a private, but I've absolutely no privacy.* The pain returned.

Marching off the Plain in early February, now that was a great experience. We felt so proud, so disciplined as we headed to the trains. Amazing what a few months of training can do.

He thought about the crossing from Avonmouth to St-Nazaire.

We had no idea where they were taking us, but the food sure improved once we arrived in France. God! That British stodge was horrid. Three days in the railway freight cars and only five hundred miles. Three days on a Canadian train will take you six times as far and a lot more comfortably.

He winced at the pain as he smiled at his memory of the soldiers pronouncing Ypres as Wipers when they arrived to join the British First Army.

I have to remember not to smile for a while, but the Brits were even worse with the pronunciation.

I guess they were desperate for reinforcements; we went straight into it, into the trenches. We had no battle to prove ourselves, but it still gave us confidence knowing we were trusted to hold the Front Line. What a relief to finally be moved back from the trenches at the end of March. That break at Estaires made me feel almost human again.

After the break, on the 15th of April, the Canadians took over the Allied Front Line to the northeast of Ypres. Following the launch of a German offensive on the 22nd, the division became deeply involved in the Second Battle of Ypres and in the first effective use of chlorine gas in battle.

That was so awful. David winced from the pain of both his wounded face and his memory. *Watching all the troops along the left side fall when the yellow clouds came. They had no warning, no way to fight it. So many of them. So many.* He shuddered.

The Canadian 7th Battalion was to the right of the French Colonial troops in the front line trenches when the Germans launched their first gas attack. Both groups took heavy losses, the French retreated, but the Canadians stood their ground. Word quickly spread around their trenches: "If another gas cloud comes, piss in your handkerchief and breathe through it. The chemicals in your urine will neutralise the gas."

So strange, desperately needing to pee but daring not to lest I needed it. Then the idea to piss in an empty Maconochie tin and save it. God! That Scottish stew was horrid; even piss would improve it. I wonder how Fritz is eating. Surely, it can't be as bad as Tommy's rations.

The Germans had begun advancing toward the four-mile-wide gap that had been left by the French retreat. The Canadian 8th Battalion, from its position in reserve, was immediately mustered and ordered forward to push the Germans back and hold the line.

Mid-evening of the 22nd, David had taken a grazing shrapnel wound, and he was moved back to have it sutured and dressed. Because he was fresh from a day's rest, he answered the call for volunteers among the lightly wounded, to join the members of his battalion's Headquarters Company when they moved forward late on the 23rd to reinforce the 8th Battalion and assist them in holding the line near Saint-Julien.

They had scrambled to hold off the Germans in the face of further gas attacks, without additional reinforcement and with no support on either flank.

I wonder how the rest of them fared. So many had already fallen. So few left.

His pain grew sharply.

Let me get back to thinking of the mountains, of climbing... Pleasant thoughts.

Chapter Five

Roeselare, Belgium — 26 April 1915

David's lip, chin and cheek were sutured, his scalp wound was rechecked, and he was given some Aspirin tablets and a pass to go home to recover. His orders required him to report to the field hospital in Roeselare on the 4th of May to have his sutures removed. The clerk gave him a receipt for his rifle and told him he would be issued a replacement at the arsenal after he returned from sick leave.

The clerk had also explained the sick leave chit gave him passage on the train to Müllheim and the orders gave him passage back to Belgium.

Don't even know if Müllheim is home, but they accepted it.

He had been told to take the train to Ghent, where he would find a connection to Brüssel, then through Liege to Köln.

Need a map so I can sort out where I'm going.

In Ghent, he got off the train and walked through the station and out the front. Across the street was a bookstore, where he bought a copy of Justus Perthes' *Taschen-Atlas vom Deutschen Reich*, the 1908 edition of the Pocket Atlas Germany.

Probably find a more recent edition in Germany, but this will do.

Back across the street, he sat on a bench in the station's waiting room, opened the atlas to the index and found Müllheim. Then turning to the Württenburg u Baden pages, he ran his finger to E-1.

There it is, just to the east of the Rhein. He measured the distance from the scale. *Twenty kilometres north of the Swiss border. I've always wanted to go to Switzerland, to the Swiss Alps, and this is a great time to do it; they're still neutral in this war.*

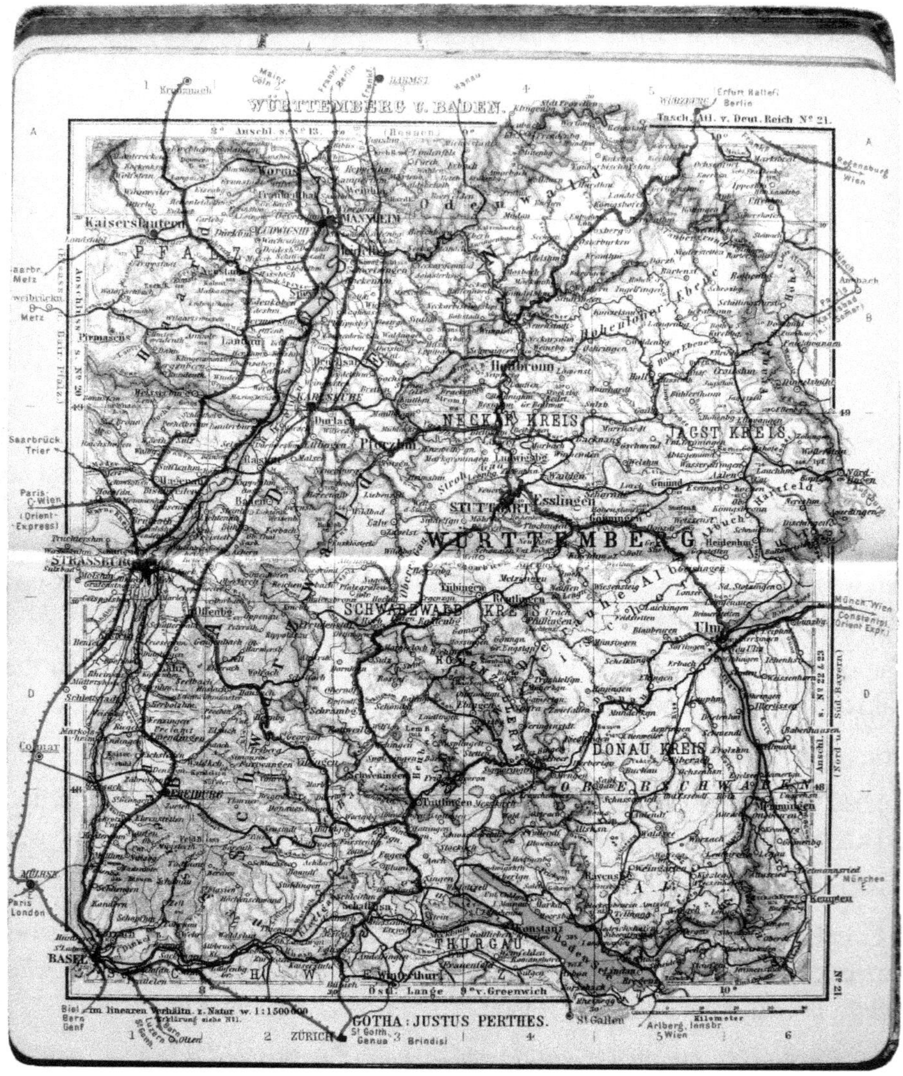

An interesting thought. An alternative to finding my way into France.

He looked up to see if anyone was watching him. *Seems normal. Reading, talking or sleeping.* He looked back down at the atlas and ran his eyes along the French border.

The whole thing is the Front Line now. Where would I cross? How? Does it still make sense to head there? He looked around the room again. *I can get back to the regiment as easily from Switzerland as I could from France.*

He nodded, closed the atlas and continued thinking, staring blankly into the room. Besides his own small fold of Belgian Francs, he had found a small wad of Reichsbanknoten in his new pockets. There was a thicker wad of notgeld, but when he had tried to pay for the atlas with it, the shopkeeper told him he'd give only fifty percent, so David used some of his own Belgian Francs.

Try again in Germany.

He shook himself from his thoughts, reached into his pocket and pulled out the wad of emergency notes to examine.

Most of these were issued in Wattenscheid. Probably get better value for this flimsy scrip closer to there. So where's Wattenscheid?

He opened his new atlas again, turned to the index and looked it up.

There, to the north of Köln.

He ran his finger along the rail lines from Brüssel to Frankfurt.

Goes through Liege to Köln then up the Rhein. Köln's likely a good place to spend this scrip.

His train arrived in Köln, and he got off to go shopping, visiting several stores near the station before heading farther into town. He bought heavy wool trousers, two wool shirts, two pairs of socks, a pair of heavy walking shoes, a hat and a small rucksack.

He also picked up a few other things as he worked to get rid of the wad of notgeld; a pocketknife, a small pair of scissors, a mirror, a roll of surgical tape, rolls of gauze and a small bottle of rubbing alcohol, among other small items. On his way back he saw a metzgerei and bought a half dozen links of landjäger.

Conrad often talks about how delicious these are, how much he misses them. Wonder what he's doing.

But his mouth was still too sore to eat anything but soup, so he had three bowls of linsensuppe and a beer in a gasthaus just along from the station. Before he boarded his train to Frankfurt, he exchanged the last of his Belgian Francs into Reichsmarks.

Didn't get much for them, but farther away they'd be worth even less.

It was well past dark when he arrived in Frankfurt. He played dazed and confused when he asked the clerk at the ticket wicket for connections to Müllheim, Baden. In the atlas index, he had seen two other Mülheims, both with a single l rather than a double.

He was told he had missed the last train of the day. *The next one is 0630 tomorrow. Must remember to change at Offenburg.*

When he had asked where he could spend the night, he had been directed to a waiting room with long wooden benches. He decided not to dig with further questions, but he was surprised there were no hostels, shelters or volunteer support services for the troops.

The YMCA run great support services behind our lines at Estaires and Ypres. Great morale booster. Welcome relief when we fall back from our trench rotations. That makes sense — long way from trenches here.

The waiting room was crowded, but he found a space on a bench along the far wall and sat. Drained, both physically and emotionally, he sat there for a long while running his situation through his mind.

It's working. I've made it this far. Many had stared at his bandaged face as he travelled, but he had acted aloof and managed to avoid engaging in conversations. A few he had needed to divert with hand gestures to his bandages and a mumbled, "*Schwer zu reden.*"

Thankfully, they all seemed to understand it hurts to talk. Now only if this annoying kid would... It's not the kid; it's the parents who are annoying.

As he tried to relax, he was repeatedly pestered by a young lad in lederhosen and tethered on a leash.

He needs a shorter leash — no, he needs stronger parents. Doesn't look five yet; closer to four, but he controls them.

David finally stood, shouldered his pack and walked out into the evening to get away from the kid wanting to play with his face dressings.

After walking for the better part of an hour, he went back to the station and was relieved to see the annoying family had left. He spent the night on a hard wooden bench, wrapped in his greatcoat, pleased it was large enough to also wrap his new rucksack. His wounds added to the discomfort and he woke frequently to check the time from Josef's wrist watch — *my watch now.* He had no trouble making the early train southward.

In Offenberg he easily found his platform in the small station. He boarded the connecting train, and he remained aboard when it stopped in Müllheim, having in mind a story of needing to visit his fraülein in Lörrach if he was questioned. He had been surprised at how lax security had been once he left the area near the Front. He hadn't been questioned. He fit in as part of the scene.

So many wounded soldiers travelling.

During his study of the area in the atlas, he had seen the border between southern Germany and Switzerland was the Rhein as it wound downstream from Schaffhausen to Basel. But at Basel, there was a strange bulge of Switzerland across to the north side of the Rhein, and for what appeared on the map scale to be about five kilometres, both banks of the Rhein were in Switzerland. He had travelled up the river all the way from Köln and he knew it drained the high Alps. It was broad and moving and likely cold, so he headed toward the bulge of the border.

I'd much prefer to walk across the border, rather than to try to swim across.

When he got off the train in Weil am Rhein, two armed soldiers stopped him and asked to see his hundemark and his orders. After a cursory check, they were satisfied and waved him on.

Makes sense. They'd be watching near the borders for deserters.

He put his papers in his pocket then walked through the town, following signs to Lörrach. The Swiss border was only a hundred yards to his right as his route led him beyond the last houses. The narrow gravel road turned to follow the base of a hill, and now only a split-log fence separated him from Switzerland.

Three German soldiers stepped out from the small copse beside a sharp bend in the road and stopped him. He handed his sick leave chit, orders and weapon receipt to the one who had asked for identification. Then he took the postcard from his breast pocket and mumbled, *"Fraülein im Lörrach,"* through his heavily bandaged mouth.

The soldier looked at the papers and read the postcard. Pursing his lips, he hefted his crotch up and down a few times before he slapped David's shoulder and handed back the documents and the postcard, saying, *"Weitermachen, Glückspilz."*

Their loud laughing chatter receded behind him as he headed up a curving rise beside a forest grove covering the steep slope to his left.

So I'm a lucky devil, they think — the fraülein trick worked.

After a quick look around, he stepped off the road and into the trees.

About fifty feet up the slope he stopped and sat on a moss-covered fallen tree. He took out his atlas and studied the page again, thought for a while, then slapped his knee.

Time to do it.

Quickly changing into his new clothes, he put on his walking shoes, emptied the uniform pockets and the boots and cached them in the hollow of a tree. He unwound his head wrappings to check the appearance of his face dressings in the small mirror, then removed the one on his cheek. The gauze was more yellowed than bloody. He replaced it with a small piece from his new roll and held it in place with surgical tape.

Won't need the head wrapping for this.

He checked his appearance in the mirror, then with his rucksack slung over a shoulder, he headed back down the slope toward the road. He heard bells ringing and peered down through the trees in their direction, looking for the source of the sounds. Then he heard a gunshot.

He stopped short. Paused to listen, then with the movements of a stalking cat, he slinked silently down the short distance to his right and into the crotch between the steep hillside and the trunk of a large oak.

Coming down the road from the direction of Lörrach were three armed soldiers. One of them began talking to the leader of the three-man patrol coming up from the direction of Weil, the patrol which had stopped him. They met just up the road from his tree and stood looking across the fence into Switzerland as they talked.

He was a little too far away to get the details of the conversation, but he did hear enough to tell him another deserter had been stopped. Then he heard another gunshot. After a brief discussion, the patrols turned and headed back along the road.

David waited for a long while before he dared move. He pondered his options. Just across the road from him, on the other side of the fence was Switzerland. Face down a dozen yards into the Swiss field lay a dead German soldier, still warm.

Chapter Six

David leaned back against the slope and let his eyes wander up the trunk of the tree, thinking of his immediate options.

That so easily could have been me. I need to slow my heart rate, slow my mind. I need to act, not react.

With care not to crack the dry twigs underfoot, he moved back up the hill, found his cache in the tree hollow and changed back into his uniform. He sat on the log and looked at the watch on his wrist.

Ten past five. Not much more than an hour of daylight remaining.

Unaccustomed to having one, he removed it to wind and to more closely examine it. The dial read: *Hans Wilsdorf Geneva*

On the back was engraved:

> *on Retirement to*
> *Major Corcoran O'Byrne*
> *from the officers of the*
> *Royal Dublin Fusiliers*
> *30 August 1912*

So it seems Josef is a watch thief, a grave robber, but now so am I. Looks like the Major re-enlisted, or maybe he gave this to his son when he sent him off to Belgium. When I get out of this, I'll have to send this back to its proper home.

He strapped the watch back onto his wrist, took the atlas from his rucksack and looked at his surroundings in the dim light. He was in the southwestern corner of Germany, in the Schwarzwald, a large area of hills and low mountains rising, it appeared to him to a bit below 1500 metres.

Feldberg is the highest elevation I can see, marked at 1492 metres, could be 1493. Difficult to read the small print in this light. Whatever, it looks like the highest point on the map.

He pulled out the postcard with the rendering of the valley which ran east from Müllheim. The prominent peak in the background was labelled Belchen.

Strange. It's an attractive peak, but I can't find it mentioned on this map.

The area of mountains was framed by the right-angled bend of the Rhein as it turns from flowing west to flow north as it passes Basel.

Along the margin of the map, the latitude read 48° directly beside a large town named Freiburg. The main body of the range looked to him to be about a degree square. He remembered Conrad telling him, "A degree of latitude is 60 nautical miles or 111.1 kilometres. I have no idea what that is in the miles you use here in Canada."

I wonder what Conrad is doing.

The Black Forest mountains are lower than those he knows in the Columbia Ranges and the Rockies.

Less than half the height. More like the ones on southern Vancouver Island and they're at almost exactly the same latitude.

The hachures on his map showed rather gentle hills, cut with streams. Then it became too dark to see the map comfortably.

We had a big moon, a bulging half on Sunday when I left the trench. Captain told us it'd be full on Thursday... Captain... Fuck! Sniper shot to the head. Officers are so easy to target with all the fancy lace on their sleeves. So stupid.

He closed his eyes, shook his head, then started calculating the moon phases in his mind.

This is Tuesday, it should now be up, two days to full, rise a bit over two hours before sunset. It should be well around toward the south by midnight.

He sat thinking for a while in the fading light.

Appears they have trip wires and bells strung along the border. Won't be able to see them in the dark. Likely trigger lights at night.

He looked at the area around him, then down the steep slope.

Probably safe to stay here the night. They're complacent with their set-up down there.

With the postcard as a bookmark, he put the atlas back into his pack. In the groove between the slope and the log, he made a bed from gathered duff and laid a side of his greatcoat on top of it. He curled onto it with his ruck-sack as a pillow and pulled the other side of the coat over him as a cover.

The sun woke him. He remembered nothing since lying down.

Slept straight through. Face still very sore. Fuzzy mouth, very thirsty.

He lay still and listened. Then he sat up and listened more intensely, stopping his breathing to reduce noise. He sipped the last bit of water from his canteen. *Damn! Should have refilled this.*

He moved up and sat on the mossy log to gather his thoughts.

Rounded south slope, likely dry with no streams.

He examined his dressings in the mirror, then wrapped gauze around his face and head and checked his reflection again. Satisfied, he looked at his watch as he wound it.

Twenty to eight. Time to find some breakfast.

He crossed the slope westward toward Weil am Rhein, sensing it would be better to stay off the road along the Swiss border.

Wiser to come down out of the trees around the bend after the road veers away from the border, closer to town.

Just in from the edge of the trees, he stopped and sat to survey the scene and ponder his situation.

I'm still on sick leave. My papers are in order. My story makes sense. These facial bandages still gave me license to slur and mumble my German. Such a strange dialect here, not like the German I know. Not Conrad's Austrian accent. I can always fall back on the stunned act. The shock of the exploding shells.

A horse was drawing a waggon toward him. After it had disappeared behind the trees before the bend, he stepped out and started walking along the road toward Weil am Rhein, turning to ask for a ride as the waggon approached.

He sat on the bench with the driver all the way into town, pantomiming rather convincingly, he thought, that he had a wired broken jaw. Through clenched teeth, he mumbled thanks as he got down from the waggon when it turned toward the market. He continued a few blocks to the train station, hoping to find water to drink.

There was none, so he continued along to the first gasthaus. The frau who served him said the tap water was not healthy to drink, and she suggested either the Gerolsteiner or the beer. The bottled water was more expensive, so he had a half litre of beer while he waited for his breakfast. He had explained to her in a mumbling slur that he could eat nothing but very soft. She suggested scrambled eggs, and he said six.

His thirst was still there, but the frau had no suggestions except more beer or the Gerolsteiner. Since he had much to do and needed to keep a clear mind, he bought a bottle of the water.

Strange. It tastes like it stood too long in an iron bucket full of crushed rocks. Quenches my thirst, though.

With the remainder of the bottle in his pack, he walked back to the station and boarded the first train north. His sick leave and orders were ready in case he was asked for a ticket.

Nobody approached or questioned him when he got off the train in Freiburg, so he headed into the shopping district. In a hiking shop, he bought a collapsible Primus, some nesting pots, two half-litre tins of kerosene, a tin of matches a flint and steel and a larger rucksack. He managed to get rid of the last of his notgeld.

With no idea what to do next, he took a room with a bath for two nights in a gasthaus across from the station. He let his instincts and his impulses lead him.

Ideas and plans will evolve. I've done it this way for much of my life, and it's always worked well.

Finally, he had some privacy and a bit of comfort to care for himself. He bathed, then cleaned his wounds. He had nothing to shave with but wasn't concerned. The dressings on his cheek and jaw had been an excuse, but it made sense to continue growing it.

It would look silly shaved around the wounds. How old is this stubble now? Have to figure out what day this is — Should have looked at a newspaper. Friday the 23rd I went back to the line, Sunday the 25th I got hit, Monday the 26th transported to hospital, Monday night on the bench in Frankfurt, then last night, Tuesday night on the hillside. It's now Wednesday the 28th. Whiskers are now five days old, going on six.

The stitches had put his lip back together well. It was still quite swollen and tender, and though red, it didn't appear infected. The hole in his cheek had also been mended well, and it was much better looking and less tender than his lip. He examined the lines of stitches.

Looks like I'll have some large scars. A beard should hide them.

He checked to see how much he could open his mouth.

Still very painful more than half an inch. Moving it at all is painful.

He tongued through the gap from the two missing teeth and felt the rasp of stitches in his gums. The doctor had said his jaw wasn't broken.

Sure feels it. Badly bruised, he said. Awkward to eat for a week or so.

"Serious looking bandaging to continue my ruse," he mumbled to himself as he stood in front of the mirror wrapping his face in gauze. Pleased with the appearance, he dressed in his new clothes, put on his hat, and slinging the small rucksack over his shoulder, he headed out again, taking his sick leave chit, rifle receipt and orders with him, in case he was questioned.

In a hardware store, he bought a piece of oiled canvas two metres by three, a small bottle of boiled linseed oil, some sisal and hemp line, two large darning needles and a card with a selection of smaller ones. He added spools of strong linen thread, two of them very thick.

With terse two and three-word sentences, which he hoped his bandaging excused, his communication worked well.

No need for grammar, mumble the words. They want the business.

In a book shop, he bought a hiking guide published by the Schwarzwald-verein, the regional hiking club's 50th-anniversary issue. The clerk in the shop showed him a selection of topographical maps of the Black Forest, also published by the club. From this, he assembled a series to quilt the entire southern part of the range.

He bought a litre of beer, another bottle of Gerolsteiner, a huge piece of soft butter cheese and a loaf of softest bread he could find. His small rucksack was crammed full, so with the roll of canvas under his arm, he returned to his room in the gasthaus.

Chapter Seven

Freiburg, Germany — 28 April 1915

Maria sat on a sunny bench in the hospital's garden, and as she ate her lunch, her mind was increasingly filled with thoughts from the lectures.

I must talk with Mama about this. She's told me so much about me, about my body, but never about men. Always told me to ask as soon as I became curious.

Maria shook her head and laughed to herself.

Funny, she asked me again last month if I needed to know more. I didn't then, but I certainly do now. I'll ask her tomorrow.

Nearly half past noon, David thought as he glanced at his watch after locking his room door. He took off his shoes, wiggled his toes and then massaged his feet. The new shoes were still rather stiff, and he had a red area on the back of his left heel. Not yet a blister, but looking like it wanted to become one shortly.

Have to be more careful, I'm going to need my feet rather seriously for the next while.

On his train trip away from the Front, he had seen many wounded German soldiers, apparently heading home on sick leave like him. Others, the ones with missing feet, hands, legs or arms, some with combinations of these, he hoped were going home on discharge. He was thankful he still had all his parts, most of them still working very well.

Need to keep them that way.

He wondered how many had made it back from the line that night outside Saint-Julien. He had seen so many fall, so many others taken prisoner. *If captured by the enemy, your duty is to escape.* He repeated to himself the words of the Prisoner-of-War lecture from his initial training.

But I'm not captured by the enemy, and that's another thing I want to keep as it is.

David laid out all his possessions on the narrow bed, unloading his pack of freshly acquired items and unpacking the larger rucksack.

The Fritz uniform has worked superbly until now, and it still has some days of life, but after next Tuesday it becomes a liability.

He turned it in his hands and examined it.

If this uniform fails to show-up in the field hospital in Roeselare on the 4th of May, it will be AWL. This is Wednesday afternoon, it still has just under six days of life remaining. Do I still need it for anything? Can it take me anywhere useful from here?

Instead of answering his question, he unfolded and laid out the topographic maps of southern Baden and the Schwarzwald, quilting them together on the floor to give him a sense of the region. It was crisscrossed with hiking trails, most interlinked and assembled as circuits or as through routes. He cross-referenced the maps to the pages in the guidebook, studied the terrain away from the trails and looked at the dozens of small communities scattered throughout the area.

He took his sick leave order from his pocket and examined it. "I need some black ink and a pen," he mumbled to himself. "One with a broad nib."

Pulling out his scissors, he snipped the stitching holding the sleeves into the greatcoat. Then he undid their seams and rolled out the cloth. He snipped the shoulder seams of the coat and laid-out the flat pieces of heavy felted wool material, playing with panel placement as he slowly assembled a shape, which with very little cutting was closer to rectangular than anything else. It measured a little under two yards by nearly a yard and a half. He spent over three hours stitching it together with the darning needle and heavy linen thread.

Shortly after three o'clock he took a break and had some lunch. He pulled the core from the bread loaf and sliced pieces off his cheese and washed these down with nearly half of his litre flask of beer. There was a sign in his bathroom warning that the water was not safe to drink.

Spending millions of dollars trying to take over Europe, and they can't even supply safe drinking water to their own people. I need to quench my thirst, but the bottled water is more expensive than the beer. The alcohol addles my mind, maybe that's what's wrong with Fritz.

Eating was a little less painful than he had expected and he was pleased with the progress of his healing. He went back to work, separating the tunic and trousers into their panels and assembling another puzzle. Then he stitched together a second large rectangle.

I need some smaller buttons, he thought as he started stitching a large buttonhole in the wool sheet from the uniform. He hadn't finished it, when he muttered to himself, "Why am I doing it the hard way? Tie tabs will hold the pieces together more easily." He cut strips from the tunic lining, stitched them into ties and attached them to the peripheries of the two large panels of cloth.

He assembled his bedroll and tested it. A heavy felted wool outer and a lighter wool liner.

Wonderful how wool stays warm even when wet.

With the bedroll bundled, he stuffed it into the bottom of the larger rucksack, then he gathered the brass regimental buttons, flashes, badges, pins and the few unused scraps of cloth from the uniform. He removed the brass badge, buckles and top spike from the stiff moulded felt helmet and stomped on it to flatten it. All of these he wrapped in the piece of brown paper which had bundled his guidebook and maps.

Other than this bundle and the bedroll, his Fritz uniform was down to a shirt and a pair of boots.

I think I'll keep both.

After locking his door, he went down to the dining room, where he sat in a back corner quickly devouring a bowl of soup and a stein of beer while waiting to see what would come from the kitchen. He had explained to the fraülein serving him that he couldn't eat anything hard, and she had said she would bring some soft things to eat. David had finished his soup and beer shortly before the beautiful young woman returned with a plate of spätsle and a piece of braised pork which was so tender he was able to mash it with his fork. He ordered another stein of beer.

He enjoyed watching her gracefulness as she approached his table.

Love the way her breasts move at the top of her bodice as she walks. Now as she bends, ready to spill out.

He watched her place the second stein on the table and caught sight of a nipple.

Now both, just sitting there. So close. Oh, God!

He moved his eyes to her face and smiled as she straightened up, and he said, "Du bist sehr schön." She smiled and winked, blushing lightly as she thanked him, then headed toward a waving arm across the room.

Her blond hair, with a slight tinge of red in it, was twisted in a loose tail twined with thin pink and red ribbons. He smiled as he watched it. Sometimes it trailed down her back and other times she wore it draped over a shoulder to tease the top of her breasts as she moved.

I would love to be doing that.

He shuddered lightly and continued to watch her.

She seems interested in me. Her movements, her air. Daren't do anything to risk compromising my precarious position.

It was a tough decision, particularly with the second stein of beer. He hadn't been with a woman since the week before he had left the Salisbury Plains in early February.

Maybe just sympathetic about my wounds. Her body movements and that wink tell me it's more than that. Could be simply I'm the only young man left in town. Young men are scarce. If they're fit and healthy, they're off to the Front. My God! She's so beautiful.

After rearranging himself under the table, he got up, thanked her and went back up the stairs to his room. He undressed, lay on his bed and did something he hadn't had the privacy to do in a very long while. Relieved and relaxed, he cleaned up and fell asleep.

He slept comfortably, in a real bed for the first time since the end of his short leave in January. In the morning, he soaked in the bathtub, another luxury he had missed. He swelled at the thought of the fraülein and enjoyed himself again.

Living in cramped tents with dozens of others leaves no opportunity to do this. God, she's gorgeous.

After a breakfast of scrambled eggs and several cups of coffee, he took his small pack and went out walking, trying to break-in the heel of his left shoe. He had rubbed linseed oil into it and placed an oil-soaked remnant of cloth on it overnight. It was a bit softer, but he thought his own heel still needed more. In a *tuchladen,* he bought some remnants. One, a very soft piece labelled *Flanell* and another slippery one labelled *Seidenatlas*, which reminded him of one of his mother's silk-satin dresses.

Farther along the street, in the Badischer Wanderungen Ausrüster just off the Hauptstraße, he found a pair of heavy wool trousers with a placard indicating they had been made of the same weave of wool that Roald Amundsen had worn to the South Pole in 1911 and that Ernest Shackleton had taken to the Antarctic in 1914.

He looked for a long time at a carbide lamp and a metal box of crystals, but in the end, he opted for a folding candle lamp and a paper bundle of seven squat beeswax candles.

At Freiberger Schreibwarenladen he was pleased to find a broad-nibbed Waterman pen identical to the one he used at university. After adding a bottle of black ink and a small notebook to his purchase, he headed out to find lunch.

He paused at a patio table in Münsterplatz and sat admiring the intricately carved red sandstone of the Gothic cathedral. The daily street market was winding down, and waggons were being loaded.

He sat and enjoyed the scene and ordered a stein of beer. His jaw was feeling a little less tender, and he could open his mouth a bit wider without too much pain. He described his eating predicament to the frau when she arrived with the beer. She said the Oberländer is tender and knöpfl need little chewing.

The sausages were delicious, and he taught himself some new ways to eat without causing too much pain.

These knöpfl are like the little squiggles of fried pasta that the beautiful blond had called spätsle last night.

He felt himself stirring.

My God, she's so gorgeous.

He pictured her in his mind and encouraged the swelling to continue down his thigh under the table, enjoying the feel of his trousers as he slowly moved his leg side-to-side.

What a captivating essence she exudes.

He enjoyed the sun and his thoughts, and although the food was very tender, he took a long time eating and had a second stein of beer to help quench another of his thirsts.

The church bell struck two shortly before he arrived back at the gasthaus. He went upstairs to his room and pulled out his new pen and ink and loaded the reservoir with the eyedropper.

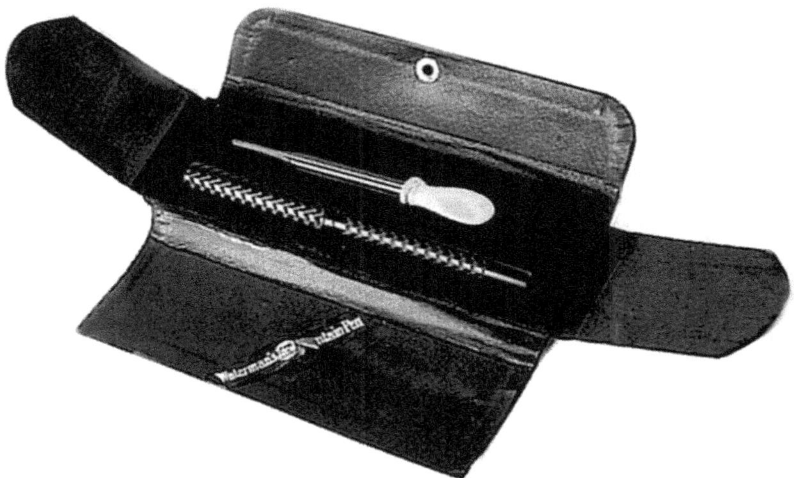

Inside the front cover of his new notebook was a calendar for 1915. He underlined 25 April, the Sunday evening he had left the trench. He stroked out the days which had passed using his memories of their nights. Sunday night unconscious in no-man's-land, Monday night on a hard train station bench, Tuesday night on a hillside above the Swiss border, Wednesday night in a proper bed.

Michael Walsh

Today's Thursday, 29 April. One more comfortable sleep, then...

He started writing a diary — cryptic notes written in truncated and abbreviated German, with no need for grammar or even spelling.

Comfortable with how the pen writes, he changed the end date on his sick leave chit from 3 May to 13, giving him an additional ten days. He couldn't see any easy way to change the date on his orders to report to the field hospital in Roeselare on the 4th. There wasn't enough space in front of the four, so he tore the paper into tiny pieces and tucked them into the bundle with the remnants from the uniform.

Now he had an altered sick leave chit in someone else's name. That person was due back in Belgium on the 4th. He had no identification papers, but he did have the hundemarke to match the regimental number on the chit.

So funny they call them dog marks. Looks like we're not the only ones who think they're curs. Have to hope anyone who stops me for identification is stupid.

He looked again at the chit.

But this whole war is stupid. What's it about? Why are we maiming and killing each other? So incredibly stupid.

Chapter Eight

David sat on the narrow bed with his back against the wall as he studied the sections of the map sheets to the south and east of Freiburg.

Probably the best idea is to keep to the unpopulated areas as I work my way across the Schwarzwald. Stay high as I aim toward what seems should be a less popular area to cross the border.

With the map's latitude scale, he measured the distance across the mountains from Freiburg to the large bulge of the Swiss border across to the north side of the Rhein at Schaffhausen. It looked close to half a degree, thirty nautical miles, or about fifty-six kilometres as the crow files.

But I'm not a crow. There'll be many twists and turns along the way, many ups and downs.

He noted that Feldberg, the highest point in the Black Forest, is a broad plateau in the centre of a web of high ridges. He ran his finger across the high land, and then along a trail leading up toward it from a little to the east of Freiburg.

Looks like an elevation gain of 1100 metres to the plateau and a distance of almost twenty-five kilometres.

The line from the summit of Feldberg to the closest bulge of Swiss Schaffhausen measured thirty-seven kilometres, and he saw that once the elevation was gained, the interconnected ridges remain above 1000 metres for most of the traverse. *Must be places which would be difficult to effectively patrol. Must be good hiding spots to camp.*

He figured there would be few out walking and hiking along his intended route this early in the season. Besides, the war will surely have taken all the fit and adventurous. To be safe, though, he prepared and outfitted himself to do the entire route off the trails and to stay far away from them wherever possible.

The guidebook was new last year, surely all of them are marked.

The contours and hachures on the map sheets showed the tops to be gentle. There were many streams cutting the slopes along the entire route.

Drinking water will not be a problem up there.

Satisfied with his route, he refolded the maps and set them aside, then rolled out the large piece of oiled canvas, two metres by three. He folded it in thirds across its long axis, then creased the ends of the folds. With the tip of his knife, he pierced eight holes around the periphery of the sheet, about an inch in from the edges, one on each corner and one at each of the four creases.

He began sewing cringles like he had learned in the sailing club while he had studied at University School. Part of the club instruction was sail-making, maintenance and repairing.

What I need is a palm to make pushing the needle easier.

He looked at his watch. *Twelve minutes past four, 1612 Army time,* he thought as he put on his shoes, took his small rucksack and went out.

It took him nearly half an hour to find Walder Nähenden Geschäft from the conflicting directions he was given when he asked for *Leder Nähzubehör.* Inside he bought two more darning needles, a stitching palm, thick cotton thread and a small block of beeswax. On his way back he stopped at the *metzgerei* he had seen and bought a dozen pair of landjäger. He had sucked on a small piece from the stash he had bought in Köln and loved the flavour, and he knew with jaw getting better, he would soon be devouring it.

David stopped in the *Gemischtwarenhandlung* two doors along and had the grocer bag half a kilogram each of lentils, split peas, rice and barley. He mumbled to the questioning frau that it was for soup; he was due back in Belgium and was getting ready. She reached behind, picked up the remains of a large ham, placed it with the bags and said, *"Hier, nehmt diese Schinken. Suppen brauchen ein gutes Stück Fleisch.*" She added a small bag of peppercorns and a box of salt.

He thanked her for the ham and the seasonings and pulled out some coins to pay for his dried goods. She wrapped up the groceries in a piece of brown paper and tied the bundle with a string. She refused to take his money, explaining her three sons are at the Front in Elsass.

Back in his room, he continued stitching the cringles, now much easier with the palm. At 1835 he finished the eighth and last one, then laying out his entire kit on the floor and on the bed, he did an inventory.

The folded oiled canvas would serve as a groundsheet, a windbreak and a roof when pitched and tied to the trees. The altered greatcoat and uniform would be his bedroll, which can be rolled into the waterproof canvas and lashed to his rucksack.

He had a stove and cooking pots, a candle lantern, matches and a flint and steel in case the matches got wet. The sore red spot on his heel had improved, and he assumed it was from the earlier rubbing in Josef's large boot, not from his new walking shoes, so he added the boots to the small accumulation of things to discard.

His topographic maps covered more than his intended route, but he decided to keep them all, just in case he had to change plans.

Much easier to carry too much than to go without something that might later prove critical.

Besides the spare topographic sheets, the pocket atlas also stayed. For food, he now had eighteen pairs of landjäger, small sausages in links of two, pressed to a half inch by an inch in cross-section before drying.

He had two kilograms of other dried goods; rice, peas, barley and lentils, and there was the large piece of ham, probably still four pounds of flesh on the bone.

With cryptic German abbreviations, he made a list of items to pick up in the market in the morning in Münsterplatz: cooking onions, turnips, carrots, other winter vegetables. Cabbage only if there's no other choice. He was nauseated by thoughts of the reek of stewing and pickling cabbage from his Saxony neighbours in Trail.

I'll add dried fruit if I can find some, plus a careful selection of apples and anything else fresh that hadn't spoiled over the winter. Eggs, I need eggs.

Again he reviewed his inventory in his mind.

I have three shirts, three pair of socks two pair of wool trousers. I need a woollen pullover and a warm jacket.

He counted his remaining money.

Forty-eight Marks and some loose Pfennig, easily more than enough. Eggs are only ten Pfennig a dozen, I should be able to find a pullover and jacket for less than twenty Marks.

He penned another cryptic line in his notebook.

Trying various placements, he packed the large rucksack, arranging it for convenient access and doing another inventory. Everything fit except for the roll of shelter and bed, which he strapped across the top of the pack. The small rucksack was empty, waiting for its fill of market purchases in the morning.

He removed the dressings from his wounds and examined them, then following a relaxing soak in the bathtub, he reapplied his face bandaging and dressed. After putting the boots and paper bundle of uniform scraps into the small rucksack, he locked the door behind himself and headed down the stairs. His watch showed sixteen past seven.

1916 Army time. That makes much more sense than AM and PM.

The dining room was rather quiet as he passed out into the street, but he saw the young blonde in the back. He swelled at the thought of her as he walked through the small shopping district around the station and out toward the edge of the city, toward a garbage dump he had seen in the afternoon while searching for the leather supply shop.

After tossing the boots and the bundle onto the heap, he continued along, then quickly looped back toward the gasthaus.

The beautiful blonde fraülein served him again; even warmer this evening. She recommended that instead of beer, he have some of the local wine from the Kaiserstühl, *"Es ist ein köstlich frischen Wein..."* She told him about the wine her father had grown and made before he was killed in September in the war.

"Ich würde es gerne versuchen. Ich sage euch aber, ich weiß nicht, Wein..." David explained he had never had wine, but he would love to try it. She brought him a glass, a strange looking thing with a small round bowl sitting atop a knobby stem, which reminded him of a miniature version of his mother's gâteau Saint-Honoré.

She poured a small taste for him, then watching his face as he savoured it, she described what he should be tasting. *"Es hat eine schöne frische Geschmack..."* Even with his mouth wounds, he recognised the taste of apples, spring flowers and spices.

He nodded and looked into her eyes. *"Ja ich sehe es. Es verfügt über einen öliges Gefühl..."* He agreed and added that it has an oily feel in his mouth, and the smell reminded him of falling rocks in the mountains. He told her he liked it a lot and would have some with dinner if she told him more about it and how it's made.

She returned with a half litre carafe, and after pouring a glass of the wine for him, she began by talking about the passion that had been put into producing it. She introduced herself as Maria and told him her father and two brothers had been killed in the war, so most of last year's crop rotted on the vines. She works here in the evenings after her studies to make enough money to keep them going. Her mother works with the wine, trying to keep the small business from collapsing and until they can find a way to get back to their family roots in Switzerland.

They chatted frequently during his dinner; the dining room was near empty. He ate slowly, not solely because his mouth was sore, it had improved appreciably. His dawdling was to enjoy watching her, to enjoy her graceful movement, her lively spirit and her captivating fragrance. He stayed at the table long after he had finished eating to continue the conversation. When Maria had completed her duties at eleven, she suggested they go upstairs to his room.

Chapter Nine

David and Maria stood in the room and hugged for a long while, silent. She rested her head on his shoulder, looking at his dressings and asked if his wounds hurt. *"Sind Ihre Wunden schmerzhaft?"*

"Viel besser jetzt." He told her much better now, then he looked into her pale blue eyes and told her she was absolutely gorgeous, so beautiful. *"Sie sind absolut großartig, so schön."*

She smiled up at him and blushed. *"Du ... Du machst mein Körper kribbeln."*

He was pleased he made her body tingle and thought it a good sign.

She blushed more deeply and bit her lower lip. *"Ich will mit dir Sex zu haben. Kannst du mir beibringen wie?"*

David grinned in amusement at her innocence. Then the reality sunk in. She was asking him to teach her how to have sex.

Oh, God! Is this a dream? A virgin? Need to be gentle with her.

After suggesting they be quiet as they enjoyed, he began unlacing her bodice, and she followed his lead, undressing him. They stood admiring each other for a short while, then they joined in a passionate hug, shuddering as they did. He led her to the bed.

Oh, God! Control, David. Take your time. Ease into this.

He used his hands until she begged for more, telling him she wasn't at the fertile time of her cycle. They conjoined, and after a gentle but passionate twenty minutes, they lay entangled in each other.

She quietly spoke, sharing her story of moving to the Kaiserstuhl just to the west of Freiburg when she was nine in 1905. Her father had seen a promising future growing wine in the complex mix of soils on a volcanic plug at the edge of the Rhein plains. Now he was dead, her brothers too. She missed them, she missed her Unterhallau friends and her grandfather back in Küsnacht.

It was a long and convoluted story. She seemed to be reliving pieces of her past. When it appeared she had finished her catharsis, he asked her where Küsnacht is.

"Lass uns wieder spielen, dann werde ich Ihnen sagen." She said she'd tell him after they played again."

He didn't argue.

Several minutes later, at the height of another orgasm, Maria panted, *"Oh God! — So intense!"*

"Pleased I can bring you so eas..."

Shit! Slipped into English. Dumb move to be doing this, David. Should have walked away again.

"I knew it." She panted. "Your accent — reminded me of Grandpa in Küsnacht — Knew there was something different about you when you came in last night." She giggled. "Guess that's now the night before last, isn't it?"

"You're British!"

"Mama's parents were. They moved to Switzerland after they were charmed by it on a tour in the early 70s. Mama was born in Küsnacht not long after. They all made me learn English and French, besides the local German. I grew up with it and it's what we speak at home."

"Küsnacht again. Where's that?"

"On the lake six kilometres from Zürich. It's where we're trying to go if we can get out of Germany. Do you know where Zürich is?"

"A big city in Switzerland; the banking capital."

Surely she has no love for Germany after what they've done to her family.

"I'm heading to Switzerland tomorrow."

"But it's impossible to cross the border now. It's closed."

"I'm going over Feldberg, along the ridges. It's full moon now."

"That's what we are planning to do, but Mama said it was dangerous in the winter and early spring. We're ready to go now, but waiting until late May when the conditions are better. Maybe you can take us with you." She peered into his eyes. "Could you do that?"

David's head was racing with conflicting thoughts.

I need to slow my mind, look at things more quietly. God, she's gorgeous. So innocent, so passionate.

"I need to think for a short while. To be quiet and look at the situation." He made a gentle thrust with his hips and smiled. "I'm still here with you." She responded with a deep sigh, a quiet moan and her own gentle movements.

He ran his hands down her back and felt her firm buttocks as she lay on him.

Lean, trim, firm. She seems very fit... Barely winded with all that exercise. God, what a magnificent body. But the wilderness, the mountains are not for the unfamiliar, no matter how fit...

"Do you know the mountains? Are you familiar with wilderness? It's completely different up there."

"We were always up there, hiking and climbing, that and working the vineyards. Mama is strong and fit."

Alright, David, you've already blown your cover. May as well explain.

"There's something I must tell you — I'm a Canadian soldier escaped from the Germans in Belgium and trying to get out of the country before they catch me." He paused to think.

Would two women make me appear less conspicuous? Likely would.

"How quickly can you and your mother get ready? I had planned to buy vegetables in the market early in the morning, and some warmer clothing when the shops open, and then heading up."

"Everything is ready; it just needs to be gathered and packed. We can meet you part way up the Schauinslandweg, at the trail junction two hundred metres above the valley."

"I still need a thick woollen pullover and a warm jacket. Have you any at home that'll fit me?"

"We've a lot of spare men's clothing now. We could bring some and leave earlier — no need to wait for the shops. What a horrible thing the Kaiser has done to us just because he wants more land."

"You'll have to dress warmly. It'll be freezing most nights up there. Wear men's clothing, not women's. Are you sure your mother will come at such short notice?"

"She's desperate to get out. We'll both have to hold her back."

They were still entangled, still connected in an intimate cuddle through this entire conversation. She kissed him, lightly stroked the back of his neck, gently rocked her hips and felt him expanding. She trembled at the sensation, rotated her hips more vigorously and from the back of her throat found a voice, "Pump me full of energy again. I've not done this before, and I so enjoy it."

He began a slow rocking of his pelvis to match her churning. "I'm delighted to be introducing you to one of my favourite activities."

As they were relaxing again a very enjoyable while later, he asked her, "How far is your home from here?"

"Not far out. West toward the Rhein, before the village of Gottenheim, under an hour's walk. I should be going."

"Does it make sense for me to walk with you, to take my pack, take everything with me? We can prepare to leave from your place. Is there a less busy route from your house to the start of the hills, or do we have to come back through Freiburg?"

"Come, let's get dressed, I'll take you home. We've lots of vegetables in the root cellar, lots of food in the pantry. From home, we can go south, around the west of the city through a quiet area of vineyards and farms. Then there's a trail across the slopes to the Schauinslandweg junction I was talking about."

"My lip is still quite sore. Otherwise, I'd be smothering you with kisses." They shared a long quiet hug, then slowly unplugged, quickly cleaned themselves and dressed. He shouldered his big rucksack, she took his small empty pack and led him quietly down the service stairs and through to the empty kitchen, using the shaded candle from his room to light their way.

Maria lit her candle lantern, put her school books into the small pack, and in the light of the full moon, she guided him down the back lane and into the street. She took his hand and led him out of town with the moon now off to their left.

"I know this route well. I've done it twice each day for months."

They talked quietly as they walked hand-in-hand along the road. He told her the story of his misadventures after leaving the trench to help deploy barbed wire. He talked of his life in Canada before the war, of his climbing in the Purcells, the Selkirks, the Bugaboos and the Rockies, and he shared with her some of his memories of wonderful experiences, free and wild, exploring up in the mountains.

After a fifty-minute walk, she unlocked the front door, entered and headed immediately down the hall. "Mama! — Mama!" she called as she opened the door to her mother's bedroom.

"What is it, Sweetheart, are you alright?" her mother asked as she opened her eyes and lifted her head off the pillow.

"I am very alright. We are very, very alright. I've recruited a Canadian mountain guide to take us over the ridges to Switzerland. We're leaving before dawn. We need to start getting ready."

"What are you talking about? Have you been drinking?"

"No, Mama, I'm completely sober. You need to get up. You need to come meet David."

"What time is it?"

"It's almost one thirty. We need to leave well before four to be into the trees before dawn."

"Is this real? Tell me I'm not dreaming again. I've dreamed of this so often these last months."

"It's real, Mama. Put on your housecoat, come meet David."

"Please call me Rachel," she said as she shook his offered hand a short while later. "You've been injured."

"Four days ago in the trenches in Belgium. Our position was overrun, and I ended up on this side of the German lines."

"Your injuries... Do they need treatment?"

"I've had them cleaned and stitched. They seem to be healing well and don't appear infected. I'm trying to get out of the country before I'm caught. I'm heading over the Schwarzwald to Switzerland."

"Bad time to do it. The weather's unstable this time of the year, and it's still freezing up there at night."

"I've spent years exploring in the Canadian mountains, up in the glaciers and snowfields. And you? Maria told me you've spent a lot of time hiking up there."

"Two dozen years, late spring through early autumn. I know much of the area like the back of my hand. The last years, it's been mostly family rambles for a day or two at a time, but earlier, we explored a lot more widely."

"I'd planned on leaving first thing in the morning. I'm packed and ready, need only a jacket and a pullover and some vegetables."

"We've those here. Lots of men's clothing." Rachel looked at him and nodded her head. "And Maria said we could go with you? Would you want to have us hamper your free movement?"

David looked at Maria, who had remained silent.

Such a beautiful woman. God! So passionate, yet so innocent. She sure loves rooting. Can't believe she's not done it before.

He shuddered, then looked back at Rachel. "It might make me seem less suspicious if I'm with a couple of women. It would help me blend in."

Rachel nodded, looked back and forth between Maria and David, then nodded more vigorously. "Let's get started." She stepped toward David. "You're certainly a handsome lad. A handshake isn't enough." She rose to her toes, kissed his unbandaged cheek and gave him a warm hug. "Come. Let's get ready."

They continued their introductions as they began rummaging through drawers and closets for a heavy woollen pullover and jacket for David and warm, comfortable clothing for themselves.

"I have lentils, split peas, rice, barley — half a kilo of each and a large ham, probably two kilos of meat left on the bone. And three dozen landjäger," he said as he unloaded the food from his pack and laid it out on the kitchen table.

"It will it take us only three days to get across," Rachel said.

"Yes, if we're alone up there and the weather is good, but if we have to sneak around or we're delayed by conditions, it could take a week or longer."

"Maria, pack a lot of cottons, we may need them. Don't forget your knickers, pack some for me too — lots of soap also," Rachel said as she opened the back door. "I'll be in the root cellar."

"Have you a tent or a sheet for shelter? What about bedrolls?" David asked Maria.

"We've a small hiking tent, two layers of sailcloth. It works well in the rain if the layers are kept apart. We have a piece of painted canvas for the ground, and Mama stitched up thick wool blankets with soft flannel linings. We were ready, just waiting for conditions and weather — maybe we were waiting for you."

Rachel came in lugging a bulging cloth, holding it by its corners. She laid it out on the table and spread it open. "Maria, go gather the eggs, see what the hens have given us this morning. Leave the gate open and let them free, someone will give them a home, perhaps a pot. What time is it?"

"It's a bit beyond two thirty," he said after looking at his watch. "I love your energy and your enthusiasm."

"*When your rescue boat comes by, don't simply look at it.* That's what my father said when he cautioned me before I first headed out in the little sailboat on the lake. *Then after you've climbed aboard, don't just sit there. Help with your rescue.*"

"He sounds like he was a wise man."

"Still is. He didn't move to Germany. He still owns and runs the sailing school in Küsnacht."

They juggled the load into three large rucksacks and put water and snacking food into his small one and strapped it onto the top of his pack.

They shared a huge omelette with thick slabs of ham, grilled bread and mugs of coffee. Then at a quarter to four, Rachel locked the house door behind them and they headed off.

The moon was now quite low in the west, and they had its light over their right shoulders for nearly an hour and a half before it dipped over the high hills across the Rhein.

Chapter Ten

It was starting to get light, but the sun was not yet up as Maria led David and Rachel along the trail angling upwards across the side of the hill. As daylight increased, David pointed to the trees. "I'm surprised by the symmetrical appearance of the forest. The trees here are lined up in rows. So different from the natural forests back home. It looks as if these slopes have been planted like crops."

"The story I've been told," Rachel said, "is the trees were stripped from the hills here and floated down the Rhein to the Netherlands, first to build trading ships for the East Indies, then for pilings and shorings to build in the low lands in the river deltas. Well over a century ago they ran out of easily accessible trees and somebody, I can't remember who, but someone organised a replanting program. There are still some wild, original patches of forest, but mostly high up where the trees were too small and remote to be worthy of harvesting. Also, higher up are many open meadows where forests once stood, barren land where the forests haven't yet been able to regenerate."

The trail was good, and they were the only ones on it. "Today's Friday," Rachel said,."Most people are working, probably be the same tomorrow, but Sunday will be busier."

"It looks like it's possible to be across on the far side of Feldberg by evening." David glanced at his watch. "It's twenty to eight. We're almost to the junction with Schauinslandweg, according to that sign. From my memory of the map, it's about three more hours of uphill grinding to reach the top of the ridge."

"We would make it from the centre of Freiburg to the ridge top in under three hours," Rachel said, "but that was with light packs for summer picnics. We've already gained almost two hundred metres. The sign at the junction should show the el —"

Maria put up her hand, stopped and turned to the others with her finger to her lips. She pointed to the side of the trail and quickly headed behind some bushes up the slope. David and Rachel copied her movements. They sat in silence half a dozen feet up the slope and watched a nine-man squad of soldiers with rifles and large rucksacks heading up the main trail ahead of them, talking loudly and laughing as they went.

"We're likely fine," Maria said after they had passed, "Mama and I have proper German papers, and David, or rather Josef, has a sick leave chit and face bandages. He's off hiking with his fraülein before he heads back to the Front. The story sounds good to us, but it's best we not have to test it on them."

"I think it makes sense to avoid them," David said. "It's hard to guess what they report and what they do with the reports. It's best not to press our luck. We can hope the other squads are as undisciplined and noisy as this one, you can still hear them." He looked around. "This is a good time and place for a break, anyway. We've been going steadily for nearly four hours."

"I wonder where they're going. Does it make sense for us to head up the slope off the trail?" Maria asked.

"The going will be slow and tiring with all the undergrowth, uneven ground, rock outcrops, gullies, windfalls." David pointed at the slope. "It would be like mountain approaches in Canada, where there are practically no trails. We'll go half the speed and get twice as tired."

David continued talking, more thinking aloud, while he tried to analyse their situation. "Let's instead sit here for a nice long break and then head up the path staying well behind them. From the appearance of their packs, they could be heading up to relieve a watch post on the ridge. They were going at an army pace, so we won't have to slow too much to stay out of sight behind them. We'll have to be careful with lines-of-view across the open fields and on the switchbacks, but we should be able to stay out of their sight as we follow them up the trail. It's unlikely a squad will come down until this one relieves it." He looked at each of the women. "I've rambled, but does my thinking make sense? What else should we consider?"

"They might be heading to the new club refuge below the crest of the ridge, I forget its name." Rachel took another sip of water, then continued. "A short distance above it is a fire lookout tower with views across to Belchen to the south-west and Feldberg to the south-east and the high ridges connecting them."

"We can follow them up to about a hundred metres below the top," Maria added, "Then head left across the slopes in the remaining patches of old forest. We'll be able to stay below the shoulder of the ridge and out of their view. Then we can head up a bit and take a line through the trees over the saddle to remain out of sight. At that point, we'd be five kilometres from them and heading away."

She paused as a smile filled her face. "There are some patches of wild, unspoilt forest up there, short, squat trees, very old trees. Near the crests of the ridges, there are many wondrous ones, bent and trained by the high winds. It's an enchanting area which most people miss by staying on the trails."

After they had given the squad half an hour, they re-slung their packs, stepped back down to the trail and headed the remaining thirty yards to the junction. They paused and listened.

"You lead this time, David," Maria said, then added with a giggle. "I want to watch your bum. You've watched mine all morning."

"Have you two been friendly?" Rachel looked into Maria's eyes with a knowing smile and a wink. "I thought you might have been. Aah, to be young again."

"You're not old Mama, you're barely into your forties, and your body still looks as if it were twenty. There are lots of men in Switzerland for you. They haven't gone to war."

"Get your bum moving, David," Rachel said with a laugh. "You've two young ladies to lead to Switzerland." He looked up the trail, then with a waggle of his butt, he led the way along it.

They had to stop thirty minutes later to watch the Germans zigzag a series of switchbacks in the fold of a shallow open gully. Twenty minutes later, with the last of the squad over the shoulder, they continued up, moving quietly along the set of switchbacks, unable to see beyond its top. Near the head of the gully, David heard voices, so he paused and whispered, "The squad's stopped for a break. Let's take our packs off and have another one ourselves."

They continued up in spurts and stops as the squad hiked slowly for fifty minutes and took a ten-minute break. David, Maria and Rachel did the distance in half an hour, so they had half hour breaks at a time to relax and nap. It was slow progress, not much more than half the speed they had planned.

As the time for the noon break approached, they could see the rounding back of the end of the ridge above them. To the left, off to the east, they looked across the slopes heading toward Feldberg. As they left the trail and headed into the trees, Rachel estimated their elevation was around 1200 metres. "We're about fifty metres below the top of the ridge."

Although it was more difficult moving, they made better progress, partly because they had stopped climbing, but mainly because they moved much faster than the Germans. David led a route across the sidehill, into and out of gullies and out around ridges trying to maintain the elevation they had gained. He had learned the knack for sensing the easiest line, going around rather than up or down.

His years of mountain exploring had taught him that on a traverse, each foot of elevation he lost and needed to regain, meant having to carry his body weight and the weight of his pack down and then back up that lost foot. The freshest climber, the one with the best apparent endurance, is simply the one who has taken the care to maintain the elevation that's been gained and not to casually squander it. Maintain the elevation until it is no longer needed.

At ten to one, they were more than a third of the way across the slopes at the head of the broad north-facing cirque on Feldberg. There were still substantial patches of snow in the bottoms of the gullies and at the bases of the steeper outcrops.

They stopped for lunch beside a tumbling little stream in a small grove of ancient pines. "Feldberg sure looks disappointing as the highest peak in the range," David said as they sat on the soft forest floor, "I guess it lives up to its name, Field Mountain, a broad high field."

"Besides Belchen, which has a little bit of shape," Rachel said, "none of the mountains here look like mountains. When we cross to the other side of the ridge in a short while, we'll see real mountains." She looked up at the blue sky. "It should still be clear enough to see the Alps spread out across the entire southern horizon. I miss them *so* much."

They drank the fresh cold water from the stream and broke pieces off the dark loaf of rye bread, slathered them with fresh butter and cut pieces off the ham. David's mouth was feeling better, though he couldn't open it much and chewing was still rather painful in the hinge of his jaw. He had thought of taking the dressing off his lower lip to make eating easier.

The stitches are now four days old, the wounds five, but I'm too hungry to pause.

After they had finished eating, Maria snuggled up beside him and gently removed the dressings from his face. Using a cloth dampened with rubbing alcohol, she began to daub and tenderly clean his wounds. "These look good. You're lucky to have had a skilled surgeon do the suturing."

"You seem professional with this."

"I'm eight months into nursing training, I've just..."

"Shhh!" hissed Rachel, as she waved her hand and pointed across the slope.

Chapter Eleven

"Sounds like another squad of soldiers," David whispered.

"Trail ahead. Winds up through Oberried," Maria whispered back. "From Kirchzarten to the top of Feldberg. Shorter, but more open and populated. Doesn't have cover like this area."

They sat still and listened as the squad descended the trail about fifty yards across the slope from their little grove. As they faded down the hill, Maria returned to her nursing. "We can leave the dressings off to let the fresh air and sunshine do their work. Put them back on before we go to bed." She gently stroked his face. "Let me kiss your wounded lip to make it better."

"That feels much better with the fresh air, but your touch has started another swelling." He winked at her, then looked from her eyes down at his watch. "But back to important matters. It's thirteen twenty. That was likely the relieved lookout squad coming from the top of Feldberg. The timing makes sense."

"It's probably safe to head up the trail a short distance until the start of the big meadows," Rachel said. "From there we can skirt around in the trees. We'll be midway between Feldberg and Schauinsland, more than five kilometres from either lookout post. Within two hours we can be across the saddle and traversing the southern slopes, well out of sight over the shoulders of Feldberg."

"My study of the maps showed a ridge down toward the Swiss bulge across to the north side of the Rhein. Let me dig out the map."

"No need," Rachel replied, "I know the area like the back of my hand. Maria and I had been planning on heading down to the town of Unterhallau.

That's where Edom — my husband — my late husband and his family come from. They still have vineyards there. It's just across the border..." She paused to sip more water.

"There's a tongue of forest which comes down a ridge from the high lands between the little German villages and farms. The trails and roads are in the valleys on each side, but the ridge top is untamed. That's the route Edom and I would follow when we used to take the short-cut and sneak across the border to go rambling up on the high ridges of the Schwarzwald."

Her eyes wandered as her mind searched. "At the bottom of the trees is a small road, a rail line and then a line of trees beside a small river, the Wutach. The river is the border. We used to cross on the stauwehr. Downstream of the weir, the water is shallow as it runs through the rocks. We can wade across into Switzerland. Unterhallau is only three kilometres across the hills from there."

"That's the exact route I had planned," he replied. "Even the town of Unterhallau. But the geography leaves few other options, so the Germans will be guarding it closely. We'll have to be careful."

They quenched their thirsts and filled their canteens from the stream. Then shouldering their packs, they walked across the slope to the trail and started up it.

"You lead again, David, I want to watch your bum for a while more. I've never watched a man's bum before, and it's great for my imagination. You should watch too, Mama, it's quite warming."

They skirted a large meadow, remaining in the forest. The trees were much shorter and more widely spaced, but they offered good cover. They wound slowly upward, contouring around the undulating ground. At two thirty they were on their way down, angling off to the left in a gradual descending traverse.

"Wow!" He exclaimed as the broke out of the trees at the edge of a small meadow below them. "The Alps. They're hogging the entire horizon." He looked up to his left and his right, then walked across a few yards to a moss-covered log just in from the edge of the clearing. "Come have a seat, come look at the Swiss Alps."

They sat on the log and stared at the ragged line of white and dark blue which seemed to be floating above a paler blue, nearly the shade of the sky. A line of snowfields and glaciers held apart, yet together by the deep blue of the mountain ridges and peaks.

"Edom and I always wondered why the mountains are blue in the distance, but brown, grey and green up close."

"It's from the refraction of light through the air," David replied.

"I can't remember the names of the peaks over there. Edom could name every one of them. Damn you, Kaiser Wilhelm!"

"I know that's Mont Blanc over there on the right, near the end," Maria said. "It's the highest peak in the Alps, a little above 4800 metres." Then pointing almost straight ahead, she continued, "Those three ahead of us are Jungfrau, Mönch and Eiger, all around 4000 metres. How high are your mountains in Canada?"

"The highest in the Rockies is Mount Robson, a few metres short of 4000. In the north, there are peaks over 5000 metres, and one, Mount Logan almost 20,000 feet, over 6000 metres. There are large areas unexplored, particularly in the coastal ranges, and some say there are peaks there higher than 13,000 feet, over 4000 metres."

He stared at the Alps. "Let's sit and take a quiet look around and think where the Germans would set up lookout posts up here, or down below in the valleys. Let our minds wander — be creative."

He looked eye to eye, then continued, "They'll be much more suspicious of people moving on this side of the range, being close to the border. They'll be looking for men fleeing conscription, for deserters, for escaped enemy and prisoners of war, for spies, for saboteurs."

They each contributed: "There are many little villages and settlements in the valleys; their posts there would be impossible to spot. At the edge of every meadow, every field, every pasture. On every prominent spot on every ridge. Atop every rock outcrop on the slopes. Up high trees. The trails will be increasingly unsafe for us the lower we go with new hiking refuges being built along them. Of course, the fire lookout towers and ones like Roßkopfturm we saw on the way up, but we can easily see those."

"Practically anywhere. That seems the consensus," David said. "We need to be extremely alert, we need to plan every move. We're not out on a pleasure hike, we're trying to stay alive."

He told them of his experience on Tuesday afternoon above the border near Will am Rhein, starting the short tale with, "This is not to frighten you. This is so you fully understand the thinking and the actions we might run into."

They were quiet after he finished the story. He looked at his watch and continued, "It's now fourteen fifty. Rachel had a few hours of sleep last night, Maria and I had none. Those short naps on the way up helped, but we're all tired. Mistakes happen when people are tired. Let's move along carefully until we find a suitable place to spend the night. There's a line of bluffs and ledges across there on the second rib; it's a distance away, but it appears to be the first possibility. Let's go across to it; find a stream with a place to camp on one of the ledges."

Maria and Rachel were both silent as they got up and followed David back into the trees and contoured around two shallow cirques toward the rock outcrops. There was a pleasant bench running across the bottom of the rocks, occasionally interrupted by a block fallen from above. At one block, the ramp sloped down temptingly, but wanting to maintain elevation, David sidled around on a narrow ledge on the rock and saw a route continuing more horizontally.

About a hundred yards along, the line of the escarpment made an abrupt turn to the left into a gully, a broad cleft in the cliff. At the back of the gully was a thin waterfall bouncing off the rocks as it tumbled about forty feet and splashed into pools on the horizontal rock slab at the bottom. He held up his hand for the women to stop, then put his finger to his mouth in a shhh sign.

He did a slow, deliberate survey of the scene, examining the tops of the cliffs, combing his eyes through the trees, looking down the gully. After pausing his breathing to listen more intently, he moved around the corner and took a few steps along a narrow ledge toward the back of the gully then stopped and followed the continuation of a route with his eyes. Satisfied, he turned and headed back to the corner.

With a broad smile on his face, he stuck his head around the edge of the rock. "Ladies, our lodgings for the night have been arranged. Please follow me, I'll show you to your room. Mind your step, it's a very narrow corridor."

"Oh, my God!" Rachel said as she got to the corner and looked into the gully. "Edom and I stumbled onto this place many years ago. We looked for it so often after that, but we were never able to find it again. Those pools of water get warm in the sun. Our baths have been drawn for us, the sun is still on them. I hope you packed lots of soap, Maria, I'm sweaty and as smelly as an old mare in heat."

It was a delicate move around a bulge in the face, but the footing on the narrow ledge was good, as were the handholds above. Then the ledge ramped down slightly as the slab at the back of the gully rose more gradually to meet it. They stepped through the spray, the pelt and the splash of water tumbling from above as they crossed the shallow stream to a broad slab of sandstone. The broken splash of the waterfall through the millennia had carved several pools, mostly shallow, but those closer to the waterfall, rather deeper.

David tried to recall details from the geology lectures at the Alpine Club summer camps in 1913. "It looks as if we're at a junction of a gabbro and a sandstone layer." He looked up and around the tops of the overhanging gabbro faces, up to the top of the waterfall. "I think ours is the only possible approach into here."

He turned his head back down to look for a place to set up a camp, but he was too late.

Chapter Twelve

By the time David had done his geology and security survey, Rachel and Maria had already placed their packs in a perfect camp spot beside a huge block of gabbro.

He walked over to join them, took off his pack and laid it alongside theirs. "What a fine spot this is," he said, examining the setting and pointing to the tops of the cliffs soaring around them. "It appears to be well hidden from almost any angle."

Rachel nodded. "We tried for years to find it again, and even knowing where to look, we couldn't. We tried from above and below, crossed the slopes many times in each direction. No sign of it."

David wiped the sweat from his brow. "While we're hot and sticky, let's unpack and set up camp so we cool before we bathe." He examined the fallen block of gabbro. "This seems an ideal place for our shelter." He unstrapped the roll of canvas and blanket from his pack and spread it out, then said, "I'll set it up for us while you ladies unpack then go to the pools."

While the women organised the contents of the packs, David wedged the line from a corner of the oiled canvas into a crack in the rock at his chest level, then he led the line from the next corner around a flake on the back of the fallen block. Rachel came over with a towel in hand as he adjusted the line. "That's an unusual shelter."

"I thought a low sloping roof would not only make a good dew and rain cover, but also help retain our body heat. I'll tie lines from the lower two corners around large rocks on the slab. That will enclose a tight little space between the cliff face and this rock. The only opening will be a small triangle. We'll be hidden from the entrance ramp"

Rachel nodded and held up her towel. "Maria and I are off to the pools to bathe. You stay here to allow us our privacy."

A while later, as Rachel and Maria lay soaking and relaxing in the warm pool, Maria said quietly, "Mama, you've told me lots about me, about my body, but you've never told me much about boys — about men. I know you've tried, but I wasn't interested. Then I saw David and sensed his interest." She trembled. "Last night I learned I like men, at least that one over there. I don't even understand how his things work, they're so different from my little button and grooves."

"My dear little girl, my little sweetheart, I've missed your growing up. You did it so quickly. Every time I suggested we have another talk, you seemed so unconcerned. I guess I figured you already knew about men. Now here you are eighteen and beginning to learn. I'm delighted you're not shy about it."

"I'll be nineteen in September. Why should I be shy? I'm curious, though — like when I was tending his wounds, I watched the bulge as he expanded along his trouser leg. Did that mean he was interested in me, like when we put the stallion in with the mare?"

Rachel chuckled. "No, Sweetheart, not necessarily, men rise for many reasons. Sometimes when they're emotionally contented, as he would have been with your tender care. Sometimes it happens for no reason they can think of, often when they're in deep sleep and almost always when they wake in the morning."

She looked at Maria and smiled. "The good times for us are when their arisings are about us, or when they're because of us. And fortunately for women, that's an easy thing to arrange. When we're hungry, a little hint, a show of flesh, almost any little thing we can imagine to show some interest, will turn on the passion."

"I discovered that last night. I wanted a third go, so I ran my finger up the back of his neck and back down and shifted my hips a bit. It was as if I had thrown a switch, he quickly grew again inside me."

"A third time? How long were you together last night?"

"I got off at eleven, and we started to walk home at half past midnight, so an hour and —"

"My God, Maria, you've a very strong stud." She turned her head toward the shelter and smiled. "Most men need an hour and more to get it up again. Women are lucky, we can keep on going until we're exhausted. I've never been lucky enough to be exhausted by sex."

"I often have." She smiled, then trembled. "I've used my fingers ever since I can remember. Sometimes I lie in bed and rub myself to explosion over and over again until I'm too tired, or too sore to continue."

"You've a high drive like I do. Last night, did you explode with David?"

"Two or three times each time we did it. I couldn't believe what I'd been missing."

"You're a very lucky girl, Maria. I used to have a lot of trouble exploding, reaching orgasm it's called, when I was with your father. The doctor said this is common with women — speaking of father, when did you last bleed?"

"I started a week after the moon, like always. I told him I was safe. This week, we had begun studying sexual anatomy and reproduction at the hospital, so when David came down from his room for dinner the first night, I showed an interest. You know how I prefer experience to book learning. Last night he sat after dinner as we talked. When I finished, I asked him to take me up to his room and show me how."

Rachel giggled. "You've always shown initiative. I don't know what David's other qualities are or what his background is, but as a virile stud, as a kind, gentle person, and as a leader, what I see so far is impressive."

"So, Mama..." Maria hesitated. "What do I do to make it better for him? I enjoy him so tremendously — it's so intense. I can't imagine he gets the same from me. How do I make it better for him?"

"It's a complex system, Sweetheart. It's completely different between men and women. The parts between his legs are tied to his head, while ours are tied to our emotions, to our feelings."

"So what can I do?"

"You simply have to show you enjoy him. It is as simple as that. He will enjoy you more; it will boost his confidence. The more you show him you enjoy what he does, the more he will do what you enjoy. You're the leader. Women rule men by maintaining control of their dangling bits. Never forget that, Maria. Women have ruled the earth since Adam and Eve. Men mistakenly think they have."

"I play with my button and grooves." She looked down and stroked her blonde mound, which was barely above the shallow water. "Do men play the same way with themselves? I'm sure they must."

"Yes, Sweetheart, but you need to ask *him*, not me." A smile grew on Rachel's face as she thought. "He may know as little about these things as you, but being open and honest with each other is the finest way to learn. You're obviously attracted to each other, you both seem to have a high drive, and you're in a safe part of your cycle. You stay here and relax while I go talk with him."

Rachel soaped and rinsed, then stood to dry with a towel, her mind wandering to her own youth. She dressed and smiled down at Maria. "You're a beautiful woman — quick and intelligent. You deserve a fine man like David. Let me see if he's interested in calling on you."

A short while later in the shelter, Rachel sat and spoke with David. "Maria and I have been talking. First, to relieve your mind, as she had told you last night, there was no risk of pregnancy. Second, for your gratification, she told me she enjoys you tremendously. Third, she told me that except for her fingers, she was a virgin last night. Finally, she asked me to tell her how she can please you more, to tell her what excites you and to explain how you relieve yourself. I decided you could tell her better than I."

David was flummoxed, completely taken by surprise. He stared into Rachel's eyes as he tried to think of what to say. "I enjoy her tremendously as well. She has such an endearing innocence and curiosity. My God, she's so beautiful."

"You need to tell her that, David. Tell her often how beautiful she is. Women love the confirmation. Be honest with her about your feelings, all of them, the good and the bad. Sharing honesty is the finest way to get to know one another."

David looked again at the entrance to the shelter, expecting Maria to appear. "She's taking a long time."

"She's at the pool waiting for you so you can talk privately. Take a towel so you can bathe while you're there. I'll finish arranging here."

He slowly nodded as he stood, a smile growing on his face. "Thank you. I don't know what else to say. " He shuddered. "Thank you."

Maria was on her back, relaxing in the pool as he approached. "Come join me. The water is so comforting and it eases the aches."

David undressed, rising quickly in excitement.

Maria stared at his prominence. "Mama and I were talking about how it swells and lifts. She said it's often an automatic thing, not connected to desire."

"This one is definitely not automatic. Your beauty brought it on, but let's leave that for the moment. Your mother said you have questions I might be able to answer."

"Come lie beside me, let the water relax you, tell me about your parts. They're so different from mine."

"My God, you're an innocent beauty. So curious, so gorgeous and so... so endearing." He slipped into the water beside her and kissed her nose. "These wounds make kissing awkward."

"I'll clean them and apply fresh dressings when we finish here." She pointed to his shaft sticking above the water. "That's called a penis in German; what's its name in English? How do you stop the swelling when it starts? There doesn't seem room in your trousers with it this way."

"Also a penis. It's often impossible to stop. Sometimes I can divert my mind, but with inspiration like you causing it, nothing works."

"Nothing? What about stroking it like I stroke my button? That always relieves my tension. I was doing that while waiting for..." His throbbing interrupted her. "My God, it's waving to us."

"Your words are doing that, giving my mind an image of you playing with yourself." He gazed into her eyes. "But, yes, I do stroke myself for relief, though I much prefer doing it with a woman. The feeling is so much more intense, but that's not always possible."

"Will you show me how? I'm curious."

"Curious! God! That's an understatement. Why don't I instruct you how do it for me? You'll understand it better that way."

Maria followed his coaching, and a few minutes later she smiled as she listened to his breathing change, saw his legs tense and his toes curl, recognising the signs from her own self-pleasuring. A while later, she watched the pulsating geyser. "My God!" she blurted, looking at the creamy trail across his abdomen and chest. "The school lessons were well short of this. The instructor said there were many seeds released. Tiny microscopic seeds, but I never imagined this much." She leaned and kissed his forehead. "Was that pleasing to you?"

"A huge relief. Taking matters in hand is my way to quickly turn to the important things. I've always been amazed by how fast my mind clears, how fast the frenzy for relief dissipates once I spurt. My balls stop aching. I relax. I think clearly again. Speaking of clear thinking, it's getting cold. We need to finish here, get into warm clothing, finish setting up camp and start cooking dinner."

They soaped, rinsed and dried each other, then dressed. Back at the shelter, Maria looked closely at David's lip and cheek, and after dabbing them gently with alcohol, she decided they needed no further attention other than light pieces of gauze taped over them to keep them clean.

While David and Maria were at the pool, Rachel had finished unpacking and had arranged the shelter. The slab inside was thickly covered with moss and she had spread the three bedrolls on it. Ranged at the side were the rucksacks, and she had removed the food, the stove and the cooking pots and utensils.

Rachel and Maria began preparing a stew of ham, carrots, turnips and split peas in a kettle on the Primus. Once it was simmering, they all sat around the little stove and ate the last of a loaf of pumpernickel with slabs of butter as they waited for the stew to cook.

It was just into twilight when the stew was done, and as he turned off the stove, David said, "We need to finish cooking, be finished with any need for light before it gets dark. Our tiny light can be seen for a long distance and catch an eye, compromising our position. Take a good look around now while there is still some daylight remaining. Make a mental map of where our shelter is, the route to our latrine rocks, the cliff edge. Everything has to be done in the dark. There's a big moon from an hour before midnight until dawn to show the cliff edge if you need to get up."

They ate their stew in the growing dark, then felt their way across to the shelter. "It's warmer to sleep in the nude," he said. "Our clothes are damp from the day's perspiration and from the evening dew. They'll only make us colder if we keep them on. Our body heat will soon warm the bed, and if you need extra warmth, we can cuddle." He chuckled. "I think we know each other well enough now to do that."

He was the first into the shelter and he rearranged the bedrolls into a single bed. *Much warmer this way than individually.*

After stripping, he crawled under the covers and began warming the bed while he waited for the women.

Wonder what's taking them so long. Brushing hair, maybe? Her hair is so beautiful. My God, what a body she has.

Maria undressed and crawled in, nuzzling up in front of him, wrapping her arms around him, interlocking legs and pressing her breasts into his chest. He tried to keep himself down without success. Rachel crawled in behind him and snuggled her back to his.

"I feel like a piece of meat in a sandwich, a delicious sandwich. Is everyone comfortable?"

"Wonderfully," Rachel said, wriggling more firmly into his back "I haven't been this comfortable and relaxed in many months. Thank you, David. Thank you for everything you've done and are doing."

"I'm concerned about this big piece of meat pressing into my belly. Do we need to do something with it?"

"Ignore it, Maria, it's on automatic. There's no intention behind it." He chuckled. "Besides, we all need to sleep."

Chapter Thirteen

The sun had already lit the tops of the rock face above them, across on the other side of the gully, when David gently untangled from Maria and crawled to look out through the triangle. He checked his watch.

Eight thirty-five. I've slept in, Maria's still asleep.

Rachel walked toward him with a hot cup of tea as he dressed. "You had a very long sleep," she said as she passed him the cup. "You must have been exhausted."

"It's not a good idea to miss a night's sleep," he replied, and pointing into the little canvas shelter, he added, "Maria's still asleep."

"No, I'm not. How can anyone be expected to sleep with so much noise?" She giggled, then asked, "What time is it?"

"Almost quarter to nine. Did you sleep well?"

"Too well. Out of my way, I'm coming through, desperate to pee." She crawled out and trotted past them holding herself.

David reached into the shelter, pulled out the top blanket set and walked across the slab with it. "Put this around you," he said as she got up from her squat and walked toward him. "It's quite cold still, and you'll catch a chill. We all need to remain healthy." He draped the blanket around her and gave her a gentle kiss.

"These rocks are nearly freezing," she said as she began tiptoeing toward the shelter, appearing to be trying to keep her feet off the cold rocks. David swept her off her feet and carried her the rest of the way. She sighed, then as they passed Rachel, she said, "Good morning, Mama, have you been up long?"

"Almost an hour, I scampered off without the audience." She laughed. "And without a gentleman to bring a blanket for me and carry me back. Crawl inside and sit in the blanket for a while. Warm up a bit before you dress, I should have done that. It took me a long time to re-warm. I'll bring you a cup of tea."

David came back, rubbing his hands together to dry them. "I'll start cooking breakfast. What should we have?"

"There are still seven eggs." Rachel pointed to them by the stove. "I can scramble them in butter. You can slice some ham off the bone."

As they sat quietly eating their ham and eggs with thick slabs off the remains of the dark rye loaf, David was turning plans over in his mind. He set his emptied plate on the rock and nibbled at the crude ham sandwich he had made. His jaw was still sore when he opened his mouth too wide, so he took little bites. Between his nibbles, he said, "I'm thinking of going out for a careful look around, see if I can plot a safe route onward. See if I can spot Fritz or identify any of the places they may be posted."

"Fritz? Who's Fritz?" Maria asked, wrinkling her brow.

"That's the name we call the German soldiers, the whole German Army, we refer to as Fritz, individually and collectively."

"I guess it's an outside joke, then." Rachel chuckled. "Only those outside Germany would know it."

"I've been looking around. I'm now certain that the only way into this little nook, is the way we came in. The rock walls at the back and sides of the gully are too steep, and besides, they're covered in slippery growth from the spray of the waterfall." He pointed out toward the line of the Alps across the tops of the trees. "Over there, the edge of the slab drops vertically. It actually overhangs, and the little stream begins another waterfall."

He pointed to the left. "Over there, the thick stratum of gabbro juts beyond the sandstone face below it. There is no way in from that direction. No wonder you couldn't find it again. Thirty feet higher or thirty feet lower heading east across the side of the ridge and you'd walk right past it. Heading west you'd never find it."

"Besides," Maria said, "with the much easier going on the open top of the ridge a hundred — can't be more than a hundred metres above here, who would come along this way?"

"We found it when we had left the ridge to get out of some extreme north winds and driving rain," Rachel said. "Many trees were broken, some uprooted in that storm. The cliff faces, the outcrops, the ramps and the ledges led us here as we scrambled for shelter. Even in the rain, the pools were warm, and it was a wonderful refuge from the storm. We tried so many times to find it after that, but could never put together the right combination of outcrops, ramps and ledges again."

"I'll mark my route when I head out so I can find my way back in," David said a quarter hour later as he prepared to leave on a reconnaissance. "I probably don't need to go too far to survey the route and sense where Fritz may be. I should be back within half an hour."

"Wait!" Maria said. "You can't head out without a hug and a kiss."

"This stuff is all new to me," he said as he wrapped her in his arms and they stood swaying. "But enough of this," he said after a short while. "The last thing I need is to go out there with lumpy trousers. I need to concentrate, and this makes it hard to do that." He tenderly kissed her with the side of his mouth to keep from scraping her with the hard stitches. "When can these stitches come out?"

"I'll take a close look when you come back."

He hugged Rachel, then headed across the stream and along the narrow ledge to the corner. After pausing to wave, he disappeared from their view. The ramp led slightly upward along the base of the cliffs, with the trunks of large trees standing from precipitous slopes below him. He took a soft new branch on a bush. *Probably a berry bush,* he thought as he bent a loose overhand knot in its end, then undid it.

Just beyond the end of the line of bluffs, he bent a loose figure-of-eight knot in a branch, then headed straight up the slope, aiming at a broken tree and adding overhand knots on bush branches every five yards or so. At the base of the splintered tree, he looked back down the slope, recording in his mind its appearance. He looked around for other splintered trees and saw none similar.

Continuing straight up, he turned frequently to see if the splintered tree was still in view. A bit farther up, the slope rounded, and through the trees, he could see the golden grasses of an open meadow. He stopped. There were voices. He slid behind a tree trunk.

Not thick enough to hide me.

He rolled behind some low shrubs. Through the branches and leaves, he saw a platoon of soldiers loosely marched past, out in the meadow only fifty yards away, only five yards of this through his screen of bushes and trees. Another platoon followed it, and a third. He looked back to spot the splintered tree. To find safety. He couldn't see it.

A fourth platoon passed, and in the gap behind it, he slowly edged backwards deeper into the woods, farther from the meadow. He heard the faint rumble of another platoon as he turned and headed straight down to find the splintered tree.

His knots led him back down the slope, and he untied them as he passed until he came to the figure-of-eight knot. He untied it and turned left, toward the beginning of the line of bluffs and followed along their base, then sidled around the ledge on the block and continued to the corner. He looked across to the slab and liked what he saw.

Only a small corner of the canvas is visible. That can easily be disguised with a couple of rocks and a shrub.

He turned the corner and sidestepped along the ledge, reaching for high handholds at the bulge. Once he was through the waterfall, he leapt across the stream and onto the slab, and he was halfway across it before Maria noticed him, and shook with a gasp at the startle.

"We need to be much more watchful," he said without any greeting. "Quickly, hide everything from view, then inside, under the canvas."

There was a quick gathering of things which were strewn about, and the women were soon inside while David snapped a few branches off the shrubs and arranged them to cover the corner of the canvas.

"I watched five platoons of soldiers march past. They're just above us at the moment, not much more than a hundred metres higher than here. A platoon is about eighty soldiers, there are three platoons in a German infantry company, so there are at least two companies just up there," he said, pointing up at the canvas roof.

"What are they doing up here? Why so many of them?" Rachel asked.

"I hope they're up here on exercise, a training exercise, not on a search mission. There could have been more platoons go by before I got there. There could be more following the ones I saw."

"So what do we do now?" Maria asked.

"Not much we can do. Fritz has us outnumbered at least a hundred and sixty to one, probably a lot more. Likely a whole battalion. We need to make sure there is no sign of us if anyone stumbles onto this little nook. It's unlikely anyone would do the traverse over there, along the other side of the gully. It's obvious that it leads nowhere. We need to make sure we give Fritz no reason to want to cross over to here."

He pulled his notebook and pen out of the pocket of his small rucksack, opened the cover and made a mark on the calendar. "Let's do some thinking. This is Saturday, the first of May." He looked at his watch and wound it. "It's five past eleven. We're all safe, we're healthy, we're fit, we're well rested and well fed. We have a great supply of fresh running water, we even have some heated. We have a good supply of food, a cosy shelter, a warm bed and warm friends. Except that we are surrounded by Fritz, this seems to be near paradise."

"How long does a training exercise last?" Maria asked.

"I don't know about the German ones, but when we did our training on the Salisbury Plains in England, before we headed across to trenches in Belgium, they were usually two days, sometimes three. We did none longer than three days."

"I had missed that it's May already," Rachel said. "Did you also train on holidays? "Today is May Day, a holiday in Baden und Württenburg."

"War doesn't take a break for such things as holidays or Sundays. It doesn't take a break for anything," He nodded his head toward the west. "There's a lot of fighting going on across the Rhein, over in the Vosges Mountains in Alsace and Lorraine. The hills here are likely a good training area for that. Let's hope Fritz isn't going to be practising hillside tactics past our cosy little nest."

"How long can we stay here?" Maria asked. "I guess the real question is how much food do we have?"

"I probably brought enough dried goods to feed all of us for six or seven days," David said as he thought of his purchases. There's still some ham on the bone and my big piece of soft cheese. Lots of salt and peppercorns."

"I packed all our dried meat," Rachel added, "there must be four kilos of it. We're almost out of fresh bread, I have some more dried to add to David's, we have plenty of butter and two large pieces of hard cheese and a smaller soft one, a Munster. We have onions, turnips, carrots and potatoes to last for several more days, close to a week, probably. We don't have any caviar or asparagus, and our wine cellar is empty, but I'm sure we'll survive."

"What do you mean, our wine cellar is empty?" Maria looked at her mother with a wide grin. "I had some spare space in my pack, so I slid in four bottles of Dada's 1911 Bestes Fass. I didn't think you'd mind."

"Much better than leaving it there. Did you bring glasses? I probably don't even need to ask, do I?"

"Of course I did, Mama, three of the smaller ones wrapped up in all the cottons. The wine's far too good to drink from tin cups, and I didn't forget the corkscrew this time," she added with a giggle. "I also put in big bundles of dried plums, apricots and cherries and the last of the hazelnuts."

"So it looks like we're going to have to rough it," David said with a grin so wide it hurt his lip wound. He looked slowly from face to face and added, "But we're tough, we can survive."

Chapter Fourteen

Maria looked closely at David's stitches. His grin had pulled apart a short fissure in his lip, and a small bead of blood grew slowly there. She had seen the bead as it started, but before she could get to him with a piece of gauze, the blood had grown too heavy and rolled down his chin.

She laid him back, bunching up the bedrolls beneath him into a pillow for his head, then pressed the small wad of gauze against the split and held it. "You are such a beautiful creature," she said softly, "a magnificent man, a wonderful friend. I've known you for two and a half days. I feel as if I've known you forever."

He nodded slightly, almost not at all, not wanting to move his mouth. He wanted to simply melt into her care. To submit to her, to let her minister to his wounds. He had missed this since he had reached his mid-adolescence and felt he needed to reject his mother's attentions. He had often wondered why he had done so.

She had done nothing to deserve my rejection. I only pretended to her she was unimportant to me. Why? To make me seem more important? Was it to show my independence? To make me feel stronger?

When I get home, I must let her know I love her, that she is still my best friend, that she has never ceased to be. I probably avoided her, embarrassed by my maturing, probably more the shame from what I was doing with Sister Clemencia. How stupid all of that was. How stupid it still is.

David was so deeply into his thoughts he had missed Maria's questioning, or even if she had been questioning. Her voice had become rather insistent by the time he realised she was waiting for a response. He didn't even know the question or even if there had been one.

"I'm sorry, Maria, I was thinking of my mother and of how much I miss her. My mind was completely elsewhere. I don't know what you were saying or asking."

"Oh God, David... Oh, I'm so sorry to interrupt your thoughts, your memories. My question is so tiny in comparison. Here you are, half the way around the world from home, away from your family, wounded, far into enemy territory, now surrounded by enemy, and some dumb girl is asking you if you like her."

"Do I like her? What's not to like? But like is such an inadequate word for what I feel — I love her — I don't even know what that means, but it says it better."

She squeezed his hand lightly, but the worried expression was still on her face. "I'm so sorry for interrupting your thoughts of your —"

He raised his hand to interrupt. "I need to be here, to be here in the present, not daydreaming of other times, other places. I would rather be here than anywhere else. Trying to be anywhere else is a waste of time and a big waste of energy. We miss what's here, what's now. We miss the experience of the present, we miss seeing opportunities as they arise. So, thank you for bringing me back."

"I love your way of thinking. I love your energy and your spirit." The concern melted from her face as she spoke. "Men usually keep their thoughts and their feelings, hidden. You — you're wide open, so easy to understand, so easy to be with."

"I'm delighted you think so..." He paused. "You're pressing rather hard on my lip. How's the bleeding?"

"Sorry, distracted." She lifted the gauze and looked. "The bleeding has stopped. It was a tiny rupture in your dry lips. I'll leave it open for now. You'll have to remember not to smile so widely, not to stretch it too much again. How long have these stitches been in?"

"This is Saturday, I was stitched-up Monday mid-morning, so five days now. Did the wound reopen?"

"No the wound's intact, and the stitches can come out now. Five days is sufficient for facial lacerations, longer than that can cause more suture scarring. The blood supply to the face is greater than other parts of the body and healing is faster. Elsewhere, a week to ten days is more normal." She stroked his short whisker stubble.

"I have a small personal kit, tweezers and nail scissors which will do a fine job. I'll start with your cheek, but I'll have to be careful not to mistake beard stubble for stitches," she giggled. "How old is the beard?"

"A bit over a week now. I last shaved on Friday after my bum had been stitched-up."

"Your bum?"

"I got a small rip from pieces of exploding shell, and I was moved back behind the lines to have it repaired."

"I'll have to look at that. I've not seen your bare backside, only your front. Your front is so intriguing to me, I never thought to check elsewhere."

"You're making me swell, Maria."

"What? So simply?"

"I can never predict what pumps it up. Sometimes has a mind of its own."

"Can it wait until I've done your face? Or should I start lower down toward your butt?"

"My father frequently reminded me it's necessary to start at the bottom and work up." He looked into her eyes and chuckled.

"Off with your trousers, then. Mama, take his shoes off and pull down on his cuffs. Let's get to work."

He undid his belt, unbuttoned his front and lifted his butt to help Rachel tug his trousers down. He rolled over as she finished.

"It's so long, lots of ragged tears. So many stitches all over the place. Looks good, though, there's no redness, no swelling." She leaned to smell the wound. "Smells clean." She kissed his butt cheek.

"The medic at the ADS said it was mostly shallow, a few chunks of meat missing, but not serious."

"What's ADS?" Maria asked, as she continued to examine the wound across the top of his left buttock.

"I don't exactly know. It was the second place I was walked to from the trench. The first one was the RAP, Regimental Aid Post, where I was examined, bandaged and accompanied farther back."

"Is it sore?"

"No, not really. Just a bit tender. I looked at it when I got my room in the gasthaus. Difficult to see back there, even with my little mirror. I removed the bandages and daubed it with gauze. There was no blood, not even the yellow oozing which I still had on my face. I soaked in the bathtub for a long while, then taped layers of gauze over it. After another soak in the tub on Thursday evening before dinner, I left the dressing off. It had been totally clean."

"It looks good. There's some puckering from stitches which bridge missing flesh, there's scabbing on the shallow scrapes, but I think the stitches can come out. That high on your buttock, there is little movement, little to stretch and reopen the wound. Our instructor said there'd possibly be a bit of bleeding and oozing as the stitches come out. Maybe a bit of pain. This must have made a mess of your trousers."

"Ripped the entire seat out of both them and my union suit."

"What's a union suit?"

"Underwear, a soft wool suit the Army issued me for extra warmth under my trousers and shirt. I ordered replacements for it and for my trousers from the Quartermaster. One of the stretcher bearers taped-up the seat of my trousers as the medic was stitching me back together. He did a terrific job on them, taping mostly inside."

Maria knelt between his legs and dabbed the wound with alcohol. She lifted the first stitch with tweezers and snipped the thread. "Tell me if this hurts," she said as she tugged gently with tweezers on the end of the suture to dislodge it. "We practised with stitches on oranges in school, but this is my first real one. They said some will be difficult to get moving, but this first one was easy."

"It's a strange feeling, almost like a little tickle inside."

"At school, we were told to start by removing every second stitch to make sure the edges of the wound stay together." She continued along the longest laceration, leaving half the sutures in place. Then she began removing stitches from the side tears, finished them and worked her way back along the long tear. "Your butt looks really good."

"Yes, I thought it had healed well when I looked at it with the little mirror."

"No, not the wound, David." She giggled. "I meant your butt. You've a beautiful butt. I'm curious, though, these balls dangling and wagging around down here between your legs; they must get in the way when you walk, when you move. Where do all your dangling parts go? Women have such a tidy arrangement."

"I've never thought about it — I guess I simply let them do what they will — except when moving to sit down. I learned long ago to hand myself an automatic little heft as I do, to prevent sitting on tender things. Are you done back there?"

"Done except for the admiring, a cleaning with alcohol and some taping. Then we can start on the other side."

She finished the cleaning and put the tape directly onto the wound. "The tape will hold the edges together, keep the area clean and prevent chafing on your trousers. It'll hurt a bit when it's removed, and we'll have to be careful with the scabs, but this is the best way to do it in our current circumstances." She finished applying the tape, then kissed both butt cheeks and said, "Roll over, let the nurse examine the rest of you."

Rachel had been watching and admiring her daughter's nursing. "You two need privacy. I'll go —"

"It's not safe outside now with Fritz wandering through the area." David shrugged his shoulders. "Besides, I've nothing I'm ashamed of having you see. What about you, Maria?"

"I have nothing to hide from Mama."

"What about you, Rachel?"

"I love watching you two interact, but you need your privacy. I'll roll over and see if I can catch up on sleep."

After Rachel had turned her back, David rolled over. Maria put her fingers under his balls and lifted them, rotating them to examine and study. "Tell me about these things. Yesterday when you got out of the warm water to dry, they were dangling nearly half way to your knees. By the time we began to dress, they were up almost out of sight. Now, they are somewhere in between — they act like a coblenz."

"Coblenz? I'm familiar with the city, I went through there earlier this week, but I miss the analogy."

"It's a toy, a pair of wooden discs on an axle that you play with and spin to roll up and down a string, like this." She demonstrated.

"A yo-yo? We call it a yo-yo. Yes, I guess they are like that. They go up and down to regulate their temperature. I learned they need to be at a cooler temperature than the rest of the body, so the yo-yo, the coblenz is the regulator. When it's hot, they hang low."

"How low do they go?"

"I don't know, I've never checked, though the left one is always lower. I know how high they go, though. Let me show you." He worked his left one up inside his pubes, then did the same with the other. She was left holding an empty bag.

"This is very stretchy skin," she said as she pulled it.

He took hold of it and stretched it across his thigh and let go. They watched it sit there a while before beginning to retreat. "Watch this." He tensed his abdominal muscles, and the two balls popped back out into his sack, pulling the stretched flap off his thigh.

"You love your body, don't you? I love your familiarity with it."

"It's the only one I've ever explored closely. Yes, I enjoy it — I enjoy how it works. I figured out long ago I can't expect to know anyone else unless I know myself first. I've spent a lot of time alone, learning about myself, about how I work. Physically and spiritually."

He paused to look at her, tilting his head. "Maybe it's time I start learning about someone else. I've been physically close to women, but I've never been emotionally close to any. Other than a few parts, I know nothing about women. Learning about you seems a great place to start."

"We can start by doing something about your swelling here."

"But that's me, not you. I want to learn about you."

"But it is me too. It's a huge part of my interest, of my curiosity right now.

I've not seen one before. Well, never a man's. I used to see the tiny ones on my brothers when we were young, but I had no idea these things grow so much. I've never examined one." She held it, then moved it around as she observed, sliding the skin on and off the head and studying its structure and action.

"Besides my brothers', the only one I'd seen before yours was in the strange drawings in the anatomy book at school this week. The bodies were drawn sliced in half like a hog at the butcher shop. I couldn't recognise anything familiar on the drawing of the woman, and I assumed the drawing of the man was as misleading. That was a big part of my curiosity a couple of nights ago."

She smiled at him as she pushed it down to his belly and watched it spring back, then pulled it down toward his knees and let it pop back up. "So your penis is very much about me at the moment. See, you've already learned something about me. That I'm curious."

"You're certainly not shy, either. You're confident and self-aware."

"I'm also hot and completely wet. Let me get a bit more comfortable." She took off her shirt and the camisole under it, undid her trousers and slid them off. "Do you mind if I sit on you while I examine your cheek?"

He throbbed at the sight of her nakedness. "Please, go right ahead, you're the nurse, you seem to know what's best for me."

"Just lie still," she said after she had slipped him into position. She slowly moved back and forth, taking a closer look at the stitches in his cheek and then moving back for a wider view, then a closer one, then wider.

Maria's examination routine slowly increased in speed. After a few minutes, she tensed. Her buttocks quivered and her breathing grew deeper and quicker. Random twitching shook her body, she threw her head back and opened her mouth wide, let out a roar, scrunching her eyes. Her whole body quivered, then convulsed and again, and again, and again.

Her hands kneaded the bedroll as her head dropped and hung while her chest rapidly expanded and contracted with deep breathing. When it had slowed, she lifted her head, leaned down to kiss him gently and went back to her slow examination of the stitches in his cheek. A closer view, a wider one, closer, wider...

After two more cycles of cheek examination and two more gentle kisses, she asked him, still lightly panting, "What can I do to help you?"

"Nothing else at all — this is truly exquisite. I've been holding back for you, allowing you play. You let me know when you're ready to finish, and I'll be right there with you."

"Let's do it this time, I'm familiar with all your stitches now." Maria giggled, then together they slowly climbed to a huge shuddering release. She collapsed onto him, and they lay gasping with wide smiles on their faces.

"Careful you don't tear your lip again," she panted as she tenderly stroked his face and lightly ground her mound against him, shuddering anew.

Chapter Fifteen

"I never imagined such a thing was possible," Rachel said after a few minutes. "Such incredible passion, such beauty, such pure animal freedom and enjoyment... Sorry, I couldn't help hearing."

"I had forgotten you were here, Mama. I had forgotten there was much else other than David and me, there were times it was so intense that David wasn't even here."

"That's interesting — I wonder if Fritz is still up there. What time is it?" David pulled his left arm out from under Maria's collapsed body. "Five minutes past noon. If they're like the French and the Belge, they'll have stopped for lunch five minutes ago."

"Unfortunately, they are not that predictable," Rachel said. "The Germans will work until the task is done. The French, though, will stop a hundred-hour-job five minutes before final completion if the clock intervenes."

"Mama, can you pass me two pieces of cotton, we're rather messy over here." Maria giggled, then continued, "I must get on with nursing. I've a wounded soldier here in need of care."

David and Maria pulled apart, and she wiped him with one piece of toweling as she sat on the other. "This is still so large, how do you hide all this in your trousers?"

"It'll go down a bit more, it's been up for a long time, and has had some heavy exercise. Usually takes a while longer after this kind of treatment."

David stuck his head out through the triangle and looked around. The sun was coming directly into the gully, and all the pools were bathed in its rays.

He leaned out farther and looked across at the entrance ledge. It was empty. He scanned the tops of the cliffs and still saw them as being impossible to approach safely. He looked at his watch again as he unbuckled it. *Twelve past noon.*

He pulled back inside and smiled. "Bath time. A quick dip, a soap and a rinse. I'm going to rinse under the waterfall."

He and Maria scampered out. The sun had heated the dark sandstone and gabbro, the entire nook was wonderfully warm, almost hot. Rachel hesitated, then shrugged, undressed and joined them. Six minutes later they were back in the shelter, dried and dressing.

"Let me do your cheek stitches," Maria said. "Properly this time."

"That was very proper the last time." He chuckled. "You'll now need to do it improperly."

She carefully snipped and pulled out the stitches and wiped his cheek with an alcohol-soaked piece of gauze. "We're down to your last roll of this, but we won't need so much after..."

There was a series of cracking sounds above them, followed by loud voices, guttural German voices. Excited voices, then more cracking and a scream. There was a sharp crack and thud close beside them and the sounds of falling rocks and branches. Voices came from above again, *"Oh, mein Fick! Leutnant Herzog!"*

David knew it was impossible to see in on the nook from above, but still he was cautious as he poked his head out through the triangle. Ten feet in front of him was a man in a German officer's uniform. There was a growing pool of blood on the sandstone beneath his head. He was still, face down, his neck at an impossible angle. The strange-looking wood and leather case, which was fastened to his belt, was skewed onto the middle of his back.

Looks like his pistol holster.

He scanned the cliff tops again, listening to the sounds of cracking and rustling tree branches, snapping of shrubs, dislodged rocks. One rock hit the edge of the canvas and bounced off.

A small one, fortunately.

The excited voices continued above. He looked again at the body, paused for a few moments, then crawled out.

He unclipped the cased weapon from the officer's belt and held it out toward Maria, who was in the triangle watching. She stepped across to take it from him and picked up the clips of ammunition he had removed from the pouches. After a pause, David dragged the inert body the six feet to the brink of the slab and rolled it over, listening to the dull thud as it hit the next ledge, barely audible over the chatter of voices and breaking branches on the cliff tops.

"Wir kommen von unten. Bleiben Sie ruhig," called a concerned voice from above. The cracking and twig snapping continued, moving away from them as the sounds gradually faded.

David quickly looked around, picked up the lieutenant's spiked black leather helmet, examined it, then dropped it over the edge before he turned and scurried back to the shelter.

"Was he dead?" Maria asked.

"Must have been, his neck appeared snapped. Regardless, after his last fall, he's dead now, and we're still alive. We'll have to remain quiet while they search."

"They said they were going to come from below."

"That's their only logical choice. And they have the time. This is likely a training exercise they're on, but even if it's a patrol, they'll pause to find their missing and injured. Even in battle, an effort is made whenever possible. Fortunately, they've headed across that way," he said pointing to the rock wall beside them. "We're safe for the moment. There's no way into here past the cliffs on this side, and the line of bluffs will lead them below us when they head back across to the stream."

"What if some have gone around the other side," Maria asked.

"We have a few minutes before the first of them could find their way into here. I'll find a way to cover or disguise the blood over there and the trail to the edge. You two rearrange our camouflage to make it appear more natural. Grub out more bushes to place beside the rock to make the shelter impossible to spot from the corner. Quickly, we have only a few minutes."

After they had finished and were back inside, David picked up the strange-looking weapon. He had not previously seen anything like it. He flipped the hinged wooden top of the case and pulled out a long-barrelled pistol. After he had made sure it was unloaded, he read the stamped name:

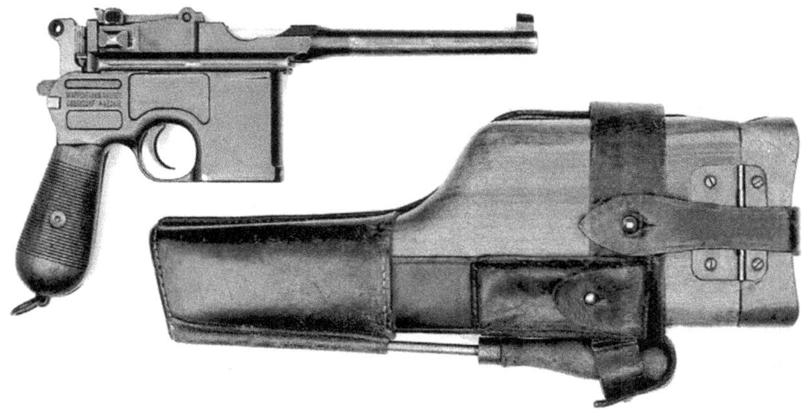

WAFFENFABRIK MAUSER
OBENDORF A NECKER

He slid the carved oak case out of its leather harness and examined it. A fitting on its small end clipped into the metal frame of the pistol's handle, converting the pistol into a rifle. He turned it in his hands, admiring ingenuity and engineering.

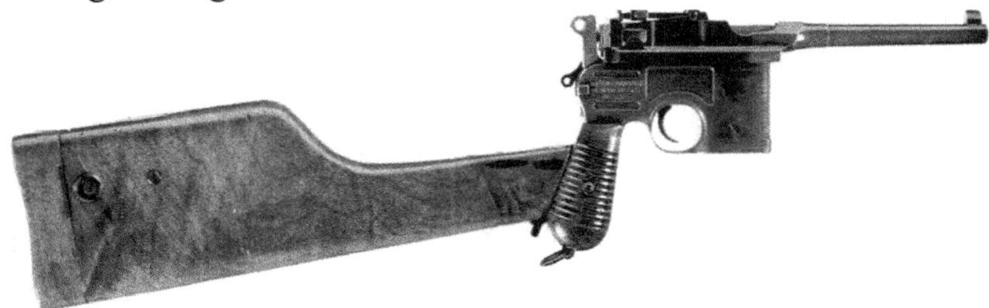

In the leather harness were a cleaning rod and a pocket with a zigzag spring. *A spare magazine spring*, he recognised. Attached to the side of the harness were two darker leather pieces, one a sheath with a long sharp knife stamped *JA Henckels. Solingen. Zwillingswerk,* the other cylindrical and containing a three-section collapsible brass telescope.

David familiarised himself with the gun's operation, cleaned it, flipped the safety lever, loaded it from a ten bullet clip and stood it against the rock just inside the edge of the canvas. "It's semi-automatic, we need only aim and work the trigger. We have five clips, fifty bullets, so we can hold off Fritz here for a while if it comes to that, but I hope it doesn't. I hope we don't need to use this."

After he had finished with the gun, Maria removed the rest of his cheek stitches. Then they sat quietly, leaning against the rock, gnawing on pieces of landjäger. His jaw was working better now, but he was surprised to find it easier to chew on his wounded side.

Probably to do with the levering or twisting of my jaw. The stitches are irritating my gums, but this flavour is too delicious to stop.

The discomfort finally caused him to stop eating. Still unfamiliar with the geography of his two missing teeth, he ran his tongue around and explored, trying to count the stitches in his mouth. Most were too fine and close together for that, but he did count three in the new gap from the missing teeth.

As he was concentrating and running his tongue around, Maria had been watching him. "What's wrong, David? You appear concerned."

"Nothing — I'm exploring to find what the damage was inside. I haven't done it before — guess it's been too sore until now."

"Let me look." She turned and knelt in front of him. "Open wide, let me see."

"I can't open wider than this. Still too sore back in the hinge."

She gently pulled his lower lip down. "I didn't realise you had stitches on the inside. Many fine stitches. I guess I should have examined more carefully when —"

They heard excited voices below them, over the lip of the slab. The soldiers had found their officer. They were about thirty feet below them, at the base of the cliff a few yards away. Fortunately, the splashing of the waterfall erased the sounds of their quiet talking.

There was a loud voice, bellowing like the sound of a drill square sergeant. It broadcast to the searchers across the slopes that they had found Leutnant Herzog. That he was dead. To tell the *Feldwebel* they would be bringing his body up to the top.

"That is very good for us." David pointed out toward the precipice. "They've found him, so the search is finished. They'll likely feel spooked about this area, probably go well out of their way to avoid it."

"What about the weapon?" Rachel asked, seeming quite concerned. "That's an unusually fine piece. Won't they search for it?"

"Possibly for a short while, then someone in authority will dismiss it as having fallen off his belt and bounced farther down the escarpment. I left the ammunition pouches unfastened, so they'll likely think any clips he had there had fallen out in his tumble, so we're safe here for a while."

"I'm still trembling a bit much to go back to examining your lip just now." Maria looked at her shaking hands. "Let's sit here and be thankful we're all safe, see if we can relax — see if I can relax."

They sat quietly in their private thoughts with their ears finely tuned to the slightest sound. There was none but the murmur of the water cascading down the face and splashing onto the slab.

After a few minutes, she looked at him and said, "I need to get back to work. I hadn't realised your lip was so damaged. It must have been incredibly painful."

"I missed most of the intense pain — I lay in no-man's-land for many hours unconscious. It was almost dawn when I came to, having lain there on the ground for ten or eleven hours." He continued the remainder of the story that had brought him to Freiburg.

"What a horrid thing the Kaiser has done to us all," Rachel said. "Get back to your nursing, Maria, we've got to make sure our young hero mends properly. He needs to lead us the rest of the way to Switzerland."

Maria knelt in front of David again and tenderly probed at the outside of his lip. "It looks very good. Still some swelling, but clean and sweet smelling. Does this hurt?" she asked, pressing gently at the end of the wound, almost at the point of his chin.

"The bone is tender underneath, but there's little pain in the flesh."

She moved her finger up along the line of sutures, asking him to let her know where there was pain. She got to the line of his lip, and he said, "It's numb there. There is almost no sensation." He ran his tongue across his lower lip and then down inside. "The numbness is only on my lip, down the inside," he paused and ran his tongue down again. "Down farther inside there's good feeling."

"Please let me know if this hurts," she said as she carefully pulled his lip out and down.

He said nothing as she pulled and moved it side to side, then put a finger in behind it and gently squeezed with her thumb. "No pain? Not sore?"

"Just a bit tender, but it feels surprisingly fine. I'd much rather have you doing this than anyone else. What do you see in there?"

"It appears we can take out the stitches up your chin to your lip and tape it. The ones in your tooth gap can also come out. I'd like to keep a few of the inside stitches in place a while longer, and also a few on your lip. The split from your smile showed it's quite fragile at the moment with its dryness." She ran a finger along it.

"It looks like your lip had been sliced completely through to the gum line, then down your chin. I don't know if the doctor used deep suturing to hold the internal structure in place, But looking at the rest of his fine work, he probably did, and they're probably absorbable. What do you think?"

"You're the professional here, I'm simply the patient."

"I have almost no training with this, but what I sense seems right. Mama, I need your opinion. Come look at this. Rinse your hands with the alcohol first."

Rachel repeated the examination, pulling, probing and squeezing, and then said, "I think you're right, Maria, it's probably safer to keep a few of the inside stitches and some of the ones in the lip in place another day or so. Do you need help?"

"You can hand me the scissors as I need them and take the removed sutures from me." When she had finished, she wiped his chin and lower lip with alcohol and cut a small piece of tape, rounded its corners and applied it over the scar.

"With the apparent internal sutures, it's safe to remove the stitches from inside the lip. Leave only the two on top where the skin has dried. I wish I had some Vaselineöl to moisten there."

"What about the stitches on the inside of my cheek? They irritate my gums when I chew."

"What? Let me see.." She ran a finger around inside. "There's a vee-shaped line in here, same as the outside. The outside looked so cleanly repaired, I didn't even think to examine inside. That was a terrible wound. Your face had been ripped to shreds."

"It was quite sore for a while, but it's so much better now."

She ran two fingers inside, gently pressing against her thumb from outside. "Is this sore? Does the pain increase when I do this?"

"Not so much anymore. Tender is a better word. A bit strange."

"You're so fortunate to have had a skilled surgeon do all of this, rather than have someone tie you up like a pot roast. I think we can also safely take out all these stitches. Leave only the two on the lip. What do you think, Mama?"

"You're much more the expert than I am with this, Maria. And it appears to me you're also quite the expert with other body parts," she added with a giggle.

"I'm just beginning to learn, Mama." She giggled back.

Chapter Sixteen

Maria finished removing the stitches, all but the ones across the rounding of David's lip. She gently cleaned the inside of his mouth and tenderly kissed him. "I've got to get your lips into good working order, I want to enjoy them."

He ran his tongue around the inside of his lower lip, through the gap in his teeth and again up and down the line of toughened tissue, the scar lines inside his mouth. "This is so much better. I hope you don't mind if I practice using them on you as I regain control."

"Oh, please do. Can we go lie in the sun? Would it be safe?"

"There hasn't been a sound from Fritz for a long while now. Not since they lugged Herzog back across the slopes. It seems their camp is on this side of the stream, likely near the top of Feldberg. Much better than it being on our entrance side. How long ago was that? When they left. I've lost track of time. I've been luxuriating in all this caring attention."

"Has to be close to half an hour, now," Rachel said. "We haven't heard a sound, not even above us. They must have done a wide skirt around this place."

"Let's hope they keep doing that," he said as he removed his watch and began unbuttoning his shirt. "Last one out in the sun is a — is a — is the last one in the sun."

He shuffled out of his shirt, kicked off his trousers and stripped off his socks. Maria had already crawled past him, stepping out of her trousers as she ran. He watched in awe as she spread her arms and twirled around, spinning on quick little steps. Rachel soon joined her, and they ad-libbed a *pas de deux* in the sun.

David stood entranced for a long while before he picked up the top set of bedding, and without taking his eyes off them but fleetingly, he walked to the spot he had calculated the sun would leave last. He spread the blanket and sat enjoying the girls gracefully play.

Such beautiful creatures, this is more like the way people should interact. This is so far from the hatred, the violence, the mayhem of the war.

His mind continued spinning.

War is so stupid, What's this one about? A family feud? A grab for more land? Kaiser Wilhelm is King George's cousin. They are both grandsons of Queen Victoria, yet here is Wilhelm causing the deaths of hundreds of thousands of young men, mostly men, but also many women. Why? Pride, mostly. Too proud to back down from a bad decision last year in —

"You're off in a dream world again, David," Maria said, rubbing her sweat-glistened body against his as she sat beside him on the blanket. Her chest was heaving, juggling her breasts as she puffed to regain her breath from the dancing. "Where have you gone this time?"

He looked at her and shook his head, "I was hypnotised by your graceful movements, the both of you, together, unfettered, free, joyous, beautiful expressions of life, magnificent creatures moving in harmony." He stopped himself short of continuing into the darker thoughts which had followed.

"We had an enchanting dance, so carefree. That's what life is meant to be, carefree, uninhibited, sharing. You should have joined us."

"I'm not a dancer, at least not on the floor, though I've been told by people who've seen me climbing, that it's as if I'm dancing on the rocks. I prefer that type of dancing — it's also free and unfettered — we need to get out of this damnable war."

She gave him a hug and a light kiss, then lay beside him, and patting the blanket, she said, "Come, lie beside me, let's get some sun. It's beneficial to your wounds."

David sat looking at her, then he shifted position, turning to sit beside her knees as he scanned up and down her body, from her face to her thighs, slowly caressing her with his eyes, looking without pausing anywhere to examine as he continued up and down slowly. He watched each time he returned to her face as it grew into an increasingly sublime expression.

"That feels so good," she said. "I've not thought of being massaged by eyes. Where did you learn that? It makes me feel so... So tingly all over."

"I learned it on the first of May in 1915 in a little nook in the Black Forest, inspired by an absolutely gorgeous woman."

"But you do it so well."

"I'm very inspired." He nodded his head toward her blond mound. "Tell me what you know about this exquisite part of you. What do you call it? I love the short hair-do, I love the way the little pink flaps peek out."

Rachel rose and pointed to the pools. "I'm heading for a soak to offer you two a little more privacy."

David and Maria watched her walk across the slab, and when she was out of earshot, David commented, "She has an amazing body for a woman in her forties. Firm, fit and... but back to this collection of delicate folds." He nodded to it. "So beautiful."

"I don't know what it's called in English, but I call it my button and grooves. In our textbook at school, it's called a *weibliche Scham*, that's such an awful name, *woman's shame*, for such a wonderful part."

"In English, it's called a *vulva*. I was curious and looked it up in a medical book in the library when I was on leave in Bristol. It comes from the Old Latin word for roll or wrapper. The drawings and pictures made them look mundane, not in the least inviting. Yours is so beautiful, but I must say, I've never looked closely at one. Every girl, every woman I've ever been with has been too shy to let me look closely."

"Maybe that's where the German name comes from. But why the shame? I like mine, it makes me feel so good."

"I like it very much as well. Where does it feel the best for you?"

"Here, on my little button, the book labelled it *Kitzler* — that's the German word for *tickler*. And it certainly is. It's extremely sensitive, so I can't rub it directly too much, it becomes too intense. I have to move the skin around it and only occasionally touch it directly with a wet finger, not a dry one. There's a wonderful source of slippery wetness once I get going," she rolled a knee aside, "down here inside the bottom of my lips."

"What if I licked it? Some of the Army fellows talked about licking. My saliva is slippery, and my tongue is soft."

"I'm sure I'd like that, probably love it. Would you want to do it?"

"I would love to, but let me study the geography first. It's such a wondrous combination of folds, and I've never been allowed to examine one closely before. This is exquisitely exciting for me; I hope you know that." He leaned close and shuddered. Such an intoxicating aroma. These flaps are so delicate and soft."

"They're also very stretchy, like your wrinkly pouch. Look." She ran a finger between them to separate, then pinched her right one and pulled it out. "I can stretch this one about five centimetres, the left one a little bit more."

"Are they sensitive?"

"Deliciously so. I sometimes close my legs and run my finger lightly along the parts which stick out, tickle them gently for a long while, dreaming, then a few firm strokes of my button sets me off."

She lifted her other knee and spread it down. He lightly pulled the small pink flaps apart and examined how they joined in an inverted vee, attached to the sides of her tickler toward the apex of her rounded lips. "You're so beautiful down here," he said with another light shudder. "You're so beautiful everywhere. I'll try not to scratch you with my whiskers and stitches."

After their intimacies, David and Maria joined Rachel and the trio spent the middle of the afternoon variously baking in the sun, cooling off under the spray of the cascade, rewarming and soaking in the shallow pools, having cold body massages from the pelt of the heavier flow falling in the narrow main stream of the waterfall, and enjoying warmer ones from each other.

"I wonder how much longer Fritz will remain up there exercising?" Maria asked.

"We don't even know if he's still there," David replied. "Though it would seem strange to come all the way up for only a few hours. It was shortly before 1100 when I saw the platoons marching past, coming across the fields.

How long does it take to climb from the valley to the saddle with a heavy pack?"

"It's about a thousand metres up from the valley and about a dozen kilometres," Rachel said. "We'd take about four hours."

"So the platoons, the companies could easily do it in five," he said. "Unless they were marching from an overnight camp along the ridges to the west, they were just arriving. A six o'clock start is not unusual. Early starts are part of the exercise."

"What about the dead officer? Won't that stop their exercise?"

"No, Maria. Injuries, no matter how serious, won't stop an exercise. Death and injury are a part of the game. War is a serious game, a deadly game." David shook his head. "I much prefer the games we've been playing here."

"How long will the ex —"

Maria was interrupted by the sound of a gun firing. Then another followed by many more. They seemed a long distance away, then came the echoing from the hills.

"Sounds like target practice. The shooting is too regular for anything else. It reminds me of the target practices at Valcartier and on the Salisbury Plains; the same patterns of sounds."

David carefully looked around, up along the top of the cliffs, both sides of the gully and across its back. He again confirmed it was impossible to see in. The slopes rounding back from the vertical precipices were too steep to approach, too slippery from the layers of wet vegetation, lichen and slime. Leutnant Herzog had demonstrated it was dangerous to approach their little hideaway from above.

"I'm going to check the view from the corner. See what Fritz would see if he found this little nook."

He got up and walked to the stream, crossed under the spray and sidled along the narrow ledge, edged around the bulge and stood at the corner looking into the gully.

Nothing of the canvas is visible. Except for the two beautiful women laying on the blanket, a cake of soap and some towels, I see nothing to suggest anyone is there. My God, she's so gorgeous. So innocent, so endearing, so horny.

The opposite side of the gully looked impossible to pass. It was obviously a blind end. He looked down at the waterfall at his feet, and he watched it splashing onto next slab, down where Leutnant Herzog had landed after his second fall.

He froze.

Holding his breath, he slowly plastered himself back into the rock face. With his chin tightly to his neck, he looked down and couldn't see them.

I'm now out of their line of sight, hidden by the slab.

He saw Maria and Rachel watching him. With his elbows kept back, he slowly put a finger to his lips and pointed down with the other hand, moving both hands to emphasise their messages.

With slow, calculated moves, he eased around the corner backwards, crouching to ensure he remained out of sight from below. At the bulge, he stood to manoeuvre past it and scramble back into the waterfall. He paused there under its cold pelt, trying to regain his calm.

Chapter Seventeen

"Two soldiers. Probably searching for Herzog's gun. Back inside ladies. Look around carefully. Make sure there is no trace of us. I'll grab the blanket, Maria the towels, Rachel the soap over there by the pool. What else is there?"

Once they were back inside, David said, "The shelter is completely invisible from over there. The gully looks impassible from the corner. The ledge is tricky, and it offers no temptation to continue unless you're seeking a perfect hiding place and a delightful spa."

"What's a spa?" Maria asked as they began dressing. "I love the way you flip your trousers to flop your penis inside."

"Mineral springs, hot springs. The relaxation and health resort built around them. We have some fine ones in the Rockies. Radium Hot Springs just starting. Banff Springs Hotel, such a marvellous place, an immense castle-like hotel built up in the mountains. I was there at an Alpine Club event two or three years ago."

"This would be a much better spa if Fritz would go away," Rachel said, as she leaned against the base of the rock face. "There's a town in eastern Belgium named Spa, I was told that's where the name comes from. Here, they're called *baden*. This whole area of Germany we're in is the Grand Duchy of Baden. There's a town north of Freiburg, I guess it's a city, named Baden-Baden."

"Baden, those are baths in English, aren't they? We went down through Bath on our way to Bristol a couple of times on leave when we were training on the Salisbury Plains. Stopped there for a night the second time. They said the Romans established baths there in the first century, eighteen or nineteen hundred years ago."

"Looks like we're not the first ones to enjoy bathing and luxuriating," Maria said with a laugh.

"Probably goes back thous..." He paused, put his hand up, then pointed to the gabbro block, toward the entrance to the gully.

They heard the scraping again. David reached across for the weapon, flipped off its safety and sat at the edge of the triangle. Relaxed, but ready.

"Helmut! Helfen, helfen Sie mir. Ich schlüpfe," came a desperate voice from close in front of them. There was a louder scraping, a scream, a hollow crack, a dull thud and a splash, followed by a clatter of falling rocks below.

David had quickly glanced out around the block of gabbro, sensing the source of the voice would be too concerned to see him. He saw the soldier hanging by his fingertips to the edge of the ledge below the bulge, on the slippery wet rocks in the splash of the waterfall. Then he had watched as the fingers lost their grips. First, one slowly, then another, followed quickly by all of them. He watched as a trouser leg snagged on a spike of rock just into the fall and spun soldier sideways, slamming his head onto the lip of the slab before he disappeared.

"Horst!" came the cry from below. *"Horst! Mein Gott! Horst, nicht du auch."*

David sat at the edge and listened, staring intently at the entrance ledge with one eye barely around the corner of the rock. He ran the scenes of the past several minutes through his mind.

Then he repeated them quietly for the women to hear, "I had seen only two soldiers below when I was at the corner, but I had taken little time to look. Horst had called for help from Helmut, not from anyone else. Is that Helmut below us now? Or is Helmut on the entrance ramp? I've heard no other voices, heard no other sounds. Is that Helmut below?"

Before either of them could answer, there was a loud, breaking voice from below, bellowing up the hillside, telling whoever that Private Smidt was dead, that he needed help to bring up the body.

There was no reply, his voice most likely lost in the noise of the continuing target practice. A minute later, with still no reply, the voice from below bellowed again, then they heard loud sobbing.

"That's Helmut down there. Maria, could you hand me my small mirror? It's in the side pocket of my small rucksack, the left one."

She brought it to him, and he said, "Lean back against the rock. Put your head here, like this." He adjusted her position and kissed her, then got up and moved back out through the triangle. After gathering a few small stones, he paused to look closely at the entrance before continuing along the base of the cliff about five feet.

He stood the mirror on the slab, looked at the angles, tilted and swivelled it. "Tell me when you have a view of the entrance."

"It's too low, all I have is the slab, lean in back a bit — more — a little bit more — there. That's the ramp. It looks like the edge of the bulge. Yes, I see the light colour below the bulge. Twist it a bit toward you — oops, the wrong way. More, a bit more... Stop. Back a tiny bit... There, I now have a view from the slab to a couple metres above the entrance. Hold it and I'll watch now." She giggled.

David carefully placed his gathered rocks behind the mirror and two at the bottom front. "I need a small bush to disguise this, how's the alignment? Does it need any adjustment?"

"Still perfectly centred."

He pulled two small boughs of needles off a pine and carefully arranged them around the mirror, breaking the impact of its hard edges and screening it from easy view from across the gully.

"That's ingenious, where did you learn that?" Maria asked as he came back in and sat in the viewing position.

"It's another of those things I learned on the first of May 1915 while relaxing at a spa in the hills of the Black Forest with two beautiful women," he said with a wide grin.

"Watch you don't split your lip again. You learn so much while relaxing at spas —magic with a mirror, eye massage, an alternate use for the tongue..." Maria drifted off dreamily.

"Did you enjoy that?"

"You saw how quickly and often I exploded. You must be joking. Next to you rooting around inside, I've never had anything so intense. Let me rephrase that. Next to you doing anything, I've never had such intense feelings. Physically or emotionally."

"Sex for two is much better than for one, I've always thought." He looked at his watch. "It's twenty to five, I'm going to check over the lip to see if I can spot Helmut."

He leaned over and kissed her. "These lips are working much better, feeling much better. Thank you for your excellent nursing."

He checked the mirror, delighted at how well it worked, then crawled out through the triangle and slowly walked toward the brink, stopping six feet from the drop. Moving his head slowly back and forth, he tried to safely catch a glimpse below. *Nothing.* He moved a few inches farther and bobbed again.

Still nothing of Helmut.

Finally, about four feet from the brink, he caught movement and got down on all fours to move slowly forward. He craned his neck and saw Helmut, a young lad barely needing to shave, slinging two rifles and slowly dragging the lifeless Horst across the slope, angling downward toward the left side.

Toward our safe side.

Back in the shelter, he explained what he had seen. He checked the mirror again to make sure the entrance ledge was clear, and the mirror was well-masked by the screen of pine boughs. He stepped out and pinched a sprig off a bough and brought it back into the shelter. "Do you know the secret of pine needles?"

"They have secrets?" Maria asked.

"Only to those who haven't taken the time to look enquiringly. These needles are bundled in pairs like the Scots pine we have at home. Other species of pine have three, four, five or six needles bundled together. The Ponderosa Pine has three needles, the white pine usually has five. It doesn't matter how many needles are in a bundle, pull them together like this." He ran his fingers from their base to their end. "They form a thin, spiralling cylinder of two, three, five, however many equal segments."

He handed the needle bundle to Maria, and she ran her fingers along the two needles, pulling them into a thin cylinder. "Amazing, where did you learn this?"

"From pausing to observe and to think. There's a lot of wonderful quiet time alone in the mountains, and we can learn much if we keep our eyes and minds open."

"The twist, what's that from?"

"My thought is it comes from the Coriolis effect, from the force of the earth's rotation, though I've not confirmed this."

He put up his finger. "But, let's get back to here, to our present situation. Let's pull out the map and guidebook. We haven't even checked where we are and what's around us."

After he had unfolded the map sheet to the appropriate panels, he said, "Let's play a game. With eyes only, quietly trace the route you think we've followed. Determine where you think we are. No talking. When everybody's ready, I'll count *one, two, three, go*, and we'll all put our finger on the spot we think we are. This will be fun, but it's also a serious game. It'll give independent opinions we can discuss."

They examined the unfolded panels, traced with their minds where they thought they had come, examined the contours and hachures. He looked from face to face at the smiles and nods when he asked, "Ready? Alright, one, two, three, go!"

Three fingers piled one atop the other. "So, the discussion now is: What if we're all wrong?"

"Hard to be wrong," Rachel said, "there is logically nowhere else we could be."

"The route we followed up and then across, the edge of those large fields, the distance below the saddle, the two broad ribs, the cirques, the stream, the lines of bluffs... I cannot see how we could be anywhere else but here." Maria tapped the spot on the map. "Was this little game another of your ideas dating back to May Day 1915?"

"You're getting good at guessing, Maria," he said with a grin. "It's much better to pay heed to your senses than to try to tell your mind what to do."

He opened the guidebook and placed it on the map sheet. "Here's a trail going down from the top of Feldberg through Brandenberg to Todtnau." He looked at the scale diagram. "A little over two hundred metres across the slope from us. Helmut probably came down it from the top with Horst to search for Herzog's gun."

"With so much gentle slope all around here, I'm surprised Herzog led his troops into this line of bluffs," Rachel said.

"Maybe he was another of those aristocratic buffoons like some of the British officers who make bad decisions for our armies." He paused and looked at them. "I led you into here, but that was to find a place to hide."

"I'm so glad — we're so glad you led us into here." Maria looked across at her mother. "We would most likely have been spotted with so many hundreds of soldiers wandering around out there. Even in this hidden nook, we've been visited twice. At least twice we know of."

Chapter Eighteen

"We should think of cooking dinner," David said, looking at his watch and winding it. "It's almost five. We have about an hour and a half of daylight left before we have to turn off the stove. Though I much prefer eating later, we need hot food for the night. The sun will soon be around the edge of the gully, and it will cool quickly."

"I can put together a big stew in short order. Carrots, turnips, onions, diced sausage then diced potatoes to thicken," Rachel said. "I'd love to brown the onions first, but the aroma might carry too far. Hold the garlic also. Safer to do a blander stew."

Maria pointed to a block of gabbro. "That rock over there, we can set-up the stove behind it, it's hidden from the entrance and not much more than two metres from here. We can sit inside, keep warm and out of sight while it cooks."

"And we can sit back enjoying cheese, crispbread and wine while we wait," David smiled and shrugged. "This is a spa, after all. Dining is rather refined at spas, from what I've seen. I'll try to convert a piece from that splintered tree trunk into a cheese board. You girls get dinner going."

"Have you something to cut it with?" Rachel asked.

"I have a folding knife. We have Herzog's sharp blade."

"I have a wire saw, a surgical bone saw in my pack. We use it to cut firewood up here when we're camping. I'll get it."

"Oh, my! That looks familiar," he said as she handed him the coiled piece. "Conrad had one exactly like this. He told me he got it from a surgeon from Vienna whom he used to guide in the mountains. We used it a lot in the valleys and up the ridges."

"Edom was given this one by one of his good wine customers, a surgeon from Freiburg..." Rachel paused and looked into David's eyes. "So who's Conrad?"

"An Austrian mountain guide, I met him in the mountains four years ago. The Alpine Club had brought him in to help expand its programs, summer climbing camps, instruction, guiding and so on. The club was newly founded, and he had a lot of spare time, so he climbed mostly solo until we met."

"So that's where your Austrian accent comes from," Maria said. "I was wondering."

"Yes, a wonderful friend. I learned so much from him besides the German. I wonder what he's doing now with the war..." David shook his head. "But, to present things. We have much to do."

They all went to work.

David examined the short piece of shattered tree trunk lying at the edge of the slab. He looked up to see where it might have come from and saw clinging to the cliff a thick, broken trunk with a ring of new branches reaching up toward the light past its splintered head.

Might have blown apart from a lightning strike, could be simply a windfall, but whatever the cause, it was a few years ago. The wood is now nicely seasoned.

He selected a section of a long tapering splinter and cut it off where it was about six inches wide and a little over an inch thick. With the saw a foot farther along, he made a second cut, and another foot farther along, he made a third. He had two foot-long slabs an inch and a quarter thick, one tapering from about six to seven inches wide, the other more regular.

As David sawed, he had thought of Conrad.

Strange. He's the only person I've been close with since Sister Clemencia. The only one I've felt free around... The only one I've allowed near is more the point.

He moved to a flat area of sandstone and sat to begin easing the slab's edges and corners. He then sanded the gently arched top face of the larger slab of wood.

The only one I've allowed near until Maria. So strange. Such a different closeness, though. So wonderfully different. Intimate. So many unfamiliar feelings, emotions...

He shook his head, looked at the slab, tapped the sanding dust out of it, blew it off and washed it under the waterfall. He presented the new cutting board to Rachel, saying, "It's a bit rough still, and too late for the onions, carrots and turnip, but it'll make it easier doing the sausage and potatoes."

"That was quick." She flipped the board around in her hands as she examined it. "You could do well selling these in the market, I've seen worse there."

"Back to the grindstone." He looked at her and chuckled. "We'll have a cheese board in another five or six minutes."

"The stew will be another half hour or more. Maria has the wine chilling under the waterfall. Bring it over when you come. She's inside, digging out the glasses, the cheeses and the flatbreads."

A while later, after taking a sip, David picked up the bottle to read the label. "Tell me about this. Its aroma and flavours are even more complex than the one the other night."

1911er Kaiserstuhl Gewürztraminer
Kabinettwein Bestes Fass
E. und R. Meier
Gottenheim, Baden

"The 1911 is one of the finest vintages in the region in many years, and it was our first one of any size." Rachel gazed into her glass and sighed. "The vineyards were finally maturing, the vines were then six years old. We made spectacular wine that year, from both the Riesling and the Gewürztraminer..."

"So that's how that's pronounced, guh-voorts-truh-mee-nur," he said looking again at the label. "What's Gewürztraminer?"

"It's the grape variety, it means spicy Traminer, which is another grape variety, this one is its spicy cousin."

"It certainly is. The smell reminds me of my mother's baking. But there's also a lot of fruit. A complex smell."

"You should smell ginger, cloves, nutmeg and cinnamon among the spices," Maria said as she swirled her glass and held it to her nose. "Peaches and apricots also. Swirl the glass like this to coat the inside of the bowl. You'll get a bigger aroma."

He swirled and nosed again. "Wow! I see all those." He took a sip and looked up. "I really like this. It smells so sweet, but it has such a crisp flavour, not sweet at all. Not like that insipid stuff they call tea south of the border... Wow! I love this."

"It was my first wine," Maria said. "My first wine that wasn't watered-down. We had it on my sixteenth birthday, soon after we had begun harvesting the 1912. I much prefer the 1911, particularly from this barrel — I miss Dada so much."

She set her glass down, tried to staunch the flow of tears, then gave up and let them pour down her cheeks as she sat staring blankly. Her shoulders twitched, then she surrendered, allowing deep sobs to convulse her whole body.

Leaning over, she pressed her head against her mother's shoulder, under her chin and continued sobbing, gradually more quietly. Rachel ran her fingers through Maria's hair and hummed a soothing tune into her ear, rocking with her gently.

Maria slowly calmed and lay there for a long while before she said, "Thank you, Mama. You haven't hummed Pachelbel to me for many years, not since before we left Switzerland... That seems so long ago now."

"We're almost back there again, Sweetheart," Rachel said. "So close I can almost taste it."

"Taste — that's what we need to do," Maria said, as she sat up, leaned over and kissed David, then continued, "I'm so delighted you like Dada's wine... Sorry for the outburst, but I do miss him so much."

He put his glass down, wrapped his arms around her and said nothing as he gently kneaded her back with his hands.

"Cheese..." She shook her head. "We have a delicious selection of cheeses: Munster, Appenzeller, Gruyère, Butterkäse, all laid out on a nice board — an old family board we picked up at a spa in the Black Forest on a May Day back in '15. We also have knäckebrot. It will all go wonderfully with the wine."

She picked up her glass, looked at it and continued, "I'm running low, who's hogging the bottle?"

With glasses replenished, Rachel introduced and described the cheeses; two hard ones from Switzerland, a crusted soft one from the Vosges mountains across the Rhein in Elsass and a soft buttery-sweet one from Baden.

"Your cheeses are so much more delicious than the one I had chosen," he said. "Such wonderful flavours. Wild, complex flavours. They're so different from the bland cheddar we had in England and the boring things they fed us in Belgium."

Rachel got up twice to stir the pot and to add more water to the stew. On a third trip, she took the stew pot off and put on a lidded pot of water to boil for tea.

They leaned back against the rock, which was still slightly warm from the day's sun, and enjoyed their second course with spoons from deep bowls. David got up and turned the stove off when he heard the rattle of the lid as the water came to a boil. He dropped in the tea ball, brought the pot over and continued with his stew.

As they sat sipping their tea and nibbling pieces of dried fruit, Rachel said hesitantly, "You seem rather experienced and casual with sex, David — you're still young — I don't know if you're even out of your teens. I'm curious."

"I'm twenty. I had formal training at school."

"Formal training?" Maria asked in close harmony with Rachel. They all laughed.

Maria was the first to continue. "They do that in Canada? They don't even talk about it in school over here."

"It was private tutoring after class."

"Private tutoring?" Again asked in harmony.

"I was taken aside by one of the nuns when I was a few weeks into my tenth school year. A Catholic school. I had just turned sixteen, and she told me I needed additional work after school to improve my grasp of some subjects."

He took another sip of tea. "Partway into our first session, she told me she had noticed how I sometimes had trouble hiding myself in my trousers. She asked me if I needed assistance with learning ways to handle it." He looked at them, waiting for a response as they sat in silence with strange expressions he couldn't read.

Each is different, both unfamiliar to me.

"I guess I simply let it happen. I spent a lot of time after school taking private tutoring from Sister Clemencia. She started by hand, then by mouth, then a few sessions later, she hoisted her habit. She was quite young, probably not much more than twenty, and she was very hungry. Her mother and grandmother had forced her into the convent to finish her schooling, to become a novitiate and finally to take her vows as a nun."

"Why did she go along with their wishes?" Maria asked. "Why didn't she stand up for herself? Simply leave the convent when she realised... When she..."

"She talked about how it would ruin the family image, destroy her mother and grandmother if she left. As the second daughter, the tradition was that she become a nun, so she had crossed her fingers during the vows, hoping for a later escape. That's four years ago now — I wonder if she's still holding herself captive."

David paused and stared into his tea mug. "It's strange thinking back to that now. She was so embarrassed about having me look at her. Shame had been deeply drilled into her head, so I had to close my eyes and try not to touch her except with my..." He shook his head. "I guess I was too weak to refuse, and I allowed her to use me. No feelings but the physical ones. Great sensations they were, but so confusing. I'm probably still confused by it all."

Chapter Nineteen

David, Maria and Rachel sat for a long time after the last of the tea had been drunk, and they entertained themselves by telling stories from their pasts. It was just past eight thirty when there was a quick drop in temperature, which they all knew was the signal it was about to begin raining heavily.

The sounds of the advancing thunder had grown louder for the past twenty minutes or so. "Everybody up and out to pee," he said, "We're going to be pissed on from above very shortly. Probably our last dry chance before bed. We don't have to go far; the rain will rinse it away."

The three barely made it back into the shelter before the downpour began. As he stooped through the triangle, he said, "Be careful not to touch the canvas. It appeared properly oiled, and it should hold well against this, but let's not give it any excuse to leak."

Later they sat listening to the sounds on the canvas as the huge raindrops turned to sleet then quickly to hail. It was pitch black, and he couldn't see his hand even a few inches from his face, except in the fleeting light of the lightning. Some hailstones had bounced off the slab and in under the edge of the canvas. He flipped the side of the bedrolls farther in under cover.

"Fritz won't be out in this. It's probably safe to light the candle lantern to see how the shelter is holding against the thunderstorm. What do you ladies think?"

"The light won't carry far through the deluge," Rachel said. "Besides, I can't imagine anyone stupid enough to be wandering around near these bluffs in these conditions. I think it's safe while the storm continues so heavily."

David was feeling around in the back pocket of his large rucksack for the folding lantern, a candle and a tin of matches when the inside of the shelter lit up. He looked around and saw a small cylindrical lantern and Maria's yellowed face smiling at him from the shadows behind it.

"Guess we don't need mine." He chuckled. "Let's take a look around, check if water is coming in anywhere."

The rock walls beside and behind them were overhanging, and except for one small water runnel off the gabbro block, they were dry. Water at the bottom of the runnel flowed down the slight slope of the slab and out into the wetness beyond. The canvas was dry inside but for the two damp lines running along the creases, which had been caused where he had folded it for packing. There were no drips from them.

No drips, yet.

They checked the slab at the upper side of its gentle slope. Dry, except for scattered hailstones which had bounced through the small gap between canvas and rock.

"I think we can safely crawl into bed, snuff the candle and let the sounds of the storm put us to sleep," David said as be began undressing. "Looks like we're rather tight here." He got into another delicious sandwich and was quickly asleep.

The light of the moon woke him. It was still. The front had passed, the sky was filled with stars, and the moon had just rolled into the gully, showing the slab white with snow. He looked at his watch, fascinated with the way the hands glowed in the dark.

A bit after four; I've already had seven hours sleep.

The bed felt completely dry. He was sandwiched between two beautiful women, warm, comfortable and contented. His mouth, cheek and butt felt so much better.

Now all we need is to remain safe until we can escape from Fritz and get to Switzerland. He fell asleep again wondering how long the German exercise would continue up there.

The next time he awoke, the sun was lighting the tops of the trees which poked above the void at the edge of the slab. He was still in his cosy sandwich. He gently lifted his left arm and glanced at his watch.

Almost seven thirty. Another three and a quarter hours sleep, I guess I needed it.

Rachel stirred behind him, kissed his shoulder and whispered, "Good morning."

Maria whispered, "Good morning David. Seems our handsome prince is finally awake." Then stopping her whispering, she continued, "We don't have to whisper anymore, Mama."

"How long have you girls been awake?"

"Long enough to get warm again after our little trip outside." Maria giggled. "What time is it?"

"Half past seven. How deep is the snow?"

"Less than five centimetres," Rachel replied. "It should melt quickly once the sun starts warming this nook."

Maria lifted her head and kissed David's cheek, then worked across to his lips. "Mama explained that your stiffness isn't for me, that it's simply a normal morning thing. Is your penis always stiff like this before you awake?"

"Ever since I can remember. I guess I don't even think of it anymore, it's just a normal thing. I read the cause is the pressure of the full bladder on the prostate."

"What's the prostate?"

"A gland about the same size as one of my balls, but located inside between my bladder and the inner end of my penis. It's the source of most of the fluid that —"

"The inner end of your penis? It goes inside you too, not only inside me?" She giggled.

"Here, let me take your hand and show you." He rolled onto his back, spread his legs and guided her willing hand down and behind his balls.

"Run your fingers along back here, you can feel how far back it goes before angling in."

She ran her fingers along, then sat up, making a tent of the covers as she did. "I've got to see this... My God! You're hiding another big piece back here behind your balls. Can you reel more out from inside?"

"It doesn't reel out from inside, it's anchored there, and the whole thing expands with my excitement. It thickens, grows longer and stiffens."

"My little button expands and becomes firmer when I'm excited. I've often wondered why."

"It pumps full of blood. The excitement trigger causes blood to fill it until it can't expand any more, so it becomes rigid, the veins bulge out... Anyway, the prostate surrounds the tube which comes from the bladder, and makes nourishing fluid for the sperm which comes up through tubes from my balls. It's mixed together and then pulsed forcefully out through my pee hole when I have an orgasm."

She ran her fingers, her hands and her eyes along his entire length and back several times. "That's a hand and a half long. What a complex plumbing system nature has designed,"

"And packaged it so beautifully," Rachel added as she looked on with fascination.

"Speaking of plumbing, I really do need to go. Where are my shoes? Stand by to rewarm me when I come back."

David was hanging rather limply as he stooped back in through the triangle. "That was a quick deflation," Maria said as he kicked off his shoes and crawled again between them.

"Two things — the release of pressure and the cold. Both cause a quick drop. But feeling your flesh on mine and thinking of you has already stopped the fall and reversed it."

She reached down, encircling him with both hands. "Let me feel it grow... It's throbbing."

"Part natural and part me doing it. That's one of the tricks Sister Clemencia taught me. Do you know Morse Code? I can send you a message."

"What's Morse Code?"

"I know it," Rachel said. "I did telegraphy before I met Edom. I should teach you some day, Sweetheart. You squeeze my hand with what you feel, and I'll translate for you."

Rachel read Maria's pulsating code and repeated aloud each word as it was completed. "Please — tell — Maria — I — love — her."

Maria kissed him softly on his cheek, nibbled his lip, and giving his penis a gentle squeeze with each syllable, she quietly said, "I love you. Je t'aime. Ich liebe dich. Ti amo."

She looked up into his eyes. "I wish I knew other ways to say it, knew other ways to show you how much I love you. I first saw you on Wednesday evening, got to know you Thursday night, now it's Sunday morning, and it seems I've known you my entire life."

She brushed her lips gently across his. "I love you, David. I love you so deeply, but until I met you, I had little understanding of the meaning of the word. Now I'm beginning to know its wonderful feeling."

Chapter Twenty

David lay in the bed with Maria and Rachel for a long while after he had rewarmed, waiting for the sun to come around and into the gully. He occasionally sat to get the mirror angle right so he could monitor what the sun was doing across on the far side of the slab. By ten o'clock there were small patches of dark sandstone appearing across the slab where the sun hit it, and there were wisps of vapour rising from increasingly large areas.

The entrance ledge was clear of snow, and he was pleased to see it also clear of Fritz. "Our automatic snow removal system should have the slab cleared by noon," he said as he lay between them again to rewarm. "I should put on a pot of tea, we should have breakfast while we wait."

He slipped his feet into his shoes, grabbed the billy and picked his way through the sodden slush to the stream, trying not to splash. The air was already warm in the nook, and he enjoyed the sun on his skin as he dipped the billy full of water. He set-up the Primus a short distance outside their shelter, but far enough away that if it flared up or tipped over, they'd be safe.

Back inside, he told the girls about the tent which had burst into flames from a knocked-over stove at the O'Hara camp in 1913. "It had happened so quickly. Fortunately, other than minor burns on the tent owner's hands, there had been no injuries. Little of the tent or its contents had survived. We cannot afford to injure ourselves or to lose or damage any of our belongings."

As they nibbled on Appenzeller, landjäger and knäckebrot and sipped their hot tea, they continued telling each other stories while they waited for the snow to melt.

At 1030 they heard the resumption of target practice up on the ridge top, its sharpness well muffled by the trees and the cliff faces above them. "So Fritz is still up there," he said, "I wonder for how much longer." He remembered to wind his watch.

"What's that?" he asked with a start, raising his head quickly.

"Sounds like an engine — it's getting louder," Maria replied. "It sounds like a flying machine."

David nodded. "An aeroplane. They sometimes fly them over our trenches to photograph the enemy positions, movements and strengths. I've heard they're also used to telegraph the fall-of-shot details to the artillery for them to use in aiming their guns."

"There's a *flugplatz* in Freiburg." Maria shrugged her shoulders. "I don't know what they're called in English, I guess a flying place."

"They're called aerodromes," he said.

"The first time I was there was a few years after we had moved from Switzerland. Dada took to watch a big balloon ascend and drift off above the valley. It's over on the north side of the city, near my nursing school. We hear them flying every day now. Every day it's not raining. I think they're training fliers."

The sound had come from well above them, back toward the ridge top. It grew louder, seemed to be directly up the slope from their nook, then the sound changed pitch, still quite loud, but moving away from them now and slowly diminishing.

The rifle firing stopped. The sound of the engine suddenly stopped. No, not quite, there was just a faint putter. They listened to it for half a minute. Then it stopped.

"That's the sound they make when they come back down onto the grass. I sometimes walk over to the field and watch them on our lunch breaks. It sounds like that one came down up there on the meadows."

"Why would they want to come way up here?" Rachel asked.

"Could be bringing the General up to look at the exercise and to inspect the troops. Maybe they're flying Herzog's body back to the valley for burial.

The officers get a lot better treatment — the others are usually buried where they fall."

David paused for a moment, then continued, "I've been fascinated with flying machines, with aeroplanes ever since I can remember. Other than the balloons, the dirigibles and other inflated devices, the world's first powered flight was in France in 1890, four years before I was born. That's where the French word *avion* originated."

He smiled as he recalled, "My great uncle, my mother's uncle was there when it happened. He had been working with Clément Ader for several years in Castelnaudary. At Christmas, when I was five, thinking now, that's 1899, he had shown us a photograph he had taken of a machine, which to me looked more like a bat than anything, as it soared into the air powered by a small steam engine. He was so proud that he had helped Clément build the engine and boiler.

"Five years later, I protested to my school teacher, Sister whatever-her-name-was, I can't remember, she hadn't impressed me — doesn't matter. She told us when we had returned from Christmas that a man had finally for the first time flown a powered machine off the ground. I told her my uncle had helped Clément Ader do that getting on fourteen years before in southern France, in 1890. She told me to stop lying. I insisted it was true — I didn't want to lie, so when I didn't give in to her, I was strapped until both my hands bled..."

"Strapped?" Maria asked, barely cutting off Rachel.

"Catholic school punishment. Our fingers were grasped and bent back, then our palms were whipped with a thick, wide leather strap. The nuns continued until our hands turned red, some until they hinted at bleeding, some continued it longer."

"Sounds sadistic. Unusually cruel."

"I was stubborn and a free thinker, and we were not allowed to be free thinkers and Catholic — except by a few like Sister Clemencia; she was so different."

Maria felt him swelling as they cuddled, talking. "I sense you still enjoy her," she said as she pressed herself closer.

"Memories — hair-trigger response to the thoughts of the physical experiences. There was nothing emotional, no kissing, no caressing, she didn't allow that. I had to keep my eyes closed when she was undressed, but I learned to peek through squinted eyes. Most of the time she preferred me to just lie back and let her do what she wanted. It's interesting looking back at all of that now... Strange. I've not examined this closely before... Such deep emotions with you, but with Clemencia, there were none, only physical."

He paused to take a sip of tea, then continued, "Old experiences linger, but these last few days with you I've had feelings, sensed emotions I didn't know existed. I'm overwhelmed. Sharing you here with your mother's permission and encouragement takes me into realms I've never imagined. I cannot think of anything more exquisitely pleasurable. It's so innocent and shameless, so guilt-free and so non-Catholic."

"I often wondered about the guilt which seemed to consume our Catholic friends," Rachel said. "What was that all about?"

"We were told from the age of comprehension that we were evil. That we were born damaged. Born with sin. We were all guilty and our sins had caused Christ's death."

"What a fucking aberration," Rachel said, "so asinine."

"Asinine — I cannot think of anything hinting at ass and Catholic without thinking of buggering priests. My mother forced me to be an altar boy. At fourteen I was molested by one of the..."

He shook his head. "But back to the flying machines, I remembered the teacher's rebuke so strongly. For the following many years I focused on demonstrating that the bicycle makers from Ohio made fraudulent claims about being the first. The Wright brothers were late into the game of flying. More than thirteen years late. Weisskoph in Boston had flown in August 1901, the French, Germans, Spanish, Swiss, Brazilians, and I don't know how many others had all flown long before that, some more than a dozen years before."

"What in God's earth gives the Americans their license to fuck with history?" Rachel asked.

"I started wondering that myself in early 1904 as their system of creatively rewriting history overrode reality." He shook his head.

"I had a wonderful time at the Alpine Club summer camp in 1913 at Lake O'Hara. There was a rotund Texan in the group. A boastful, big-talking

Texan. He bragged of his climbing. Hah! What a fraud. He had trouble climbing out of his tent. He had insisted on having the pack horses lug his personal tent and other gear up to the camp. It was beneath him to sleep with the others in the large camp tents." David shook his head.

"He was by far the biggest boaster, exaggerator and liar I've ever heard. He regularly boasted that the US of A was the first, the biggest, the best with everything. When he told the story that the Wright brothers were the first ever to fly, I lit into him.

"I loved listening to Billy Foster, Al MacCarthy and some of the others whose names I can't recall just now. They all ripped into him also. I was eighteen then, almost nineteen, but my stories from my uncle were confirmed and celebrated. Conrad added more facts to set the Texan's twisted history straight. I finally felt vindicated.

"Then the buffoon Texan derided Canada as being nothing but wilderness and Redskins. Billy said, *That's because we haven't slaughtered ours like you did. Your government put a big bounty on your native people, offered big rewards for killing them.*

"I laughed when the Texan countered, *But they were in the way of progress, hampering the development of our great nation.* What a buffoon he was." David finished his reminiscences of the 1913 ACC camp and said, "Sorry ladies, just venting some emotion."

"You don't like America do you?" Maria asked.

"I love it. It's a wonderful place, beautiful geography from what I've seen. Unfortunately, the portion of North America which lies to the south of Canada is filled with USAians, filled with so many greedy people, many of whom seem to have their government by the balls."

"That's an interesting expression. I've not heard it," Rachel said. "What's it mean?"

"By the balls, by these things down here," he said hefting them. "They're very tender, very vulnerable, very precious. Grab them and threaten me, you've got me by the balls. I'll likely yield to your demands. Do you remember Achilles from the Greek legends?"

Maria looked at him and smiled. "The hero with the vulnerable heel. Did the grown-up version have his vulnerability a bit higher up? Now I must reread the story." She giggled.

"No, it *was* his heel, I'm just citing an example of vulnerability."

"So the Texan, how did he handle the verbal abuse?" Rachel asked.

"He was too stupid to even realise he was being criticised. He's the idiot who burnt the tent; his own tent. Burnt his hands trying to erase his mistake."

Rachel wrinkled her lip. "We've seen them strutting through here the last few years, heading a couple hundred metres up the trails into the Schwarzwald garbed in their ill-fitting new lederhosen, carrying bright, freshly carved and painted walking sticks, wearing loden hats bedecked in enamelled pins and pretending to be local."

"God bless America, few others will," David added. "They've stopped killing the Redskins openly; they're now doing it socially, and they still refuse to recognise anyone not white as people. Now the US of A is sitting beyond the sidelines of this war, making huge fortunes as their industries supply both us and our enemy, hoping the war continues. A year ago they were the most indebted nation on the planet, now they're rolling in blood-stained lucre."

Chapter Twenty-One

The sun had dried much of the sandstone slab by the time they rolled out of bed and dressed. "The pools will probably not rewarm enough today to be comfortable," David said as he looked across at them "The hail and the snow will have chilled them too much."

Maria and Rachel walked with him to the brink of the slab and looked down to the slopes below. "Still snow on the ground between the trees and on the shaded branches," he said. "It'll be slippery going for a while yet. Even if Fritz had left, it wouldn't make sense for us to continue in these conditions."

"It's started again." Maria pointed up the slopes. "The flying machine's engine has started."

The engine ran slowly for a while, then increased rapidly in both pitch and noise. "It's going back up into the air," Maria said. "They bounce along the field, gradually picking up speed, then their wings lift them off the ground. They seem so terribly fragile."

The three stood listening to the steady racket of the engine, then they heard it stutter, miss a beat, resume for a moment. There was a loud bang, a brief squeal of metal on metal, then silence.

"I know that sound," David said. "That's similar to the one Dad's motorcar made when a connecting rod let go. What a twist of metal we found when we removed the oil pan."

They listened. Heard nothing. They looked at each other, then up past the tops of the cliffs. There was nothing but clear, blue sky and complete silence except for the splash of the waterfall across from them, the gurgle of the stream and the murmur of the cascade below.

"It's going to come back down. Without the engine, there's nothing to hold it up except the air moving past its wings," he said. "The only way to keep the air passing over the wings to keep it flying without power, is to descend."

"Three weeks ago, in early April, I watched one lose its power as it was taking to the air," Maria said. "It started to turn to head back to the field, but fell sideways into..."

She stopped at the sharp snap above them. It was quickly followed by another, some twangs, the sounds of breaking trees, ripping cloth and a loud, dull thud. Then there was silence.

"That sounded rather close." He looked up at the cliffs "Can't be more than a hundred yards across there." He pointed up to the right. "Fritz is going to come back this way again, I'm afraid."

"It's on our safe side, fortunately," Rachel said.

They continued to stare up at the cliff tops. David walked out to the brink and looked from there. "Still can't see anything above the rocks from here except the ends of a few branches." Then he saw a billow of black smoke wafting across in the gentle easterly breeze, and he caught its acrid smell.

"It's afire. Smells like burning gasoline," he said as he moved back in from the brink. "Good thing the forest is wet from last night's storm. It had been dry until that. This would have rapidly spread yesterday."

"Dowsed with gasoline, it'll set trees ablaze," Rachel added. "We're fortunate there's such a light breeze. The mountains are clearly visible from home, and we've watched how quickly a fire spreads up here. Also on the slopes of the Vosges across in Elsass."

They watched the billow of smoke change from black to grey. "Looks as if the trees now burning," Maria said.

"I wonder how far back it is from the cliff tops. I can see a few sparks now in the smoke." He looked at the oiled canvas. "It might be a good idea to pack up our things, move them to the other side, across the stream. Keep them farther away from falling embers. Let's do that." He turned toward the camp.

"Take everything down. Pack as if we're preparing to leave. We may have to if the fire spreads this way and burning embers, branches, even trees fall into our nook. Let's do it."

They worked as a team, quickly striking the camp and stowing items methodically and carefully into the packs.

"I can hear the crackle of the fire now," Maria said, looking up. "A lot of sparks rising; thankfully, not falling."

David carefully removed the mirror from its supports and slipped it into the left side pocket of his small pack. "Is that everything? A quick look around. Have we missed anything?"

They hefted their packs and moved them the short distance across the slabs and laid them on the exit ledge above the stream, out of the spray. They sat on the ledge side-by-side, leaning against the wall and dangling their feet a short distance above the stream. "Now we wait," he said. "Watch and wait."

"And pray," Maria added.

"I prefer not to pray." David shook his head. "The church ruined that for me with the incessant babbling of Hail Mary and other nonsensical things. I prefer to simply think nice thoughts, think of pleasant things, let my mind wander, then totally clear. It's amazing how much more I can see with a quiet mind."

They watched streams of sparks and an occasional tongue of flame rising above the rock face across from them. The streams of sparks increased, then there were more flames. They heard the loud crack and thud of a tree collapsing and watched a swarm of sparks heading skyward. A fine black grit began settling around them. Nothing glowing; only spent sparks.

The heat of the fire carried the billows of smoke well above them. They began feeling a wind coming up the gully, an increasing wind, pulled up from below by the heat of the inferno above them. The spray from the waterfall looked confused. It wavered in the strengthening updraft, then began falling up.

"We have a place in eastern Canada called Reversing Falls. I've never been there, but here's another one," he said, pointing to the upward movement of the spray, now increasingly some of the bigger droplets.

"What's causing the strong wind?" Maria asked.

"Fires generate their own winds." He looked at her and rolled his hands like a paddle wheel. "They feed themselves in a continuing cycle. The hot air from the fire rises more quickly as the fire grows and its rising sucks fresh air in from around the fire. This fresh supply of oxygen increases the flames, the winds intensify them further, the increasing heat creates higher winds to build the fire further still. The fire keeps building, accelerating."

He looked up at the sound of another crashing tree. "I've seen forest fires back home in the Kootenays and the Columbia Valley as they danced across the tops of the trees, setting them ablaze from a distance simply from the intense heat. Trees suddenly burst into flame a long distance from the fire. We're not going to have that here; the forest is too wet, and the trees and the air are too cold for that to happen."

He saw the concern in her eyes. "We're safe here. The fire can't come into here; there's nothing to feed on, no fuel for it to burn. It's above us, and its heat will pass above us. So will the smoke." He leaned over and kissed her and watched as her face relaxed.

They sat for a long quiet time, mesmerised by the inferno as it reached the lip of the steep treed slope above the cliffs. The updraft pushed the flames up, the advancing fire was running out of access to fuel. The fresh fuel was now all upwind below it.

"Appears the rapid advance of the fire is stalled by the steep slope into the gully, starved by its own wind. It'll keep burning for a long time yet, though. Many trees are afire and likely also the underground, but it seems to have stopped moving."

He glanced at his watch. "Nearly half past noon, let's wait another half hour, until 1300, watch what it does, stay here by the water in case anything falls into our spa."

"You're very familiar with fires, David," Rachel said. "It sounds like you've been around them a lot."

"Conrad and I helped fight two big ones up the Columbia Valley when we were climbing. Amazing how much one learns about fires being surrounded by them and trying to survive. I wish we could learn more about Fritz. We're surrounded by them and trying to survive."

Within a few minutes, the flames disappeared back out of sight over the steep slope. The wind up the gully decreased then died, the waterfall lost its confusion. There was still a large billowing of light grey smoke, and a light ash began falling into the gully, almost like snow, slowly turning the dark sandstone a paler grey. A thin skim grew on the small pools furthest from the spray of the waterfall.

David carefully surveyed the tops of the cliffs opposite. He stood up on the ledge in an attempt to assess the nature of the slopes above them. "Not high enough," he said, mostly to himself, "I've got to get a bit higher."

He looked up behind their stance. "This is too steep and slippery to safely climb. I'm going to poke around the corner and climb for a better view." He leaned and kissed Maria and chuckled. "Don't go away, I'll be right back."

He sidled along and around the bulge, stopped before the corner and peeked around it to make sure the ledge was clear. Patches of snow were still on the ground.

So much warmer in the nook.

A few yards along the ledge, he turned and headed up a steep, narrow ramp sloping toward their nook. He quickly gained twenty feet, then worked across a ledge to the edge of the gully.

Above him, about ten feet higher, was the top of the cascade. Across the gully, above the cliffs, he saw a slab laid back at a steep angle, nearly treeless, but for adventurous clingers in crevices and scattered small bushes, similarly adventurous.

Beyond the steep slab were smouldering trees, a few with small licks of flames. Farther back was a charred scar in the forest with many trees still burning, most still standing, but some of them fallen. The fire was slowly putting itself out.

Beyond the burnt scar he saw movement in the trees. A squad of soldiers standing beyond the edge of the fire. He couldn't see the aeroplane.

Probably completely burned in the inferno.

He looked back at the fire, studied it for a while, confirming it was diminishing. His eyes moved back to Fritz when they caught additional movement.

Two squads. Looks like they can't do anything about the aeroplane, nor for whoever was in it. They're doing nothing but standing and looking.

He carefully retraced his route, moving backwards to ensure he remained hidden until he was below the sight line over the top of the slab. Once there, he turned and picked his way back down the diagonal, glancing along the ramp at the base of the bluffs to look for Fritz.

Back with the girls, he explained what he had seen, and he told them there appeared to be no danger of anything from the fire falling into their spa, "Nothing but ashes, that is," he said as he concluded his assessment.

"The ash fall has slowed, almost stopped now," Maria said.

David glanced at his watch again. "We're packed and ready to go, but it's well past midday. Should we risk sneaking past Fritz now and hope we'll find a safe hideaway before nightfall? Let's quietly think. Do we go or do we stay?"

A minute later he asked, "Go?" He saw their heads shake. "Also my thoughts. The going would be slippery, and we don't know where they've spread up there. Here, we know what we're dealing with. Let's set up camp where we are, get sheltered and out of sight for another night."

Chapter Twenty-Two

"Anything we could do differently with the set-up this time?" David asked as they laid their packs behind the gabbro block. "Let's stand here for a while and see if we can think of anything to improve on the layout."

The three stood looking for a minute, maybe a little more, then Maria said, "I think you got it pretty well perfect the first time. The only thing I can see is to move it over twenty, twenty-five centimetres so we won't have to hide the corner with bushes."

"That was my only adjustment also," Rachel said. "Other than adding running water, a bathtub, a commode and a bidet, I can think of nothing else to improve its excellent design."

David wedged a line back into the crack in the rock, pulling the canvas about eight or ten inches farther along and wrapped the line from the next corner around the flake again. He moved the two large rocks across the slab a short distance and tied the lower lines to them. As he did this, Maria had set the mirror back into place, popped inside under the canvas to check its alignment and continued working with Rachel to unpack and arrange.

David dribbled linseed oil along the creases in the canvas, adjusted the tension on the roof and stood back to look at it. "We're completely invisible now," he said. "Amazing what eight or ten inches can do."

"Come inside, David, let me check your wounds, I haven't looked at them since yesterday," Maria said softly from the shelter.

"I'd love to come inside," he replied with a chuckle. "I haven't done that since May Day back in '15."

"You're a quick one, aren't you? I love it. Maybe you can show me some more amazing things about moving twenty or twenty-five centimetres," she chuckled back.

"You're both very quick," Rachel said. "I'll go sit on the ledge in the sun and give you two more privacy."

He hugged Rachel when she came out, and kissed her cheek. "Thank you Mama — I hope you don't mind my calling you that, it just slipped out."

"I love it! Please keep calling me Mama. It's so much more warm and personal for me."

"Stay close to the cliff, behind the bulge, out of sight from the corner in case Fritz comes nosing around."

Maria was nearly undressed as he stooped in under the canvas. "I'm getting into my nursing uniform before I prep the patient." She looked at him and giggled. "Please be patient."

"You are such a beautiful woman, Maria. Beautiful dressed in grubby, baggy men's clothing, beautiful dressed only in your skin. Beautiful as an image in my mind. You have a beautiful mind, such an open mind, you hide nothing. You have a beautiful wit, a beautiful spirit. You're all my images of a beautiful woman."

"I have difficulty absorbing all this. Difficulty understanding it. I've never been close to a boy — to a man before I met you. Well, except for the gangly dimwits I was forced to take a few turns with on the dance floor at the graduation party last year. Other than that and wonderful talks and hugs from my father and some frolicking with my brothers, I don't know men at all." She shrugged.

"Mama told me you're a very special man. Not the normal, not like any she has ever seen. She told me this morning while you were still sleeping that you're a very rare bird and I would go through my entire life finding no one near as fine. Also, she told me not to tell you this, but I guess I already have. You know I can't keep my thoughts inside. I don't want to."

"You're the special one, Maria. I'm just me. Just me being the only me I understand. I don't even know what I am, who I am, what my purpose is. I've pondered these things since I can remember. Sat high on mountain ridges and on many summits thinking, trying to understand why I'm here. Do you know why you're here?"

"I've spent so much time deep in my thoughts, lying awake in bed trying to comprehend my purpose. All my school mates quickly dismissed me, told me to stop being so serious. I had no close friends in school. Really, no friends at all. I was the only one I had to talk with, the only one who could answer my questions."

"I didn't then, and I still don't now know the answers."

"I don't know them either. That's our attraction, why we fit so well together."

"Speaking of fitting together, shouldn't we rearrange ourselves along that line of thought?" He looked down and smiled. "I see I'm up for it."

They lay and coupled. "This is a much more intimate conversation," she said as she slowly rotated and flexed her hips.

They flowed their conversation through a broad range of topics as they continued their gentle movements, Maria interrupting occasionally to enjoy an orgasm. Their intimate conversation lasted well over an hour before they both very audibly finished.

Rachel heard them from across the slabs, across the stream, close beside the pound of the waterfall. She diddled quickly to another series of convulsions, then leaned back against the rocks, smiling.

She gave them several minutes, then picked up her clothes and walked back across the slab to the shelter. "I heard it was good for you," she said with a chuckle as she ducked to enter. "It's getting chilly over there; the sun is just leaving that corner."

"We're still getting to know each other. Still trying to get to know ourselves, probably more like it. I'm sorry we took so long, Mama."

"Don't let it bother your mind, Sweetheart. Thinking of your energy, sensing it from way over there, made it so enjoyable for me. Thank you, Maria, thank you, David. Thank you so many times."

Maria examined David's wounds, starting with the one on his buttock. She gently lifted the tape, pulling some loose scabs with it and soaking the adhesive off the larger ones with alcohol. "What do you think, Mama? How does this look to you?"

Rachel examined the ragged line of the scar, running a finger along it as she did. "Is this sore?" she asked, prodding gently along the pink line and pressing the remaining scattered scabs.

"More itchy than anything, Mama. Not sore, just a little tender, but mostly itchy."

"And this," she asked with a giggle as she lightly stroked the wrinkled flesh which was draped out on the bedroll between his legs.

"That area is very sensitive. Fortunately, it wasn't wounded, but it still needs care."

"I would love to show Maria some things to pleasure you. Do you mind if I do?"

"I am your obedient servant, Madam," he chuckled. "You've got me by the balls."

"Roll over, then. We have work to do."

"Maria, you remember what I was saying this morning about pleasuring with your mouth. Let me show you what I was explaining."

David was quickly fully rigid again.

"Edom didn't have a skin covering over his head; the rabbi cut it off when he was an infant, so some of this is new to me as well. I've experience only one non-Jewish boy, but he was small even when hard, so there was not much foreskin to explore."

"Why would a rabbi cut off such a useful part?" Maria asked. "That seems like senseless mutilation. That's a huge amount of flesh to remove."

"I didn't realise how much skin is involved until I watched you slide it back and forth over his head that first day." Rachel looked up and blushed. "Sorry, I spied on you at the pool. I wanted to see how you were getting along with each other."

She slid it up and down. "I didn't realise it folds back on itself this way." She peeled it all the way back, watching carefully as she did. "That's his entire length it slides back. That's how much the rabbi cuts off, actually cuts out of the middle and leaves the raw ends in hopes they heal together. Edom had a ragged scar and his skin pulled so tight over his shaft when he was hard."

Rachel pulled the skin farther back down the shaft, to the end of its stretch and said, "That's how Edom's looked when hard. That's how a religious mutilation looks, nowhere near as attractive."

She let the skin relax, and it rolled up behind the head. "Run your tongue around here, under the rim of the head like this, Maria," she said, pausing her action not to mumble. "Edom told me this ridge was his most sensitive part. What do you think, David?"

"Around the bottom side, the wrinkled bits between the head and the shaft, those are exquisitely sensitive for me. Far more than on the other side where you are, but that's also delightful."

"Edom didn't have folds like this. His was plain with some scar tissue. You say that's the most sensitive part? Edom grew up never knowing what or how much had been taken away. We also had it done to our two sons. We went along with the tradition, with the synagogue ceremony without even questioning. Why cut it away from an infant who doesn't even know he has one?"

"Because of religion. That's the way to explain most strange traditions and aberrations." David shook his head. "Stupid, most of it."

Rachel rolled the foreskin back and forth slowly. "What a wondrous thing this is. What did we do to our sons?" She shook her head. "But let's get back to the lessons, Maria. Tongue action, that's what your father loved. I had started by taking him into my mouth, but he explained I had another part that was much better designed for that. Tongue action."

The education continued, student and instructor taking turns to demonstrate and perform lessons. The teaching aid cooperated and complied, sometimes adding experiential aspects to assist all three participants.

"These are some of the things you can do, Maria, on the days you're not safe. There's no need to burden yourselves with annual children as so many seem to do. And from what I saw yesterday, David has a wonderful way with *his* tongue." Rachel blushed. "Sorry, I couldn't keep myself from looking."

David smiled as he said, "I need to do much more practice with that, I'm just a beginner — I don't know if I understand the fertility cycle properly, though. When are the safe times, when are the risky?"

"It's a wondrous cycle, we went through it this week in school," Maria looked up and smiled. "I was fascinated by the complexity of it all. It begins with laying an egg. Women have a pod full of eggs and one is released, occasionally more than one. The egg descends toward the womb looking for seeds. If there aren't any, it waits a bit. The inside of the womb had prepared itself for the meeting, it had thickened its lining and added blood.

"Even if there is a delivery of seed, they might not get together with the egg. If they do get together, a new nine-month development of a baby begins. If the egg and seed don't get together, after only one day, the egg dies. Then the preparations, the extra blood, the thickened womb lining slowly break down. Later this is all flushed out of the body."

"My cycle is regular and predictable," Rachel said, "It follows the moon's phases. New moon is my dangerous time; from a day or two after new moon until just after the first quarter. You seem to follow the same timing, Maria — I've noticed for a long while you're always into the cupboard of clean cottons at the same times I am."

Maria nodded. "Yes, I use the full moon to remind myself I have a week before I need to step into underwear again and start folding cotton,"

"So the risky time is only when the egg is there?" David asked.

"No, much longer than that. The instructor explained that the seeds will survive for three to five days in the womb, waiting for an egg to arrive. The risk is from five days before the egg arrives, to be safer, six."

"How long does the risk continue?"

"The egg survives for only one day. To be safe we need to stop planting seeds six days before *eisprung*, the laying of the egg, I don't know what the English word is.

"Ovulation," Rachel offered.

"The problem is figuring out when eisprung, ovulation happens. Cycles can be three to five weeks long, but more usually around thirty days. The cycles can be regular and predictable like Mama's and mine, or they can be irregular and difficult to guess.

"Normally the egg arrives in the womb around the middle of the cycle, around day fourteen or fifteen in the typical, regular cycle. Day one is the beginning of the bleeding..."

"I'm amazed at how well you know all this, Maria," Rachel said. "I told you only a little of it."

"Theory from books, Mama. I looked up some things in the school library, but I became so fascinated with it when we started looking at the mechanics of it this week in class. Now I've started practising, converting theory into reality, I'm even more fascinated."

They continued with the anatomy lessons, the women turning to focus their attention fully again on the seed implanting system. Together they quietly worked on it until they got it to operate.

"Such a strong force. So many seeds. The instructor told us that in healthy men, tens of millions of seeds are delivered each time, but only one of them is needed to fertilise the egg. Was that pleasing for you, David?"

"I'm still trying to catch my breath." His body was still randomly twitching. "I feel as if I've turned inside-out, out through there."

"I think you have the idea, Maria," Rachel said. "It's really quite simple. Just watch the response, watch the little signs, the twitches, the involuntary movements. Listen to the sounds coming from his throat, sense the ones coming from his soul."

"You two are amazing. You're so open, so full of wonder and curiosity, so eager to learn, to explore, to share. I was in awe lying here watching teacher and student so deeply involved in giving and receiving instruction. I was so fascinated by the scene that I forgot it was me you were working on until I erupted. It caught me completely by surprise. I've not had that happen before. I'm still trying to recover."

"So it was pleasing for you." Maria giggled, kissing his deflating head as she towelled off his chest. "Let me examine your cheek and your lip."

She moved up, brushing her breasts across his chest as she looked at the scar on his cheek through the week-old stubble. "It looks good. The scar will be clean-edged and narrow. There's no hint of infection. The only swelling is the one I have under my belly. You surely aren't rising all the way up again, are you?"

"The feel of your breasts brushing across my chest, the look of you, your wonderful aroma, your loving attention, I have no other choice but to swell in appreciation."

She tenderly kissed his cheek scar, moved across and licked the scar on his chin, then on his lip. She sent her tongue inside and examined up and down the scar there. As she explored slowly inside his mouth, she humped her back, shifted her hips and settled onto him to slowly explore inside elsewhere.

He shuddered at the sensation of her surrounding him. "I love the nursing care in this spa. I love the examining methods. I love you."

Chapter Twenty-Three

After recovering from Maria's examination, David glanced at his watch. "It's nearly four thirty. The sun's going to leave this side of the nook in less than half an hour. After it goes, it will quickly chill, but we can light a fire in here this evening."

"But won't Fritz see it?"

"No, Mama," Maria answered. "There's still smoke and flames on the slopes above us, so our fire will fit in with the scene. Ours won't look different from the rest of the fire."

"Exactly my thoughts," David said. "I'm going to dress and go back up the opposite slope to take another look."

He checked the safety, unclipped the case from the handle, flipped the lid open and slid the pistol inside. Then slipping the case into the harness, he looped the strap over his belt and fastened it. "Just in case I've a need for protection. We have this, we may as well use it. I've been so comfortable here, so relaxed and well cared for, that I keep forgetting I'm deep in enemy territory."

After kissing them both, he checked the mirror and headed out. "The snow should be mostly gone by now from the sun. I'll likely be less than a quarter hour."

He dipped his hand in the shallowest pool.

The water's still the same temperature as yesterday. Must be a flow of thermal water across the slabs.

He examined the strata junction, smiled and nodded.

David quickly regained his previous outlook perch. The snow was almost completely gone from the forest floor, down to a few patches which had remained in the shade and in places it had stacked up from sloughing off tree branches. There were still many small fires around the periphery of the charred scar with flames licking both standing and fallen trees. Dirty white smoke rose from underground fires across the whole area.

Our little fire will fit in well. I wonder where Fritz is.

He scanned the area again, then he relaxed his eyes and set them out of focus on the slopes opposite as he sat still, waiting for motion. There was none for several minutes, then he caught movement and focused on a doe and a fawn picking their way across a small clearing in the trees beyond the fire scar. He watched in appreciation.

Then there was a gunshot, then quickly two more as both animals collapsed. Half a minute later, five soldiers walked into the clearing toward the fallen deer.

So Fritz is still up there. What bloody cowards, killing a defenceless doe and her fawn. But elsewhere they're also killing defenceless mothers and children.

He watched as the soldiers approached their kill, raising their arms and weapons in victory. The biggest man tucked the small fawn under his arm, the four others each took a leg of the doe, and they carried their meat across the slope, angling slightly upwards and then out of sight.

David retraced his route back to the bottom of the bluff and followed the ramp back along toward the gully, picking up a thick fallen branch from the slope as he went. He tossed the branch across the stream, and it landed on the slab with a clatter. Then he stood in the mirror's view until he saw Maria poke her head out from behind the gabbro block.

She ran out across the slab to the stream's edge, Rachel close behind her. Her face was streaked with tears, she looked distraught. "We thought those shots were for you. We didn't know what to think."

Rachel's face was also glistening wet with tears. "What was that about? What were those shots? We were so worried."

"Fritz shooting some meat for dinner. Looks like you both need a hug," he said as he sidled along the narrow ledge. He manoeuvred around the bulge, leapt across the stream onto the slab, took a few steps and wrapped them both in a huge warm hug.

Maria was still jerking, almost convulsing with deep sobs. "We thought you... you were... gone," she blubbered out between sobs.

"You need to keep such thoughts out of your mind." He cupped the back of her head with his hand and gently pulsed. "In times such as these, it's important to keep only positive thoughts in here. It's cold here in the shade; let's go over into the sun before you catch a chill. You're still in your nursing uniform."

The three walked back across the slab and into the sun, then he pointed to the triangle. "Inside, it's much warmer inside. You're still crying. I don't understand."

"I'm crying for relief now, not for loss, I'm so relieved you're safe, uninjured, alive." She reached out and stroked the stubble on his cheek.

"Just because you heard gunfire? We've heard a lot of gunfire the last two days. Why are these shots different?"

"You weren't here. You were out there. I watched my dreams, my expectations dissolve. Maybe my mind was too busy, it just took over and started telling me the worst. I went along with it."

"Dreams are for ideas, for reviews. Dreams are not for living. Being present, being here, living the reality of now is all that's possible. What was the dream that had devastated you?"

"I've been dreaming of spending my life with you. Since I first saw you. The gunshots put a hole right through that dream."

"But you are spending your life with me. Right here, right now. And the beauty of this is it's not a dream. All that we have, all that we can live, is the present. We can plan and have expectations for the future, but we're not there. We cannot determine what will evolve. Have you ever pondered the source of disappointment?"

"No..." She tilted her head and looked at him. "No, not that I can remember."

"Let me tell you another story. A few years ago, high on a rib in the Bugaboos, approaching the summit of an unclimbed spire, I was stopped by a nearly hold-less vertical wall. I could see the top only twenty feet above me. I tried several times to get up the wall, but alone and without the support of a roped belay, it was far too risky. A slip would be certain death. I had to give up.

"I searched for a traverse to the left. Nothing. Same to the right. I started back down bitterly disappointed. My mind was clouded. I stopped for a break at an easing of the steepness, moved around to a ledge to sit and ponder. I had expected the route would go. After I'd —"

"Route would go? What's that mean?" Maria asked.

"A mountaineering term I use; could be only Canadian. It means the route leads to the goal." He looked at her and laughed. "In this instance, it didn't, and I remember being unable to relax. I was still deeply disappointed. My mind was darkened, and I sat trying to understand why. I had expected the route would go; that it would lead me to the summit."

He looked into her eyes. "And that's the thing. I had expectations. Without expectations, there are no disappointments. Expectations are nothing other than our minds trying to project us forward, out of the present, out of reality. We can live only here, only now. There is no other time or place." He gave her a gentle squeeze.

"Emptying our minds of the future, of the past, gives us so much more space and time to fully appreciate the present, to much more fully live, fully experience. Have I told you lately I think you are absolutely gorgeous? That I love you?"

"It's all over you. You ooze it. How can I help but see? But what about planning, how do you do that?"

"Our core, our soul will guide us. Appreciate the surroundings, drink everything in. Possibilities are constantly emerging, expanding, diminishing. By being fully present, we see the evolution, we're aware of a much broader picture, of tangential possibilities, of links to still further possibilities. We don't dwell on them, we allow them to flow through.

"From every point, there's a full circle of possibilities. A hair's breadth farther along, there's an entirely fresh range. From every moment there's infinity. Always be ready to change. Change is constant. Change is the force of life. If we try to resist change, we stagnate."

He looked into Maria's eyes. "The state when all change stops is called death. Don't resist change; to do so is fatal."

"Your thinking is so deep, so clear," Rachel said. "You sound like you've lived a thousand years. Where does it all come from?"

"From inside. From climbing alone in the mountains. Wasted time, my father called it. It's amazing what thoughts come when we've no distraction when we're fully involved in being where we are, doing whatever we're doing. Not trying to design our lives, but simply fully living them."

"So were you satisfied as you headed back down?"

"Wonderfully so. After my mind had cleared, as I was preparing to continue down, I looked back up to bid the peak *à bien tôt*, and spotted a narrow layback crack a bit to the left. With a few thin moves, the crack led me onto the summit. I hadn't seen it previously, I had been distracted by expecting the rib would go."

Chapter Twenty-Four

"You should get dressed," David said as he finished sharing his thoughts. He was sitting on the bedrolls, leaning against the gabbro, Maria sat between his legs, leaning her back up along his chest, her head on the front of his shoulder. "You're making a pair of points showing you're starting to chill."

She lifted her head slightly and looked down at her breasts. "And behind my back, you're making a much bigger point that you're interested." She finished with a quiet giggle.

"You're still quite troubled in here," he said rubbing her head gently. "That was not your usual joyful and carefree giggle."

He turned his head and kissed her, moved his hands from her head down to cup and lightly juggle her breasts. "The fire in here will last. Come, let's build a different fire. Come, get dressed and we'll put together a warm bonfire for tonight."

"But what about your lump?"

"The fire there will also last. Regardless, with tinder like you, it's so easy to reignite. While you girls dress, I'll head across and start bringing in more wood to add to that short piece of shattered trunk."

"We'll gather the twigs and branches in the nook," Maria said, "and find the best place to build the fire... Thank you so much for your stability. I'm amazed how your gentle calmness — your reassuring manner — adds to my comfort, my confidence. I'm sure it also adds to Mama's."

They sidled together into a group hug. A long tender hug before David moved toward the entrance and checked the mirror as he prepared to stoop out through the triangle. "All clear," he said as he continued out. "Perfectly reinstalled, Maria."

He was just around the entrance corner when he heard a gunshot rather close above. He stopped, turned and took three quick steps back to the corner, then carefully looked around it and upwards, toward the sound of the shot.

There was a cracking sound faintly above the noise of the cascading water, then the clatter of rocks bouncing on the slab across the stream from him and continuing on downward into the trees over the brink until their noise was drowned by the waterfall below.

He continued to look up at the source of the falling rocks; watched the fall change to twigs, soil and clumps of moss. Then a large rock followed by the hooves, legs and rump of a large deer. It stopped sliding and hung there. A few rocks continued to clatter as the deer struggled.

A buck, he recognised as it twisted. *Likely the mate.*

A runnel of red came over the rock lip and slowly expanded. It grew in pulses with the struggle of the buck.

A voice came from above: *"Da ist es. Geweihen in einem Baum die Klippe an verfangen."*

Another voice: *"Wir sollten nicht hier sein. Denken Sie daran, Leutnant Herzog."*

A third voice, yelling from farther away: *"Ihr habt gehört den Major. Das ist aus Grenzen dort. Komm, zurück zum Feldlager."*

David was relieved by what he had learned from the short conversation. He continued watching the fading struggles of the buck, watched as it seemed to have given up.

Maybe building strength for a big effort.

He looked across to the gabbro block and saw the girls also watching. There was a loud crack, he quickly looked back and caught the end of the buck's fall to the slab followed by a big tree branch.

He waited for more voices from above, but there was none. The only voice he heard was his own. "Convenient meat delivery."

He sidled back along the ledge, past the bulge, sprung across the stream and went over to the dead buck, arriving just after the two girls. "Which one of you ordered the venison?" he asked as he neared with a big smile.

"I think God did," Rachel said, "I think He likes us."

"I think She does too. I have no experience at all with butchering, but I'm willing to have a go at it," he said. He looked at both of them in turn, and added, "Have either of you any experience with —?"

"Edom would always shoot a big buck in the autumn," Rachel interrupted. "I'd do the butchering. Quite similar to the goats I had done when I was growing up; we had a small herd of them for milk, cheese and meat."

She looked down at the twisted carcass. "The best cuts on a buck are the tenderloins, a pair of them inside straddling the spine near the back of the cavity. They're the muscles which provide the love thrust to the pelvis. In bucks they don't get used often, so they're very tender." She laughed. "Yours are likely very tough, David."

"Did you hear the soldiers above, what they said?" he asked.

"We heard the voices. Some of the words were clear, but the echoes and the waterfall made it hard to understand much of it, except the last one," Maria answered. "The deep yelling voice saying something about the major said it's out of bounds. Back to camp."

"I heard most of it quite clearly," he said, "I missed a few of the words, but it seems the stag they had shot had caught its antlers in a tree. There was talk that they shouldn't be here, it's where Herzog fell. Finally, the loud one, probably the corporal, shouting about out of bounds and back to camp."

"That all makes sense," Maria said, adding with a big grin, "I love the idea we're out of bounds."

"What can I do to make it easier for the butchering, Mama?"

Rachel looked around for a few moments, then said, "If we can hang it up over there near the waterfall it would be the easiest for me. Lots of cold running water to wash away the guts, to wash the carcass and to cool it."

David walked over to the face beside the cascade and studied the rock. "There's a nice crack here. I can jam a rope knot in it and hang it here. How's this spot?"

"That looks close to perfect. We can put Herzog's knife to work."

"Head up or head down?"

"I prefer head up, that's what I'm used to."

By the time they had finished the short back-and-forth, Maria had brought over two rolls of sisal line and a length of hemp. "Which do you prefer?" she asked holding them out to David.

"The thicker piece of hemp will be better. I can make a good, thick jam knot in it, a tight figure-of-eight."

He took the line, quickly turned the knot in its end and fed it into a widening in the crack a little above eye level. With a small twig, he poked the knot in deeper, then ran his hand along the line a foot or so and pulled lightly, working the knot down into the narrowing. He moved his hands another yard along the line, sat on the slab and yanked it with increasing force.

Next, he bowlined a noose and put his foot in it, stood and bounced lightly, then stepped out of it, saying, "That should hold."

Rachel and Maria had started dragging the carcass across the slab, and he assisted them with the final short distance. "What a grand team we are," he said. "No yelling, no bossing, we're simply acting in harmony."

David unbent the bowline, turned a figure-of-eight noose into the line near the upper end, took a bight near the middle of the line around the antlers, then threaded the line's end through the eye and pulled down on it to load the system. "Mama and I will take the weight, Maria, you take the line and pull the slack out of it as we lift."

Within a minute they had the buck strung-up by its antlers, its hindquarters lifted just off the slab. David took the line from Maria and turned it down on the staghorns. "We used bronze staghorns for mooring our sailing skiffs in Victoria. I'd never thought of the origin of the word until now."

"What an elegant system you've put together," Rachel said. "So simple and easy to use."

"Does this design also date back to a spa in the Schwarzwald?" Maria looked at him and chuckled.

"You know the answer, Maria. It's simply a matter of being aware of surroundings, aware of possibilities. I had no plans, I had no idea what form it would take until we finished."

He turned to Rachel and asked, "What else do you need?"

"Herzog's knife. You still have it strapped to your case."

"I had forgotten I was still armed, this thing sits so nicely." He slung the case around, flipped the catch and slipped out the knife. "This is extremely sharp. Be careful."

He slung the holster back around then gave them each a kiss. "I'm heading off to forage for more firewood. Even though we're out of bounds, I'll keep the gun with me. It's foolish to think nobody else would ignore the orders and wander over here."

"Search for mushrooms while you're out there," Rachel said. "They'll go wonderfully with our tenderloin. This time of year there should be some Austernseitling, the French call them pleurottes. Probably still some Steinpilzen, the ones they call Porcini in southern Switzerland. If we're lucky, there may even be some late Morcheln, morilles in French, morels in English. They're my favourites."

"I don't know mushrooms at all to pick them, only to eat them."

"Bring back samples and remember where you found them. Look on the dead trees for the pleurottes, they're like small pale grey or cream-coloured bracket shelves."

"I saw a lot of those on a couple of trees up the slope. I'll take my small pack. How can I identify some of the other good ones?"

"Morels, my favourites, are like honeycombs. Pointy honeycombs somewhat like little elf caps. Probably still in season up here. Search the ground, under hardwood trees like elm and oak. They range in size from a bit smaller than your little finger, mostly the size of your thumb, a few really large ones, closer to the size of your..."

"Here's your pack," Maria said as she walked back across the slab. She reached down and caressed his bulge, asking with a delighted giggle, "Is this what you were talking about, Mama? I've never seen morels this big... Now even more. My God, what a fast response you have."

David grinned, looked down, shifted himself with his hand, took the pack and kissed them again. "I'm off foraging, see you shortly."

From the corner, he slowly moved along the ledge looking for wood and mushrooms. Again, he climbed the steep, narrow ramp on the bluff to where he remembered having seen mushrooms on the trees.

They seem so slimy, but they don't feel that way at all. Appear they'd squish easily, but they're surprisingly firm.

He picked the best-looking examples into his pack, stopping when he had half filled it.

They're surprisingly light.

He looked around, spotted a stand of leafless trees up the slope. Hardwood standing against the next line of cliffs.

Let's see if there are any morels up under those.

It was a young grove, trees four and five inches through. They were leafless because they were dead, many were lightly charred.

Likely from a fire through here a few years ago. A great stand of dried firewood. Should have brought the bone saw.

Then he spotted the first one, the size of his thumb. A little honeycombed cap. It was like a loose-knit creamy white lattice wrapping a light brown core. He picked it and searched further, spotted several others and almost stepped on another as he was moving across to them. His harvesting continued for a quarter hour, finding several twice the thickness of his thumb, but mostly thumb size or a bit bigger. When his pack was full, he stopped.

He picked up two thick fallen tree branches as he headed across the ramp toward the entrance, held them on his downhill shoulder and continued to the corner, where he stopped and looked in. "Ladies, we have mushrooms. I've picked a full pack of pleurottes and morels."

They turned as he tossed the branches to the slab. "And we have tenderloin and backstrap," Rachel replied with a big smile. "We're now working on some racks of ribs to lean up beside the fire. We'll need more firewood than that."

"I was too busy picking mushrooms," he said as he sidled along the ledge. "But I found a large supply of standing fire-kill. I need the saw for that."

"We're using the bone saw," Maria said with a laugh. "Using it for its intended purpose; excising and amputating. We're nearly finished."

"Are these the right ones?" he asked as he knelt and opened the pack as soon as he hit the slab beside them.

"Mein Himmel! I have never seen so many so quickly."

"The bottom half of the pack is filled with pleurottes, at least that's what I hope they are. I also brought one of these, there's lots of them up there."

"Those are good too, März-Schneckling, March something, probably March mushroom, I know of no other name for them," Rachel said. "But they pale in comparison to the other two. Let me see the pleurottes."

Maria called from the shelter, "Hold a moment. I'm getting a cloth to pour them out on." She arrived with it, and David gently poured and finger raked the morels off the top of the pleurottes.

He pulled one out and held it up. "Is this a pleurotte?"

"A superb one. Nicely firm, yet soft. Dry surface, smooth edges. I can't believe you've never before hunted mushrooms."

"I haven't, but you're the one who found them. You described how to identify them and where to search. I simply brought them here."

Chapter Twenty-Five

As they watched the fire slowly heat from yellows and reds to greens and gradually to blues, Maria began quietly, "Mama said God delivered the meat. She said He likes us. Then you said, She likes us. I've always heard God was a He. I'm confused."

"God is all of us, all of life. Everything," David replied. "We're all part of reality. Not only He, not only She, but Us — all of us working in harmony. This is being demonstrated right here in this situation. Here we are, three people who have known each other for three days, maybe four. It doesn't matter. We've known each other for only a short time, but working together, working in harmony, each adding to the equation, we are so much stronger than the three of us acting individually." He looked into Maria's and Rachel's eyes.

"It's the greedy ones who create gods and add the confusion, add the complications. It's the greedy ones who try to get others to support them. The greedy ones distort the reality by setting up and maintaining religions so they can sit back. Sit back and be supported by the weaker ones they've scared and enslaved."

"So, the rabbis, the priests, the ministers, the preachers — they're all on the take, all gathering feathers for their nests?" Maria asked.

"Not all." He shook his head. "Not all. Some are genuinely offering their finest; offering from their reality. There was a padre I spent a lot of time talking with outside Ypres as I waited to go to the trenches again. He understood reality, dismissed the hocus-pocus, the flimflam manipulation of religion, and he agreed that many religions enslave people by preying on the weak, on the vulnerable by using emotions and guilt. Many religions seem to be little more than a way to suck the last few remnants of wealth from the weak."

"I sense you're not listed among the supporters of religion," Rachel said, "but I saw that from the beginning. You're much too free, much too open-minded, much too creative to be ensnared in those webs."

"You see clearly," he smiled, then pointing above the racks, he asked, "Do the ribs need turning? They're just starting to smoke."

Maria got up with David and they flipped the ribs, adjusted the supports and sat again.

"I love the harmony, the coordination, the acting together. No words needed. Just simply doing it together. Together. That's the power. Together. Focused and cooperating." Rachel said as she swirled the wine in her glass and looked deeply into it.

"This wine, this best barrel from the 1911 harvest, this was a great exercise in cooperation, in working together. It was a difficult harvest, ducking between the thunderstorms. Appraising the right moment for each plot, each row. Gambling together to hold out another day for the western slope, picking into the night on the Terrassen. Together."

"I've never had a taste so splendid," he said, rolling his glass under his nose. "I don't at all understand the complexity of what I'm tasting. It overpowers me, leaves me without vocabulary to describe it. The aroma takes me into realms I've never before been. I must learn more about wine. I must learn more about what it takes to produce it."

They sat almost mesmerised by the flames of the fire as they sipped their Gewürztraminer and quietly spoke, all of them offering.

David quietly added, "Here we are, calmly waiting for venison to sear by a fire on the southern slopes of the Schwarzwald. This would have been such an idyllic setting a year ago. Now we're doing it surreptitiously, close under the nose of the enemy, casually watching a large pan of pleurottes and morels cook in butter. We could be cowering in fear. I prefer not to."

"It's still an idyllic setting," Rachel said as she got up to give the pan of mushrooms a shake and a toss. "How far away is Fritz?"

"At least a quarter mile. The soldiers who shot the doe and fawn were about that far when I last saw them, carrying their meat away from the fire scar, away from us. They angled slightly upward, almost in line with the fire, so now the smoke and lingering flames up there are almost directly between them and us, and the smell of that fire will hide the aromas of our dinner... So, explain the pieces of meat you cut from the carcass."

"These two pieces are the tenderloins, the ones I told you do the pelvic thrust, the love thrust. They're wonderfully tender and deliciously flavoured. Those two larger, flatter pieces, hanging the other side of the fire, those are the back-straps. They sit on the outside of the back, run along each side of the spine. They're also nicely tender. We'll cook them a bit longer, let them cool and cut them for later. The ribs, of course, you recognise. We'll roast them even longer, make the meat between them tender, then also cut them up for later."

"What about the rest of the animal, the shoulders, the hips?"

"That's tougher meat. The muscles there get used so much more. Most of it needs braising or stewing. Long, slow cooking. We don't have the time to do that. I did skin a ham, and it's hanging in the cool little notch over by the waterfall. It will tenderise and mellow like that for two weeks or more, in case we're stuck here that long. We'll be in Switzerland long before then..."

"Mama and I dragged the rest of the carcass along the stream and flipped it over the falls. That's three dead down there in three days. I hope that's the end of it."

Rachel got up again and placed the tenderloins in the pan with the mush-rooms and moved them around to the bottom. "These won't take long. Three to four minutes between each turn, three turns, twelve minutes, a quarter hour. How are the carrots, Maria?"

"Looking good, Mama, just about ready to start to sizzling."

"I've not seen carrots done that way, cooked without water."

"It's my favourite way to cook them. Quartered into fingers and put in a covered pot with a bit of butter. Shake it from time to time to keep them from scorching. They steam in their own juices."

She took a small stick and turned the potatoes in the coals. "These are near-ly ready. They'll be done when the tenderloins are."

A dozen minutes later Rachel cut one of the tenderloins in half, looked at the deep pink colour and placed the halves on two plates then put the whole tenderloin on the third plate. Maria rolled the three potatoes out of the coals and across the slab, knocking most of the ashes off the crusted skin as they tumbled. She stabbed one with a fork and handed it to David. "Blow these off and put them on the plates, I'll get the carrots."

Rachel spooned the mushrooms over the meat, paused to cut the potatoes and poured the remaining pan juices into them as Maria forked carrots from the pot to the plates and poured the remaining butter over the potatoes.

"I have rarely dined this well at home. I can't remember such a fine looking meal in the mountains," he said as Rachel handed him his plate. "That's a big piece of meat."

"You should have no trouble with it." Rachel giggled. "From what I've seen, you're very adept at handling big meat."

"I've had venison before, but never this tender, never so wonderfully flavoured. It's always tasted gamier than this. Probably a different breed of deer from those back home."

"More to do with the season," Rachel said. "The meat is wilder, gamier in the autumn, in the mating season."

"The carrots are so sweet done this way and the mushrooms are so delicious, they add a wonderful flavour to all butter they absorbed. I've not previously had pleurottes or morels. I was too busy with the firewood to see how you prepared them for the pan."

"Morels are a bit difficult to clean. There's often grit in the folds and the grooves. For me, the easiest way is to slosh them around in a pan of water. Two or three changes of water, then toss them around in a cloth and let them dry. You still need to flick out the last few bits of dirt..." She paused to take another bite.

When she had finished savouring it, she looked up and continued. "The pleurottes are much cleaner. A few of them will need a little wipe. I like to tear them into thin strips. They tear easily and straight, starting at the rounded edge and tearing toward the stem. In strips, they crisp wonderfully in butter. The morels are..."

Maria put up her hand, pointed to the brink of the slab. They all heard it now — the growling and snarling.

"Animals fighting over the carcass," David said after a few moments of silence. "We won't be able to see them. Too dark now. What carnivores are there up here?"

"Besides us, you mean?" Rachel asked with a giggle. "There used to be wolves, some say there still are, though others dismiss sighting reports as packs of stray dogs. There are *Wildkatzen*, wildcats and foxes, I'm not sure what else."

David looked at his watch, "2110... Ten past nine. The moon is still big, but it won't rise until shortly past midnight. It should start lighting the gully a couple hours after that. Listening to the noise down there, most of the bones will be clean by then."

"Speaking of bones," Maria pointed toward the fire. "The racks of ribs need another turning and we can take the backstraps down and let them start cooling."

"Finish your dinner, Sweetheart," Rachel said, "another few minutes won't matter. This is too delicious to interrupt."

"I wonder what Fritz is eating up there tonight. Some of the stuff they fed us on exercise would better have been left for the scavengers, like those below." David chuckled. "But then, were scavengers ourselves, aren't we? Scavenging here below Fritz."

"Below Fritz only geographically," Maria added. "Far above them in every other way."

Chapter Twenty-Six

"The clouds have come down and wrapped the hillside in fog," David said Monday morning as he crawled back inside and under the blankets to re-warm.

"We saw that when we were out," Rachel said. "It often happens in the spring, particularly after a storm. Sometimes it lasts for several days, hanging on the hills until there's a wind."

"It's a few minutes to eight. Let's break camp and use this as a cover to head farther along. Good morning, ladies," he said as he rolled to kiss each in turn. "No need for breakfast, we can find a stream and pause an hour or so along for a bite."

Twenty minutes later they were through the waterfalls and moving along the ledge. "Stop there." David turned to the women. "I'll take your packs past the bulge, much safer that way; this is a tricky spot, even more now with the wetness from the mist."

He ferried the packs in three trips then coached the girls past the bulge. They all paused at the corner and looked back into their spa. "We must come back here when this war is over." He nodded and smiled. "I cannot remember a more pleasant spot."

"Nor more pleasant company to share it with," Maria added.

The trio moved quickly along the base of the bluffs. "Up there," he pointed, "That's the mushroom and firewood store."

They came to the block of rock and sidled around it, then turned and followed along beneath the lower set of bluffs, arriving at the stream again a few minutes later, below the waterfalls. They looked at the stag's remains. It was little more than a rack of antlers on a stripped skull, some scattered bones and pieces of hide; it had been well used.

David led a traverse maintaining elevation as they threaded in and out of shallow cirques and around rounded ridges. It was twenty-five past nine when he paused at a tiny stream tumbling over large and small rocks. "How's this for breakfast?"

They unslung their packs and sat on the mist dampened moss which covered the rocks. "Mama, you get breakfast ready, I want to check David's wounds." Maria ran her fingers through the stubble on his cheek. "How old is this beard now?"

"Friday evening was my last shave. This is Monday, so nearly ten days. These wounds were stitched up a week ago right now."

She pushed lightly along the scar. "Still sore?"

"No, more itchy, but that's also the whiskers. I remember in the mountains how they became itchy as they grew."

She watched the remaining stitches as she moved his lip around. "I'll take these out this evening after we've camped. They've done their job. How's the inside?"

"Feels so much better, I can open my mouth a lot wider now — the jaw hinge is so much less sore. I had no problem at all with the meat last night, but that was so wonderfully tender."

"Is this still numb?" she asked, licking his lip.

"A little, but not as much." He ran his tongue over it and caught the tip of hers. She was quickly exploring the inside of his mouth, probing the lines of his scars, checking for swelling on the inside of his cheek, feeling the other swelling with her hand.

"When the nurse is finished with her examination," Rachel said with a giggle, "I can pour the tea. Breakfast is ready."

David shifted with a deft hand move from his thigh to a more comfortable lay across his hip, adding with a chuckle, "If all medical examinations were like this, I'd be tempted to play sick or injured."

"I think it has a lot to do with the energy between you two. It's so magical watching you interact."

They sipped their tea and gnawed tender meat off the ribs. "We'll have to eat a lot of venison the next while," Rachel said. "We don't want it to spoil."

"This is delicious with the dried plums and apricots, what a great idea, Mama," David said, as he pulled a map from the flap pocket of his large rucksack.

"We've passed one road, this one," he said as he ran his finger along the folded map sheet. "The one coming from the top of Feldberg down through Brandenberg to Todtnau."

"That was easy to cross with this fog," Maria said. "Hope it continues."

"We're making excellent time, being able to use the open meadows, rather than skirting around them," he said. "We just need to stop, be still and listen frequently. Sound travels much better in a thick fog than in clear air. We can hear farther and more loudly, but we must remember we can be heard more easily by others."

"This large lake here, Schluchsee," Rachel said pointing to the map, "we need to keep to the south side of it along the ridge top. There's a broad valley and a town on the other side. The ridge is over 1200 metres elevation, unpopulated and wonderfully wild."

"Schlucht is gully, isn't it?" he asked. "Gully Lake, it sounds steep sided. Looks to be a bit over three kilometres long."

"Schlucht also means canyon," Rachel replied.

He ran his finger along the map, tracing a rather sinuous route. "Once we've traversed into and back out of this deep valley down the other side of Feldberg, we should be able to keep above 1100 metres all the way there. We can wind our way above Menzenschwand, on the broad col between it and the valley and marshes above the lake. The contours look nicely spread and even."

They had a second cup of tea and continued gnawing meat from the bones until they were satisfied. They got up, shouldered their packs and headed off again into the fog.

"It's just coming to half past ten. The fog is still holding nicely," he said as they reached the edge of the trees. "No idea how big this meadow is, we won't know until we get across. Be still and listen."

They continued along in this careful way for another two and a quarter hours, David following the lead of the land, watching the compass, maintaining elevation and monitoring their progress along the contours on the folded map panel in his hand. He figured they were at the beginning of the broad ridge running along the south side of Schluchsee.

"It's been rather featureless the past while, but the flat terrain is starting to rise. I think we may be at the head of the marshes," he said after they had paused to listen again. "Let's head along to see if the slope continues up and matches my calculations of where we are."

They continued gradually up, and twenty minutes later he raised his arm and pointed. "It's getting warmer. Can you feel the sun's warmth as it tries to burn through the tops of the clouds?" A few minutes later, after a steeper rise, blue sky appeared above them. They kept going directly up the slope and walked out of the fog, up out of the clouds.

"This is so spectacular, so wonderfully amazing," Maria said. "I've never seen anything like this. Oh, my God! I've never before walked along the tops of clouds."

"This is one of my favourite things in the mountains," David put his arms out like wings and spun around. "I love to wake in the morning and see the valleys filled with clouds below me. While I enjoy blue sky, those below resign themselves to another glum day. Come, let's continue along a bit higher, above the billow tops and find a place to stop. Confirm we're where I think we are."

Around on the south side of the ridge, he found a level patch of moss and heather at the side of a small tarn on a tumble of outcrop. "This looks like a good place to pause. It's not quite half past one," he said looking at his watch and winding it.

"What a lovely spot." Rachel rubbed her shoulders and looked around after she had set her pack down. "There's the top of Feldberg back there, the one to the left of it, Herzogenhorn and farther to the left, just peeking through, is Spießhorn. We're exactly where we were aiming for. Edom and I did this ridge many times. Down there in the clouds is Menzen-schwand with its thermal..."

Rachel stopped herself, put her hand to her mouth. "Oh, my God! I'd for-gotten about the hot spring in the rocks at the end of the ridge. I'm sure I can lead us to them. Oh, my God! Let me see the map." She was bubbling with excitement.

Her finger traced along the map to their location. She looked along the ridge, then back to the map, then back up again. "Coming from this direc-tion, we used to find it by following the top of the ridge to the start of its descent through a line of trees between two open slopes watching for an outcrop below on the slope down toward Sankt Blasien. Edom always lead, but I can see it in my mind."

She looked again at the map and ran her finger along to Sankt Blasien, then looked up and smiled. "It's many years since I've been here. I had totally forgotten about the hot pools. You wouldn't mind a hot bath tonight, would you?" Her hands went back to her mouth. "Oh, my God!" she mumbled through them.

"Thermals seem common here," David said. "Yesterday when I headed out for a look, before the shots that scared you, I checked the spa pools. They were still warm, even with the snow. I found a flow of thermal water which feeds them from the cracks masked by the spray of the waterfall. I forgot to tell you about it with all the excitement which followed."

Rachel nodded as he spoke. "That makes good sense why they're so warm. I read a newspaper article a couple of years ago saying there's a higher concentration of hot springs and thermal waters in the Grand Duchy of Baden than anywhere else in the world." She giggled. "Maybe it was written by a journalist who had been to Texas, but thermal waters are rather common here, that's why it's called Baden. Oh, my God! I can't wait... Let's go find the pools."

Chapter Twenty-Seven

It took the trio a while to find the hot pool. Rachel couldn't see Sankt Blasien down through the clouds to guide her. After a few false leads and a return to the top, she remembered how they had initially found it. "We were traversing across the side of the ridge and stopped in a rib of trees by a small stream for a drink. The water was warm. We followed the stream up the hill, feeling it get warmer."

She paused to think. "The stream disappeared above a small pool. Edom looked up the gully and thought it too deep not to have water farther above. We followed the gully upward and found another small pool of even warmer water ten metres or so higher. Another five metres higher was a large deep pool of water a few degrees above body temperature. A few metres farther up was the top of the gully. The water coming out of the rocks was much too hot."

Rachel looked at the map again. "It's about a third of the way down toward Sankt Blasien from the rounding of the ridge — it's only a hundred metres or so in elevation down the treed rib."

"Do you recognise the place on the ridge where we need to head down?" David asked.

"I can't tell now that we're back down into the clouds. Edom always led the way to it. When it was clear, we used the copper dome of the church. It's hard to miss — it's one of the largest domes in Europe. My father said only Saint Peter's in Rome and the Duomo in Florence are bigger. I can't see it, nor can I see the rock outcrop to lead us down."

"Do you think we're near the line?"

"I'm sure we're within two hundred metres one side or the other."

"Let's head back up along the ridge three hundred yards or so and descend a hundred metres from there, then spread out down the slope and walk back along parallel to the line of the ridge top."

As they descended through a steep meadow, Rachel said, "This is right, there's a meadow on each side of the forested rib." They turned, spread out and soon entered the forest. A few minutes in, they came to a small gully with cold water. They confirmed up and down the slope that the water was cold all the way along. Less than ten metres farther along, Rachel shouted, "Warm water! We've got warm running water." She climbed a few metres. "We're here. Here's the big pool."

Maria quickly descended to the spot, dropped her pack and was nearly undressed by the time David had made his way back up the slope. She followed Rachel into the pool, looking back at him and saying with a giggle, "You're the last one in again."

They sat up to their shoulders and soaked. "Doesn't have the smell of sulphur like the one in Banff," he said. "Doesn't have the luxury hotel either, but it will do just fine. Where did you set-up your camp?"

"There's a pretty little grove a short distance across there." Rachel pointed to their left. "Midway between the hot and cold running water. This is such a delightful spot. I haven't been here for many years, since before we moved from Unterhallau ten years ago. Long before that, you hadn't yet started school. We needed a break from you kids," she said, looking at Maria and smiling.

"We're only about two hundred metres above Sankt Blasien, an ancient town, said to be over a thousand years old. A monastery is how it started."

"People below must surely know about this place, it's so near."

"No Sweetheart, I don't think so. We never saw anyone here, never any signs of others having visited. It's up a rugged slope with much gentler terrain on both sides. The hot stream runs into the cold one after only twenty-five or thirty metres. It's an easy place to miss. Besides, they have a thermal down in the town and another one a short distance along the valley in Menzenschwand."

"I'm getting hot," David said, after a twenty-minute soak. "I'll head across to go sort out how to set-up camp."

"It's almost straight across the slope, impossible to miss. It will shout to you as you approach."

"I'll come help you. You stay here and relax, Mama, your joints and muscles are older than ours."

David and Maria put on their shoes and shirts, put trousers over their arms, picked up the four packs and headed across the slope less than ten yards to a flat expanse of moss between two huge stumps and a moss-covered log. They set the packs down, and he was already well up as she turned to kiss him. After a brief hug, he laid her on the moss, knelt and ran his tongue up the inside of her thigh, up past her blond patch, circled her navel and ran it back along the other thigh, then back up and paused in the middle to get more tongue practice.

Maria shortly erupted, and as her twitching calmed and she regained a more regular breathing, she said, "Inside, David, please come inside. I'm still very safe."

"We did that too," Rachel said quietly a quarter hour later, after she had watched them shudder together and then collapse limply into the moss. "We couldn't pause even to pitch the tent the first time we saw this place. That became our arrival ritual."

"Been watching long, Mama?" Maria asked, a little out of breath.

"Long enough to know you're both very happy with this place." She shuddered. "Oh, how I remember my times here with Edom." She shook her head. "Let me get you some cottons."

"I'm thinking the tent might be the best shelter, the warmest. Is it big enough for the three of us?" David asked.

Maria giggled. "We don't need much space at all, not the last few nights, anyway. But there's ample room in it for three less friendly people. The five of used to sleep in it."

"I can slant the canvas above the tent from these two old logging stumps. It will make a good rain shed if needed. This is amazingly comfortable moss."

"We cleared the stones from the bed, pulled out two big roots, added more moss and levelled it. During each visit, we improved it. I'm delighted to see it has lasted so well."

Rachel began unpacking as David and Maria lay entangled, connected and lightly panting, still coming down. She had the sailcloth tent unrolled, had the bundled lines sorted and was looking at the sections of wooden poles. "I'll leave this for you to figure out, David. Edom always did it for us. It still looks confusing to me. I'll continue unpacking."

It was surprisingly warm as they started stirring from their slump. "The cloud bottoms have lifted above us now," he said. "The air is much less damp and the clouds are holding the earth's heat in."

"We're also about four hundred metres lower than we were up on the shoulder of Feldberg," Rachel said.

"Conrad used a rule of six and a half European degrees per thousand metres. He had to convert it for his clients when he started guiding in Canada. We use feet and different degrees there, like the English. In dry air, the change is greater than in damp."

David had started dressing through the conversation while Maria continued to sit and drain onto the small cotton towel. He looked at the two large pieces of cloth, shifted and flipped them, examined the lines, picked up the thick dowelling pieces, studied the brass fittings on their ends, then looked around the small grove.

"Maria had mentioned a piece of painted canvas, Mama. A moisture cover for the ground."

"I've just now pulled it out," Rachel held it out to him. "Have you sorted out the puzzle?"

"I think I see it." Then he added with a chuckle, "But it will quickly tell me if I'm wrong." He turned toward Maria and said as he bent to kiss her, "Move your beautiful butt, you're sitting in the middle of a construction zone."

They spread the sheet, threaded the brass fittings together, placed pole ends into the cloth pockets and erected one end of the tent. He took the line from the ridge and tied it to a root while Maria held the pole. He took one of the two corner lines, put a peg through its loop and pushed it into the soft forest floor, then he repeated with the other corner. "That's one end. How does this look, Mama?"

Rachel paused and looked over at it. "Everything looks good from here. That's how I remember it during the process."

They erected the other end, adjusted and tensioned the guys, adding stronger anchors for some of them. By the time they had strung up the oiled canvas as a rain shed, Rachel had sorted the cooking utensils and the food and had a large billy of water on the Primus about to come to a boil.

David looked at his watch. "It's 1605, five past four," he said. "Still quite early. I'll lay out the bedrolls, then we can have tea. A few minutes late for the British. After that, I'm going for another soak."

As they sipped tea from their mugs and nibbled on Munster, Gruyère, knäckebrot and dried fruit, David studied the map and snaked a strip of his notebook paper along it. "With our twists and bends as we followed the contours, we came about eighteen kilometres today," he reported. Then he looked back at the map as the girls watched, quiet in their thoughts.

A minute and a half later, he continued, "The straight line distance to the border is a little under twenty-one kilometres. The safer line which follows mostly through the trees is a little over twenty-three, gradually descending about five hundred metres."

"So a day will easily put us on the rocky rib above the border," Rachel said. "We'll be in Switzerland on Wednesday."

"Let's concentrate on being here," he said. "We can concentrate on Switzerland when we get there. Being safe where we are, being aware of what's around us is the important thing."

Maria looked around slowly and said, "Anyone coming along this rocky, broken rib instead of following the easy slopes would have to be either stupid or hiding or know of the hot spring."

"We fit two of those categories," David said, and added with a chuckle, "Maybe even all three. This is my second closest approach to Switzerland. My closest was much too close. We must be alert."

As they finished their tea, David asked Rachel to describe what she remembered of the terrain. She started by saying it was a long time ago since she was last here and tried to remember when. She talked of gentle forested ridges to cross, of shallow valleys, open meadows and fields, of grazing cattle, of small farms and tiny villages.

Rachel took the map sheet and ran her finger across it, digging back through her mind as she did. "Here, this rib, it's untamed on top, broken and rocky, offers great cover very close to the border. We need to get to the top of this…" She paused, looked up, "That was 1901. We sat on the top of the ridge and talked of Queen Victoria's passing and of the new King Edward."

"I would have been five then," Maria said with wide eyes.

"No, four and a half, you weren't five until September."

They finished tea and David gathered all the food into a rucksack, tossed a line up through the crotch in a small hardwood. He thought maybe an ash, then he hoisted the pack about ten feet up and tied the end of the line to the trunk.

Maria and Rachel had looked on, quietly watching until he had nearly finished. "An offering for the gods?" Maria asked.

"No, protection from hungry forest animals. This is a routine practice at home in the mountains. Bears can't climb small trees, wolves can't jump that high, we may be visited by an extremely adventurous squirrel… To the bath."

They soaked, hauled out to cool and pleasure, soaked some more and repeated the cycle a couple of times before heading back toward camp, completely relaxed.

"Isn't this a marvellous place?" Rachel asked. "I'm so glad… Fuuuu…" She stumbled and grabbed David's arm for support.

"What is it?"

"My ankle. Rock turned underfoot. Hadn't laced my boots. Hope it's not broken again."

Chapter Twenty-Eight

David picked up Rachel and carried her the remaining few yards to the tent, and as Maria held the flap and pulled the top blanket off the bed, he continued on in and laid her on the remaining bedrolls.

"Pull the side of the blanket over her, shock may give her a chill," Maria said. "Roll this one up as big as you can," she continued, handing him the other blanket. "Go soak some towels and cottons in the cold stream. Bring them back cold and sopping."

He gave her the rolled bedroll, and she lifted Rachel's leg and put it under her calf, then gently eased the loose boot off the foot and ran her fingers lightly up each side of her ankle. "Let me know if you have sharp pain, bone pain when I do this, Mama." She increased the pressure as she walked her fingers up and down past the ankle joint. "Anything, Mama?"

"A throbbing, an ache along the outside of my foot. Nothing sharp."

"Along here," Maria asked, looking at the beginning of swelling and darkening. "Did you roll over onto the outside of your foot?"

"Yes, it rolled downhill with the rock. That's tender along there."

"Sharp?"

"No — tender is a better word, aching, throbbing. It feels hot."

"David will be here soon with a cold compress. Cooling and pressing will slow the swelling. Ease the pain a bit also. Roll onto your right side, put the outside of your foot upward."

She took the wet towels from David, folded one and put it under the ankle, folded two more and draped them over the foot.

"One more test, Mama. I'm going to push up on the bottom of your foot. First the heel. I'll increase the push gradually as much as I can. You push back as I do. Tell me if you've any sharp pain, any bone pain. Let me know as soon as there's pain." She pushed straight along the axis of the leg, being careful not to bend the ankle. "Anything, Mama?"

"Nothing but the pressure — and the throb that's already there."

"I'm going to push up on the ball of your foot. Same thing, you tell me again."

"A pull in the back of my calf, an increase in the ache along the outside of my foot. Nothing sharp."

"Did you feel a pop? A snap? Hear anything when it happened."

"Nothing."

"I don't think it's broken. It appears to be only a sprain. I'll probe my fingers along all your foot and ankle bones again. Tell me of any sharp pain or change in pain... Nothing? Good!" She looked up and smiled.

"I think you have a mild sprain, no torn ligaments, just some stretch. The instructor told us these are the most common type, turning the ankle over outward. Treatment is easy. Elevate the ankle to reduce blood flow, apply cold compresses to prevent swelling, or to slow it. We can bind it once we see the swelling isn't severe. We still have a lot of surgical tape we can use for that. The main thing is rest. Don't walk on it for a few days until the swelling has reduced."

"Damn! Damn! Damn! Damn!" Rachel cried out. "Look what I've done. Look what I've done to our dreams, to your dreams — I'm so sorry, so terribly sorry." Her shoulders shook with her sobs.

David knelt above her head, and he put a hand on each side of it, fingers running down her cheeks. "You've done nothing. It happened. I have no dreams. We need to concentrate on being here. Here is the only place we can do anything." He softly wiped her tears with his fingers.

"This may not seem to be the ideal situation, but it's the one we're in," he continued. "We can work only with what we have; anything else is fantasy, dreaming, diffusing energy which needs to be applied here, applied in this situation, not squandered somewhere off in the future." He stroked her cheek.

"Pausing here for a few days while your ankle mends might even be the best. Who knows whether there's a border sweep planned for the next couple of days which would have caught us." He wiped more of her tears. "See the interesting places the mind can take us — the current situation is far better than that."

He felt her relax, then running a finger along a tear streak, he bent and kissed her forehead. He continued to cradle her head as Maria changed the towels and applied pressure to the ankle.

"We have hot and cold running water, a wonderfully comfortable soft bed in a fine shelter hidden in an area rarely visited. We have most of the cooked venison remaining, several kilos of fresh mushrooms plus a large amount of the food we brought for the trip." He paused for a moment, then continued. "But the most important thing we have is each other — that's our greatest asset."

"Your way of thinking — I find it so amazing. Here I was a minute ago deeply disappointed that we wouldn't get to Switzerland on Wednesday. Now I'm delighted to be here."

"That's the thing isn't it?" David said. "We can't be anywhere but where we are. Yet it's so common for us to spend much of our energy trying to be where we're not. Dreaming a life, rather than living it." He stroked her hair.

"I saw many in the trenches in Belgium, dreaming of being somewhere else, talking with their buddies about plans and dreams after the war has ended. Dreaming of other places, rather than concentrating on where they were. Then bang, they were nowhere."

He kissed her forehead again and said, "I'll take those towels and cool them again."

As soon as he left, Maria asked, "Mama, can I take him inside when I'm bleeding? I'll be starting again on Wednesday or Thursday."

"It's a little messy, but if neither of you mind, it's an excellent time. Helps relieve some of the tension. Of course, it's also among the safest times. You'll need a convenient place to wash afterwards; we certainly have that here." She smiled as she reflected.

"While you kids were in school, we would do it outside on the grass, so we wouldn't mess the bed. That's why your father screened that corner of the back garden. So wild and wonderfully free..."

"Here're cold towels, what else can I get you?" David said as he passed them to Maria.

"You're so quick. One moment, take these and re-do them. I think we have the swelling controlled. We just need to keep it cooled, pressed and elevated," Maria said, handing him the three towels as she replaced them. "Let's continue doing this for a while."

"That's such a convenient stream. Be right back."

"Edom built a cosy moss bed a few metres the other side of the hot pool. It was so convenient — I didn't check, but I'm sure it's still there... Probably needs only some twig and pine cone removal, like this place did."

The girls continued their conversation in spurts of a minute and a bit as the cold compresses were changed, Rachel giving Maria tips and ideas, telling her of the games and tricks she and Edom had learned and of things which had worked well for them.

"It's such a delightful area to explore," Rachel said, "seeing what gives pleasure to him, what pleases you. The more honest you are with each other, the more magnificent the experience. Exploring together, playing like two romping kittens sometimes, driven by deep forces at other times..."

"Here's the bucket brigade again," he said, bringing in three wet towels. "How's the patient doing?"

"Nurse and patient are both doing very well," Maria said. "I think we can slow on the compresses now. I've been wrapping tightly and pressing on the towels. The swelling appears to have stopped; I think it's starting to go down a bit. We'll just keep it cooled, keep the pressure on it and watch it for a while."

"At the Lake O'Hara camp, we had a climber up at our high camp, well above the snow line with a sprained ankle. The swelling wasn't too bad, not like some I had seen. After a long spell of snow bags, it looked quite good. Conrad discussed it with some of the older men, I think one was a doctor, and they taped it up."

He moved his hands to demonstrate. "They applied surgical tape down one side, from the lower shin, under the middle of the heel and up the other side. Then another from the front of the shin, down across the back of the heel and up toward the back of the calf. A third piece diagonally the other way, making a tall X."

"That would give excellent lateral support," Maria said. "That's where it's needed. The ligament is stretched and weakened; it needs help while it mends and strengthens. Compression will also control the swelling. How well did it work?"

"He was able to apply weight within a few hours, but he couldn't walk without the crutch I had made for him. Three days later he put his boot on, and he slowly made his way along the ridge using his alpenstock for support, and continued all the way down to the base camp on the fifth day."

"Can you make me a crutch?"

"I was looking for suitable saplings each time I went to wet the towels. There are several possibilities. Probably better ones across the slope. I can make you a pair," he chuckled, "I'm not distracted by wanting to climb mountains here like I was there."

"How long did they wait?" Maria asked. "How long before they started the taping?"

"I'm not sure, I wasn't there. I had been sent down the side of the ridge to a stand of saplings in a slide scar, for crutch wood. The ankle was taped when I got back up about an hour or so later."

"How long after the accident was that — when you returned?"

"Two and a half hours — no, less. Probably two and a quarter."

"So quite soon after cooling, after controlling the swelling." Maria lifted the towels and looked, prodding the slight puffiness with a finger, watching it rebound. "Do you know where the tape is?"

"The nurse confiscated it," he said with a chuckle.

"The old tin box, the biscuit box," Rachel said. "It's in the big back pocket of my pack for quick access. That's our emergency repair kit and medicine box."

"Bring three more cold towels when you come back."

Maria applied the fresh cold towels, opened the tin box and pulled out a roll of wide tape and a pair of scissors. A few minutes later she said, "Come sit over here, David, lift Mama's leg a bit. Let's give her ankle more elevation, see if we can run out more of the fluid."

She ran her hands up the ankle. "Anything sharp, Mama?"

"No, dear, and the throbbing has eased."

"Do you remember the pattern, David? Do you want to do it?"

"I remember the vertical tapes appeared to have been pulled quite tight to offer the support. The wraparound ones needed redoing as the swelling reduced. Probably best if I pull from above. You stabilise the ankle to keep it aligned."

He rested the leg back on the roll and looked at it. "Best to roll onto your back for this, Mama. Toes up, easier to see the alignment."

He knelt and straddled her thighs, cut a half yard of tape from the roll, centred it under the back of the foot arch and pulled the ends up and then inward. "Hold her ankle, I'm going to tug. Let me know if this hurts at all, Mama."

"That looks very good," Maria said.

"Looks superb from here," Rachel said.

"Now, the first diagonal." He took another half yard piece off the roll, leaned forward and centred it on the back of the heel and repeated the sequence. "Now the third strip across the arch," he said as he applied the tape.

"That looks great," Maria said. "How's it feel, Mama?"

"It feels wonderful... Feels wonderful all over. Don't stop now, you can keep right on working down there for a long time more, I'm thoroughly enjoying watching David's three pendulums keeping time with his movements." She paused and shuddered. "He's so impressive in his nursing uniform."

"Pardon my butt, Mama; I'd forgotten we're still dressed for the hot pool." He chuckled and added, "I'm pleased to hear you're not in pain."

Chapter Twenty-Nine

David applied more tape diagonally around Rachel's foot, winding from the arch, over the top, around the heel and back to the arch to further stabilise the ankle and add pressure. As he was doing this, Maria took the towels to the stream to re-wet.

"I can't keep my eyes off your equipment, David. You're an impressively built lad. Maria doesn't know how well endowed you are. She has no comparison, but I do. I explored a fair bit before I met Edom, and I knew a lot of men — I know."

"I didn't realise until I arrived at Army camp last year and saw the other fellows in the gang showers. Didn't realise until they were pointing and staring. Until I saw they were all smaller, most of them much smaller. I had always considered this as normal. This is still normal for —"

"What's still normal for what?" Maria interrupted as she came back in with the cold towels. "Let me put these on again, Mama, then you can tell me what's normal."

She reapplied the cold compresses and looked up. "David? Mama? Who's going to tell me what's normal?"

"You go ahead, Mama," he said. "You're more experienced with this than I am."

"But you're closer to the subject than I am," Rachel said, giggling.

"Closer, maybe, but until last August in Quebec, I was completely unaware of anything of it. It had never entered my mind."

"I'm no further ahead here," Maria said. "What's this normal thing you were talking about?"

"Abnormal, Sweetheart," Rachel replied. "Abnormal is more the theme of the discussion we were having."

"Yes, but to me, entirely normal," he countered.

"But you had no basis for comparison. No norm to relate to."

"That's the thing, though. My range of comparison had been my father, my brother and me. I seemed normal."

"You come from a very big family."

"No, only one brother and one sister."

"I'm completely confused here," Maria said. "What's this about?"

Rachel reached out her hand and gave his dangle a gentle shake. "This, Maria, we're talking about this."

"That's such a delightful topic, one I'm very interested in," Maria said, "but I haven't been able to follow. What have I missed?"

"Mama, you tell her, you know more about it than I."

Maria shook her head. "Weren't we just here a minute ago?"

"Size, Maria, size. These are normally smaller. Much smaller. I didn't re-alise they came this big until I spied on you that first day. David's is bigger dangling than most men are when they're hard."

"How big are they normally, then?"

"This size," he said. "This is normal for me. This is what I grew up with, what grew up with me.."

"So that's where I came in, then," Maria laughed. "He thinks it's normal, you think it's not."

"I know it's not, and he now also knows. Tell her about your discoveries in the showers. I'd like to hear the rest of it too."

He looked at them and shrugged "My first day in Valcartier when I arrived to sign-up for the Army last August, after being assigned a bunk in the bar-rack tents, I went to find a bath. It was hot and humid, and after the four-day train trip, I was sticky and stinky.

"There were no baths, only large rooms with shower nozzles. The room was crowded when I arrived so I undressed, joined in and stood under a shower stream enjoying the cooling water for a while before starting to soap. I looked up and saw nearly everyone staring at me, so to find out what the problem was, I asked the fellow next to me to explain.

"He pointed down at me, told me I was so big. I looked down at his and could barely see it buried in his hair, so I looked at the others in the shower. Most were not much larger than my thumb, smaller than I had been as a child. Thinking some might be slow growing, I looked further and realised I'm thicker than some were long.

"I became increasingly curious during the following weeks when I had seen only one approaching my size. Most were half as long, weren't half as thick. I felt like a freak." David shook his head and offered a twisted smile.

"When I was in Bath and Bristol on my leave in January, I spent a lot of time in the libraries, reading, trying to learn more. There is so little written about such things. Almost like it's a secret."

"I guess it's because they're kept hidden, not wagged around in public," Maria said. "So, Mama, what's your experience with this?"

"Your father was also big when hard, wonderfully thick. But when soft, he was only about half as big; he doubled when excited, he grew to about the size David's is when dangling. Edom had the thickest and among the longest I had seen... Until David."

"This looks and feels perfectly normal to me." Maria hefted it and giggled. "But what is the normal size? I'm curious again."

"I read a study report in a medical journal in the university library in Bristol, which analysed several researchers' findings. Normal length ranges from two and a half to four inches and the normal erect range is from four and a half to six inches."

"How big is an inch?" Maria asked.

"It's a little over two and a half centimetres. I have an inch scale here. Two inches is the length of my little finger in a fist like this. Three inches is the length of my thumb, four is the width of my palm here below my thumb, five is from the crook of my thumb to the end of my forefinger, six is from the crook of my thumb across here to the end of my middle finger, seven is…"

"This," she said, giggling and spreading her fingers along his dangling length.

"Not quite. It's a bit down toward six." Then he added with a big grin. "It's more toward normal size."

"What's seven then?"

"Tip of my thumb to my forefinger in its widest spread."

"And eight?"

"Tip of thumb to tip of middle finger spread wide."

"And nine?" she asked, looking down and giggling.

"Only when you get me excited."

"That's an interesting thing, Maria," Rachel said, "Some grow a lot, double or more in length when they erect. Others, like David's, don't lengthen so much as thicken, they lengthen half or less. It would be rather uncomfortable and awkward for you, for the both of you if his doubled in length."

"But the size doesn't matter," David replied. "That's the theme which I heard the guys all talking. The important thing, they all said, is how well it's used. Strange, though, as word of my size spread around the company and the regiment, it became increasingly difficult for me to have a normal conversation."

Maria looked at him with a puzzled expression. "How so?"

"Few took me seriously, most of them were distracted and the talk almost always turned rather crude. It would be easier if I were a fair amount smaller, more like of the rest of the fellows. If size doesn't matter, then why were they paying all the strange attention to it? Confusing to me."

He looked at his watch. "It's now 1820. It'll be growing dark in less than an hour. I need to cut saplings and make a pair of crutches. Where do you pack the bone saw, Mama?"

"It's tied between plies in the same pocket as the biscuit box."

"I remember seeing that. How's the ankle feeling?"

"Still throbbing, but much more gently. I've had excellent care. I've thoroughly enjoyed your nursing uniform."

He looked down, shook his head and let out a deep sigh, then got up to pull on his trousers. "Let me change from nursing to woodsman's clothes, I have to go cut some timber. We should get dinner going, we don't want the stove still on too far into twilight. There's no moon tonight until well after midnight."

"I'm thinking of a thick stew of venison and barley with diced onions, carrots, turnip and wild mushrooms," Rachel said.

"The barley will take the longest." Maria added with a giggle, "I'll slip into my chef's garb and get that going."

"And what can I do?" Rachel asked.

"You can concentrate seriously on being a convalescent. Relax and rest," David said as he headed out. "You need to mend."

"So that's not normal?" Maria asked after she had heard David find the bone saw and walk across the slope.

"No dear, not anywhere near it. I met a lot of thumb-sized men and one who barely grew to thumb-size when hard."

Maria looked at her thumb. "And what was it like with them?"

"It depends on the person attached to it. I would be thrilled to have someone like David attached to a thumb-sized one. It depends so much on how it's used, so much on the passion of the person using it. Most importantly, it depends on the person. Actually, entirely on the person. Remember, it's simply a tool. Tools don't do the work. It's the craftsman's talent and passion that create the fine work."

Rachel smiled. "A thumb-sized man was how I discovered a magical spot inside... I must tell you about it. I was amazed at the magic he could do with his small tool. He wasn't Jewish, not circumcised, the only non-mutilated one I had seen until David's. God, was he long-lasting. The length of his endurance far outdid his short size."

She trembled lightly as she grinned sheepishly at Maria. "Give David a small one and I'd be no less attracted to him; he's a magnificent person.

Give David's to many other men, I wouldn't be interested except in looking at the tool." Rachel trembled again. "I do love looking at it."

"So size isn't important, then," Maria said. "I had no idea of this size thing, no reason to think David's size is anything but normal. To me, he is the normal size, normal in my experience. He's the both the smallest and the largest..." She shook her head. "I don't know what to think."

She looked down again at her thumb, laid it on her wrist and remained quiet for a long while as she stared. Then shuddering lightly, she shook her head again, looked up at her mother and said, "I'll go get the barley started."

Chapter Thirty

"Let me put this next to your arm, Mama," David said as he brought a piece of freshly-peeled sapling into the tent. "I need to measure your size."

As he laid the forked end alongside her shoulder, Rachel said in a whisper, "Seems a lot of discussion on size lately. Confusion also. Maria seems confused. Told her size in the least important thing. Told her it's the man who matters."

"Thanks, Mama, I appreciate the reinforcement," he whispered as he notched the wood with his knife beside the bottom of her heel, at her wrist and at her armpit. "We'll have the first crutch shortly."

He had cut two slender saplings about two feet below the crotches where they had split into twinned trunks reaching upward toward the light. The idea had come to him up on the ridge above O'Hara as he fumbled to assemble a workable crutch from the simple pieces he had brought up from the slide.

After cutting shallow, but effective mortise and tenon joints for the two cross pieces at the wrist marks and half an inch below the tops of the tall Y, he bound the pieces tightly together with sisal line. Then padding the top with a piece of cotton towelling, he bound it with more sisal.

"Mama, crawl out of the tent and try this," he said after about twenty minutes of work. "Let me give you a hand."

David helped Rachel to stand on her good foot as she came out, then handed her the crutch. "Give this a try, see how it works. Have you used crutches before?"

"Many years ago, when I was still in school. I broke my lower leg and ankle when I fell off a velocipede. It took a long time to mend, and I got pretty good at using crutches. I'm sure my body still remembers the process."

Rachel took a few trial steps with her left foot off the ground, then took another with it lightly taking some weight. "There is no additional pain when I step lightly. This is an excellent crutch."

"Any adjustments? Any changes you'd suggest?"

She took several more steps, moved her hand around, shifted the top cushion under her arm, looked up and down the crutch, and said, "I can see nothing to change."

"Good, I'll start on the second one. I'll need this as a pattern, and you need to get your foot elevated again. How's the swelling?"

"It seems to be good now," Rachel said as she hobbled over toward where Maria was preparing dinner. She lay on her back on the moss and placed her taped foot up the trunk of a tree.

David took the crutch and headed back toward his workplace, asking, "How long before dinner is ready?"

"Another twenty-five or thirty minutes; I'm about to add the carrots and turnips."

"The second crutch should take about the same. We'll eat when it's done."

Maria stood. "I'll go wet some towels for your foot."

"That would be nice, Sweetheart. It eases the ache, but more, we need to make sure the swelling doesn't come back. We need to get this thing working again."

David came back a little over twenty-five minutes later with the second crutch. "I lashed a stout stick between a pair of small trees down there." He turned and pointed. "That's our new latrine. It's not fancy, simply something to sit on. Squatting would be awkward with your ankle."

"The turnip is still a bit hard, maybe five more minutes. It'll start getting get dark shortly. Is it still safe to use the stove?"

"I think it's safe. When I was looking for crutch wood, I took a look from the edge of this stand of trees, out across the fields and down the slopes. I could see the church dome and the roofs of buildings in the village. There don't appear to be any roads over on that side, nor any buildings above the village."

"It's the same on the other side," Rachel said. "Up both sides of this rocky spur are steep grazing pastures. We never saw any roads or trails in them, I can't even remember grazing cattle there. I can't imagine anyone coming up in the dark."

Rachel lay on her front, propped up on an elbow with her left knee bent and her taped foot in the air with a wet towel wound around it as she spooned the thick stew to her mouth. "This is delicious, well worth waiting for. It's much better than any hospital food I can remember."

They lay around for a long while after the last of the stew was gone, quietly talking as the last of the light faded. David lit the candle in his unfolded lantern and watched it light the tall trees around them. Then he lit Maria's cylindrical lamp. "I'm taking my lantern for a walk to find out how far the light from yours extends through the trees."

He walked about forty yards until he lost sight of the last of the illuminated trees around their camp, then sitting on a log, he snuffed the candle and waited for his eyes to adjust to the dark. He was surprised by the faint glow of light above him. The few bits of light which had made it up through the trees were illuminating the base of the low clouds.

Looking back across the slope, he strained to see light from their camp, and as his eyes gradually became accustomed to the black night, a faint loom of light appeared. He lit the candle again and carefully picked his way another thirty yards toward the edge of the pasture, snuffed the candle and waited again for his eyes to accustom.

After he confirmed there was no hint of light through the screen of trees, he lit the candle again and continued to the edge of the wood, snuffing the light as he arrived. He stepped out into the pasture and saw the lamps of the town lighting the valley bottom.

Those will impair the night vision of people down there. They won't see our faint glow on the cloud bottoms.

He sat in the grass, which was now rather wet from the evening dew, and closed his eyes to allow his pupils to dilate again. After two minutes he looked back into the trees trying to catch a hint of light. There was none. The bottoms of the clouds had a faint glow from camp.

Much diminished by the glow the lights of the town puts on them. They won't see ours, let alone their own.

Satisfied, he picked his way back into the trees a few yards, lit the candle and made his way back toward camp and explained his observations when he arrived. "We're invisible from the meadow and from below, but from about fifty or sixty yards into the trees from there, our light becomes increasingly visible."

"So does that mean we can keep a candle burning in here?" Rachel asked.

"We light up the cloud base above us, but the lights from the town below mask that. I feel it's safe to use the lanterns to find our way around, but we should still be careful and put them out unless needed."

It was raining lightly on Tuesday morning when he woke. He heard big splats above him as accumulated drops fell from the trees onto the oiled canvas. He was alone in the tent, but the spaces in front of him and behind were still warm, so he knew the girls had just left.

Probably disturbed my sleep as they got up.

David checked the interior of the tent and was pleased to find everything dry.

The canvas cover is doing its job well, he thought as he looked at his watch and wound it. *It's almost seven thirty, we've slept well again.*

Voices sounded in the distance, men's voices. Many voices shouting incoherently and mixed with loud whistling. He reached for the pistol case, confirmed it was there, then quickly pulled on his trousers. He thrust his feet into his shoes sockless, laced and tied them, grabbed his jacket and ducked out through the entrance of the tent as he took the pistol from its the case.

He stood still under the edge of the canvas, just out of the light drizzle, as he looked through the screen of trees, but he saw nothing moving, nothing unusual. He paused his breathing to focus on listening, but he heard no more voices. There had been none since the first long outburst a minute or so before.

As he stepped out into the light drizzle, he sensed it was probably a thick mist. The clouds had come back down overnight and had settled into the trees. With the pistol safety lever off, he moved down the slope toward the source of the voices, taking cover behind each large tree as he descended. He heard the sharp crack of a gunshot. Then there was silence.

The snapping and cracking of twigs quite close down the slope broke the silence. He peeked around the tree toward the sound and spotted Maria and Rachel, each standing bottomless in their jackets next to large tree trunks a short distance above the latrine.

Then from down the slope beyond them came a shout: *"Großer Schuss, Heinrich, gerade durch den Kopf"*

David watched as several old men converged, appearing and disappearing through the screen of trees and mist. He listened to the rounds of congratulations as he slowly made his way down to the girls and stood with Maria behind her tree. She was shivering.

"Wildschwein, they were cornering a Wildschwein," she whispered. "We were on our way to pee when we heard voices below making noise and whistling, then on our right, we watched a line of men sweeping across the slope only twenty metres below us. I still need to pee. Even more, now I'm cold."

"Do it here. We're hidden from their view behind this tree. They're too focused on their boar to spot us up here anyway," he said as she squatted. He turned and unbuttoned his trouser front, "I have to go myself." Off to his right, he watched Rachel standing with an arched back and letting go a long yellow arc.

Strange... I've not before thought of women standing to pee. Actually, never thought about the details of their peeing.

After relieving themselves, David and Maria looked at the hunting party, then scooted across to Rachel's tree. "Now that we're all more relaxed, let's sort out what to do," he whispered. "Will they dress their kill there, or carry it intact to the valley?"

"Probably carry it down. Dress it there," Rachel whispered. "Feed the entrails to their livestock. Everybody's desperate for food now with the war. But before they go, they'll pass around a flask of schnapps, most likely kirsch to celebrate. Edom was..."

She hadn't quite finished her sentence when they heard the beginnings of toasts and laughter from down the slope.

"Edom was on several boar hunts, and he told us about the strict control. Organised noise-making from one line of men while another line advances from the other side of the slope, sweeping diagonally upward. They form a wedge and corner their prey, spooking it in the process. Only one person with a gun. Usually only one shot... Well, except for the many shots of schnapps."

They waited several more minutes, then watched four men shoulder a thick pole with the boar suspended by its lashed feet. The group slowly moved across the slope to the right, toward the pasture, the men talking excitedly as they went.

"They all look old — I guess the young ones are caught up in the war," Rachel said as they watched the hunting party retreat. "I'm sure those men want this war as little as we do."

"We were told in our training that neither side wants the killing and the destruction," David said as he ran his fingers through his hair. "I keep thinking how hard this must be for the families back home, reading newspaper reports, but not knowing what's happening with us. I wish I could let them know I'm safe."

Chapter Thirty-One

After the last of the hunting party had disappeared among the trees below them, David said, "Let's head back up the slope and into the hot pool to warm." He kissed Maria then added, "Good morning, Mama. How are the crutches working?"

"More awkward to use on the uneven ground, but I'll quickly master them in this stuff." Rachel started up the slope, using them to ease the weight from her ankle. "They're wonderfully crafted, really quite ingenious."

They arrived back at the tent, and the girls continued along the ten yards to the hot pool, while David took some towels and walked across to the cold stream to wet them.

"Keep your ankle up on the lip, Mama, elevated and out of the hot water," Maria said as they slipped out of their jackets and boots and slid into the deep pool.

David arrived less than a minute later and wrapped Rachel's ankle in a cold towel. "We've got to keep the swelling controlled for a while longer. Possibly heat will be good for it later, but now we need to make sure the swelling is controlled."

He slipped into the pool between them, and they were all quiet for a long while as they warmed and allowed the tensions of the last while to dissolve.

"I was intrigued watching you pee over there, Mama," David said, finally breaking the long silence. "I had never thought of how women pee, or from where. That's such a beautifully complex system you girls have down there, but I don't know where the pee comes out without a hose. You were squirting as far as I was."

"I'm getting a bit warm," Maria said, "Come over to the moss and I'll give you an anatomy lesson."

As they lay entangled half an hour later, still connected and along the slow descents from their summits, she quietly said, "I'll be starting my monthly bleeding down there tomorrow or Thursday. I'll have to wear cottons to absorb the flow for four or five days."

"Can we still play like this then?"

"Mama said it's fine, just a bit messy. Would you mind that?"

"Mess can always be cleaned, especially now with this abundance of hot water... Speaking of hot water, we should get back into the pool before we catch a chill."

"I've been in and out a few times," Rachel said as they slipped back into the pool beside her. "This is such a wonderful spot."

"We also did a lot of in-and-out. We explored that wonderful spot you told me about." Maria giggled. "Both of them. How's your ankle?"

"It's feeling much better. The throbbing has stopped, there's only a dull ache now, and the swelling appears to be going down. I've been playing with putting it in the pool for a minute or so, then resting it back up on the moss. The heat feels wonderful, lessens the ache, then back out, the evaporation cools it, not as much as the cold towels, but it sure feels nice. The alternating heating and cooling must be doing some good; it certainly feels so."

Maria moved around to her mother's ankle on the moss and examined it. "The swelling is definitely down; the taping around your foot is now loose." She placed one hand along the injured left side and her other hand along Rachel's shin. "The heat which was here last evening has nearly gone," she said and swapped hands. "Feels almost normal now."

"The throbbing is gone," Rachel said as she lifted her foot off the moss and put it in the water. "I'm going to do one more hot soak on it, then we should think of something to eat."

David watched the women interact, enjoying their close friendship.

From their physical looks, it's easy to see they're mother and daughter, but from their interactions, they could easily be mistaken as sisters. They treat each other as friendly sisters, as equals.

He watched as Maria moved back toward him, mesmerised by the movement of her breasts as she sidled across. "I love the way your breasts float, the way they bob to the surface."

She looked down, then up into his eyes with a big smile. "I've never noticed." She looked down at her breasts as she moved up and down to adjust her depth in the water, playing with their buoyancy for a while before turning her face up to grin at him. "I'm pleased you're looking at them."

Rachel eased lower in the water and bobbed to get her breasts as she wanted. "That's how they once were, two decades and more ago, before nursing three babies," she said with a smile. "Suckling, age and gravity all take a toll on a woman's body."

"Your body is still amazingly beautiful," he said. "I've seen many in their twenties who would love to be as shapely, firm and fit as you are. You have a beautiful body and a beautiful spirit."

"He's right, Mama — think of the thick, slab-sided shapes of our neighbours. They all seem to have gone rectangular, but you're still so wonderfully shaped, so beautifully curvy. I love the look of your body — it gives me confidence that mine will continue to be as beautiful as I age."

"As beautiful as your bodies are, your real beauty is inside," David said. "That beauty radiates from your core, from your soul. It doesn't matter what the wrapper is. Though I must admit, the wrappers on both of you are superb. But enough of these physics, anatomy and philosophy lessons, we need to have breakfast. I'm starving."

They slowly climbed out of the pool. "Lace your boots well and mind your step," he said, "Our bodies are completely relaxed, and the forest floor is wet. I'll go fill the billy for tea, Maria, you light the Primus, and Mama, you just lie back and relax. Keep your foot up. I'll get you another cold wrap?"

"Today is Tuesday, 4 May," David said, as he looked up from his notebook after they had finished breakfast. "This morning my sick leave expires, so Fritz will soon be looking for Josef Krings. It will probably take them a few days to add the name to the list of deserters. If we are spotted and questioned, my altered document is now getting dangerous to use. Though it shows another ten days left, it still has the name Josef Krings written on it, and I can't see any way to alter that. I could change the regimental number, but the name's still there."

"Let me see." Rachel held out her hand.

He unfolded the paper again and passed it to her. "It has rather strange writing."

She studied the writing for a while and then looked up. "We could alter the name to Klinger with a few pen strokes. Josef is a common name, so it doesn't need changing, but Krings and Klinger are far enough apart that it shouldn't raise suspicion. Calligraphy is one of my hobbies, so I could practice with your pen in your notebook before I make the changes on the chit."

"Great! Don't worry about messing it up," he said with a laugh. "It's worthless paper as it is, so you can only improve its value."

She copied the style of the script from the chit as she wrote Krings a few times on a page and played with ways to change it. "This will work," she said as she began altering the document.

David watched as she added a tall loop, a round loop, two short strokes and an r. "Looks as if I've changed my name again. Now let's hope we don't have to use it."

After the ink had dried, he refolded the document and put it in his notebook, then pulled out and unfolded the topographic map and placed it on the bedding in front of them. "It looks like we have to cross the stream and the road which come down from Schluchsee." He ran his finger along their lines.

"The stream is easy to cross, and the road cuts through the forest for much of its length above this village, Häusern." Rachel pointed to the map and moved her finger along to tap on Grafenhausen. "We can stay in the trees along the crest of the ridge past this high village and continue along through the line of forested slopes between the little burgs of Ühlingen and Birkendorf."

"Remembering what you know about these small towns and villages, can you imagine places where Fritz might have set up guard posts?"

"Except for the towns of Sankt Blasien below us and Häusern up the valley from it, the population is small and scattered through this area of the southern slopes. I can't see their setting-up anything this far in from the border. Much of the movement here in the hills is locals cutting wood, mowing hay, tending crops and grazing their cattle. I would think the Germans will concentrate their efforts and their guards in a much narrower line along the border where the intention to cross is much more obvious."

"They're also now sending more troops to the fronts in France and Belgium," he said. "They need to respond to the growing force we're amassing there to counter their aggressive thrust. We've stopped their advance, and I'm sure they don't like that. They might thin out their efforts along the neutral border and concentrate more on the active fronts."

"I wonder what trust they have in the neutrality of Switzerland," Maria pondered. "They've been neutral a long time, but..."

"I'm sure Fritz has spies watching for any indications of troop build-up and any signs of increasing armament," he said.

"We should be pretty safe until we get to here." Rachel pointed to the ridge above the border. "From up in the rocks here, we will have a good view up and down the valley. We'll be about a hundred and fifty metres above the valley floor, which at that point is a rather flat strip three or four hundred metres wide." She tapped the map.

"From the cover of the trees above the road and railway, it's about a hundred and fifty metres across to the tree-lined stream, which is the Swiss border. Here's a bushy slough, still shown on the map," she said, moving her finger along the diagonal line of trees. "We used this a few times when the border guards were around. It's a bit of a tangle, but it runs the entire way from the road to the stream. I wonder if it's still there. That was fifteen years ago."

"How comfortable would it be to camp up on the ridge for a few days if we had to?" David asked. "Is there water nearby?"

"There's a cascading stream coming down a gully a short distance off to the left when heading up. We always topped up our canteens there. It'll be off to the right as we come down, maybe thirty metres from the ridge top. There are huge blocks of rock along the crest of the rib, it's quite wild. I'm sure there are many little nooks which would be comfortable for camp. We never looked for camp spots as we passed; it was much too close to home for that."

"That sounds like a fine spot for our purpose." David looked at each of them, then shook his head. "But let's get back to concentrating on where we are. We have a rack of ribs and a backstrap and a half of venison we need to concentrate on eating before it begins to spoil, probably another four days before we need to go to the dried meats. We still have a large quantity of mushrooms and plenty of garlic, but we're out of potatoes, we're down to our last turnip, and we have only five carrots and six onions left."

He looked up from his notes to see Maria's quizzical expression as she asked, "Why are you always rattling off our food inventory?"

"Probably simply habit... More than that, though. I spent a lot of time exploring unknown mountains, not knowing what was farther up or around the next ridge. Decisions on whether to continue, divert or to retreat often depended on how much food I had."

Maria nodded through his explanation. "That makes so much sense... Hadn't thought of that." She looked into his eyes and shrugged. "A lot of details I haven't thought about."

David smiled at her. "It makes sense to concentrate on using all the fresh supplies first, for a couple of reasons. First to use them before they spoil and second to reduce the weight we need to pack. The dried things last longer and weigh less. So, Mama, could you design a menu for us for the next four or five days? Something to keep us going here while your ankle mends enough to move along."

"Probably a good idea to save a couple of the onions and a carrot or two to add some flavour to the sausage stews we may have to eat on the ridge." Rachel smiled, then continued. "Also some of the mushrooms and garlic. Just because we're camping doesn't mean we have to deprive ourselves of flavourful food."

Chapter Thirty-Two

After breakfast on Friday morning, Rachel pulled on her left boot for the first time since her injury. The lacing was widely spread as she did it up, but there was more than enough to tie at the top. "It's a bit tight," she said, "but it feels good to get it back on again. I'm going for a little walk."

She did a few back-and-forths in the level space between the tent and the cooking area, placing increasing weight on her foot as she did. "This thing is usable again, at least on level ground. I think a cane would be more useful than a crutch in the rougher areas."

"Coming right up," David said as he got up and dug out the saw. "Come, Maria, let's go find a cane for Mama."

"So, what's a cane look like in a tree?" she asked as they headed across the slope.

"Exactly as it does in a walker's hand." He smiled at her. "You simply have to ignore the rest of the tree. We need a rather straight branch a bit over an inch in diameter and a yard long growing at a wide angle, a right angle is ideal, off a branch or a stem about twice as thick. That's a good start."

"An inch again? How much is that? I forget."

"Let me see your hand." He took her fingers and looked at them. "Ideally we want something about the width across the ends of your two bigger fingers." He lifted them to his lips and softly kissed their tips, then continued along, kissing her other fingers.

"You have the most amazing descriptions of size." Maria smiled as she moved her fingers toward her lips and his lips followed until they merged in a deep kiss. She paused. "Here's a long stick, but it's much too thick," she said, pressing her mound into the expansion along his thigh. "I want to lick you. Do you mind if I do?" She dropped quickly to her knees and began working his trouser buttons.

He gently took her hands and pulled them away. "As much as I'd love that, we need to focus on making a cane for Mama. Later, we can go over beyond the hot pool and do something which also pleasures you." He guided her to her feet and held her in a hug. "Right now, we have other things to do."

On Saturday morning, after a final soak in the hot pool, they headed across the slope and slightly up to stay in the trees at the top of the pasture and along the traverse above Häusern. Their movement was much slower than before, with Rachel placing each step carefully, supporting most of the weight on her left side with the cane. They had redistributed loads, and her pack was much lighter than before to lessen the risk of aggravating her injury.

At 1720 they arrived at the edge of a small field with a road running across it. "Let's pause here," David said. "Pause not only for a rest break, but also to observe and listen."

It had taken almost nine hours to do the traverse to this point, with Rachel cautiously using her mending foot. "We used to take six hours, seven at the most to make the climb to the hot pools all the way from home," she said as she took off her pack.

As they sat on a mossy log a short distance in from the narrow meadow, Rachel pointed out through the trees. "That ridge across the road. That's the one I was talking about. We're almost there."

David took out the map, and they looked at it. "This road comes down from Mauchen to Eggingen." He ran his finger along the map. "The border is at the bottom of the hill, just next to Eggingen."

"There's a great view down onto the border area from the ridge top." Rachel pointed. "Not more than twenty minutes from here. We should continue so I can rest this foot — it's really throbbing."

They shouldered their packs, moved closer to the edge of the trees and paused to look and listen. Seeing and hearing nothing, they continued out into the narrow meadow and had nearly reached the road when two armed soldiers appeared around the bend, heading down the hill toward them. One called out: *"Guten Abend. Identifikation, bitte."*

David spoke quietly as the soldiers closed the gap. "If separated, continue. Camp on ridge." He stood behind Maria and slid the pistol holster farther around to his bum to hide it.

Rachel set her pack on the grass to open the side pocket for her papers and Maria's. *"Guten Abend, haben wir über die Berge kommen..."* She explained they've come over the mountain to visit friends.

David pulled out his sick leave paper and handed it to Rachel as she stood. She unfolded the three documents and put David's on the bottom before she held them out.

The young soldier took them and leafed quickly through the first two pieces, but paused at the third. He eyed the thin red cord in David's open collar. *"Hundemarke, bitte."*

Shit... Forgot about that. No name on it anyway, not like my own. Only the regiment, company and my number.

David pulled the tag from under his shirt and held it out to the end of the cord.

The soldier leaned forward to compare the regimental numbers, then stood back. *"Vielen Dank. Genieße deinen Abend."* He returned the papers, signalled to his partner, and they continued down the road.

Rachel was trembling as she leaned over to return the papers to the pack's pocket. "Take your time, Mama. Give them a chance to move away toward the next bend," David whispered as he tried to slow his heart rate.

He helped Rachel shoulder her pack, and they started walking slowly along the road until the soldiers disappeared. He glanced over his shoulder to check back along the road, then said, "Quick as we can, across the field and into the woods."

Within a minute they were in the trees unseen. At least, they hoped unseen. They paused a few yards in at the base of a steep slope and silently looked at each other, shaking their heads and trying to calm. "Too close," David finally said. "Thank God for their carelessness. But mine's much worse. I'm endangering you."

Maria shook her head. "No, you're the one in danger, not us. We have proper German papers."

"But if I'm found out, you'll both be seen as aiding a deserter." He looked back and forth between Rachel and Maria several times as his mind raced. "Worse, you're aiding the enemy, maybe a spy. The punishment is death for that." He shook his head. "Stupid... I didn't even think about that before we started. We need to go separate ways. I'm unsafe for you, deadly unsafe." He let out a big, noisy breath and shook his head again. "So sorry to have involved you in this." He let out another loud breath. "So very sorry."

Maria looked at Rachel with tears streaming down her cheeks. "Mama..." She started sobbing. "I... I don't want to continue without him. I really don't."

"Hush, Sweetheart. Not so loud, we may be heard." She put her hand on the back of Maria's neck and stroked. "I don't want to either, but wants aren't always the wisest things to follow."

"We all need to think." David took off his hat and raked his fingers through his hair. "Relax and think. We need to respond, not react. Let's take off our packs, sit here and allow our minds to quiet for a bit as we examine our situation."

"The ridge top is only a short distance above us, up there." Rachel turned and pointed up the slope. "There are many hidden camp possibilities up there among the blocks. It's late, we're tired and my ankle's throbbing. Let's find a camp spot, set-up for the night and then think. It's folly to separate at this time of day."

They climbed the hundred metres or so of the hillside through the trees to the rocky spur at its crest. "This is it." Rachel pointed ahead. "Look at those blocks. There's a great lookout along there through the trees and down a bit. From the top of a block, there's a full view over the valley and the river, the Wutach, the border, Switzerland, home. That little brook back there is the closest water I know of."

David looked around. "Let's put our packs down here and rest for a while, be still for a while and listen. If that is a good lookout over the border for us, Fritz might also be using it. While we're listening, let's also examine our situation and the possibilities. What do we do from here?"

Chapter Thirty-Three

David stood and adjusted the pistol case on his belt. "Stay here, relax and think. I'm going to make a reconnaissance of the area to find out if we're alone up here. I might be gone half an hour, don't worry. We need to be thorough."

He picked his way through the trees, over and around large blocks of rock. *Looks like a granitic intrusion,* he thought, running his mind back to his geology lectures at the Alpine Club camps.

Surrounding softer rock has eroded and left it exposed and proud. Wonderfully frost shattered through the ages. Amazing the power of freezing water.

Several good camp possibilities intrigued him as he explored along the crest of the rib, pausing often to listen. He found no sign of anyone having been in the area, no broken twigs, nothing discarded. Then he rounded the shoulder of the rib and saw the valley spread out below about five hundred feet down.

A hundred and fifty metres. I need to use metric; Maria doesn't understand the British system.

Carefully making his way down to the top of a huge block, he moved to its edge.

This must be the lookout Mama talked about.

He reclined on the warm granite near its lip and looked down. He saw the top of the continuation of the rib all the way down to the line of trees beside the road and railway. He saw the small slough was still covered with a tangle of bushes. He saw the small river, he saw Switzerland, he saw the jagged horizon of the Alps. The problem was, he couldn't see Fritz.

I wonder where they are. Surely they must be guarding this place, it's far too easy to cross. Deserters, men avoiding conscription, escaped prisoners and refugees heading out, spies and saboteurs going both ways.

He looked at the edge of a town in the valley and unfolded his map.

Eggingen appears to be a fair-sized place, probably a thousand or more people and only three hundred metres from the border. They likely have a force based there. Those soldiers who stopped us.

With his finger, he traced the Swiss border on the map and stopped at a place named Erzingen.

This town looks much bigger than Eggingen, and it's also directly beside the border and only five kilometres along. Would Fritz be based there?

He looked across the valley at the low hills on the other side, but he couldn't see Erzingen. Hidden on the other side of the ridge.

Maybe that's where the Germans are based in this area. Maybe not; there's no rail line to it on the map.

He rolled onto his back and stared at the sky while he tried to clear his mind.

Utterly stupid, David. Endangering Maria and Rachel. Should have thought of that. So stupid of me.

He let his mind wander through possibilities of how to proceed.

Don't have enough information. Don't know where Fritz is. Don't know what he's doing.

After listening for sounds, he rolled over to his belly and watched for movement below for several more minutes. There were occasional automobiles on the road, a horse and waggon, a few people walking, but there was nothing he could identify as military activity.

Tough to see detail. Long shadows this time of day.

Rolling onto his back again, he let out a deep sigh.

So strange. Don't want to leave her, even though I know I must. Never before felt this... This attraction. This attachment. Love, I guess. I've told her I love her. Rachel said women enjoy hearing that. I wonder if I mean it.

He blew out a deep breath

But what's love? I love the mountains. I love life. I love good food and that Gewürztraminer... But loving a woman. That's different. That's exclusive. One woman for life. Maybe I actually do love her that way. God, what a dangerous mess I've gotten her into. Have to find a way to get her out of it.

He turned onto his belly again to look into the valley.

Tomorrow. We'll look for Fritz tomorrow. Now we need to make ourselves safe and comfortable for the night.

He got up and began looking for a suitable place to pitch the tent and saw a few possibilities, none of which completely satisfied him.

Nothing big enough that's level. We could make do, but there must be something better.

As he ventured around to the other side of the rib to search, he felt a coolness drifting across the ridge. A small cascade of water was tumbling over the rocks in a shallow gully through the trees just beyond the edge of the granite.

He followed the line of granite up a short distance and arrived at a rather level expanse beneath a thick slab leaning against a huge block.

We won't need the tent — that's a great natural roof — a small patio also.

After checking his watch, he headed up toward the girls. Six minutes later he rejoined them and said, "There's a suitable camp ten minutes down, just before the rounding of the ridge. Our light won't be seen from below. A great lookout over the valley is a short distance beyond and around to the right. To the left, there's running water close at hand. We have a home for the night."

They hoisted their packs and quietly wound their way down through the broken granite and its cover of trees. The going was difficult for Rachel, with its mix of large steps, unyielding sloping surfaces and narrow traverses, but she followed David's slow lead without hesitation or complaint.

"What a splendid spot this is," Maria said, as she stepped around the corner onto the expanse of level granite and spotted the grotto. "This looks very comfortable and private."

"The water is across there thirty or forty feet." He pointed to the left. "And over there," he said, turning around, "about the same distance is a conveniently cleft rock, which will make a fine latrine. We can pause here for the night and think."

"How's the foot, Mama?" Maria asked as she doffed her pack.

"It's throbbing and aching. The boot is now so tight."

"Let's get you some cold towels." David stepped across to Maria as she dug into the pack to the supply. "I'll be right back. Mama, you lie back and put your foot up, Maria will remove your boot."

When he got back, Rachel was lying on folded bedrolls with her foot up on a padded block of rock, and Maria was massaging her ankle. "There's no local pain at the injury," Maria said, "She says it's only a general ache. It's quite hot, but I think all our feet are."

He lifted the foot, took a quick look, then wrapped it in the two cold, wet towels. "Doesn't appear swollen, but the laced boot prevented that. Let's just keep it from swelling now the boot's off. How's the cold feel, Mama?"

"That is such a welcome relief. Massage my calf; it's so tense. I guess I was using different muscles, or using them differently to ease the load."

"It looks like there'll be sun in here through the gap in the trees from mid-morning until late afternoon," he said as he gently manipulated her calf muscle. "Does that feel good? Do you want more pressure?"

"Wonderful. It's wonderfully relieving just like that. That was a long day, but I'm so glad we did it. Made no sense to stop part way here. This is such a marvellous little hiding place. I can't see anyone wandering through here with such easy terrain along both sides."

"Twenty feet down and thirty feet across there." David tilted his head toward the right side of the rib. "There's an ideal lookout. It's probably the one you were talking about. From there I could see the entire rib top all the way down to the line of trees beside the road and railway. The small slough is still covered with a tangle of bushes and it leads across to the lines of trees which run along each side of the river, I forget its name, the one which forms the border."

"Oh, that feels so good, the massage. The river's the Wutach. So the slough is still bushy, what about the crop fields on the Swiss side? Is there still an open stretch from the trees along the stream to the start of the forested ridge?"

"There's two or three hundred yards of open pasture on the Swiss side before the treed slope heads up the other side of the valley. Sit up, you can see the forested ridge top over there, a little lower than we are. What do you know of Erzingen?"

"A large town, a few thousand people. There's a border post there, a customs station. At least there used to be. It's right on the border."

"And what about Eggingen? I could see a bit of the town around the end of the ridge." He continued massaging her calf.

"It's not as big. Maybe half the size, sitting at the junction of two valleys. It has a small train station so that might be a place to base a border guard. But there are so many small communities like it along the border. It's a strange bulge that the Canton of Schaffhausen makes into Germany. It's like a huge head on a thin neck. I forget exactly now, but I think something like a hundred and fifty kilometres around, and the neck is only four or five kilometres across, all on the north side of the Rhein."

"That's a lot of border for Fritz to patrol," David said as he continued massaging Rachel's calf. "They may be doing random patrols, they may be watching only selected places. How stable is the border? What's its history?"

"Edom said his grandfather had told him the last border disputes were the ones around Unterhallau, just across the ridge below us. These involved many square kilometres, including some of his land. Though the area had belonged to Canton Schaffhausen for many centuries, there were still some hunting rights belonging to the Counts of something or other, and to the Grand Duchy of Baden. Finally, in the late 1830s, with some land exchanges and money, a treaty was signed to settle the border as the Wutach."

"The sun is just sinking below the ridge. It'll start cooling quickly. You keep your foot up and dream up a nice dinner for us. Maria and I will set up camp. She'll be back in a moment with fresh cold towels, and I can continue the massage after we're established."

Camp was easy to set up since there was no need to build a shelter. While Maria unpacked, sorted and laid out their possessions and then started preparing a stew, David searched through the large variety of fractured granite from the close area. He had spotted two slabs about four inches thick, one roughly triangular, about twenty by thirty inches. The other was closer to rectangular, about thirty inches by fifteen with one of its long sides curved.

He lifted each of them to test their portability, then he selected five large blocks and tumbled them into the centre of the patio and adjusted their positions. Next, he set the triangular slab straddling three of the blocks and asked Maria to help him place the heavier rectangular piece. After inserting some smaller pieces to adjust the levels and stop a wobble, they had rather flat-topped granite table.

"That looks like the shape of the houses I drew as a child." Maria chuckled. "It's missing only the chimney and the curl of smoke. Can I move the stove onto it?"

"Let's use your little house roof for the kitchen, the stove can be the chimney. We can sit around the rectangular slab."

"This should be another twenty or thirty minutes." Maria looked up from the pot. "Katenspeck Eintopf is the speciality of the house this evening, a dish designed by our Küchenchef, Mama. We're waiting for the lentils and split peas to soften."

"How's your foot, Mama," David asked. "Do you want more cold towels, another calf massage?"

"I had forgotten all about it, totally captivated by watching you two. I guess it must be fine."

In the fading light, he brought two more cold towels from the stream, wrapped them around Rachel's ankle and sat massaging her calf as the dinner finished cooking.

"The swelling appears to be well in control." Rachel flexed and rotated her foot. "The sprain seems to be mending; there's much less ache now as I move it."

"That was a long day for you. I'm extremely proud of you for wanting to push onward each time I suggested we stop and make camp. You're a very strong woman."

"We've got to keep going, we have to keep living. We can't let a little pain get in the way. There is too much energy pushing us forward. All of us."

"But not together from here." David breathed another loud sigh. "We all know it's not safe for us to continue together. I'm a huge danger to you if I'm uncovered. We won't have a sloppy soldier a second time. That was blind luck. I forgot about the number."

Maria wiped her tears with the back of her hand. "I want to stay with you. I don't care how dangerous it is."

"We need to think rationally." David took her wet hand and pressed it lightly. "This seems a rather safe spot to sort out what we're going to do. We can pause here to observe what Fritz is doing down there, sense the best way to continue from here. But let's not concern ourselves about that now. Let's be here now, enjoy this dinner and each other."

They sat around the granite table quietly enjoying their bowls of stew with a candle lantern adding a soft, flickering light from the point of the slab.

The evening hadn't cooled as much as previous ones, and David suggested it was because they were now below six hundred metres in elevation, but also there was residual heat radiating from the dark grey granite after its day in the sun.

"This dish reminds me of the pea soup we had in Quebec at least twice a week while we were training, but this one is thicker and so much more delicious. How was it made?"

"Cut a bit of fat off a piece of farmhouse ham, render it and throw in half a diced onion to caramelise, add a clove of garlic and half a carrot finely diced and a dozen or so peppercorns," Maria said. "When the carrots start to brown add water, lentils and split peas. After half an hour add half the diced ham plus torn pleurottes and quartered morels. Add water as necessary as it simmers, covered. You don't need salt, there's enough in the ham. Then ten minutes before serving add the remaining diced ham."

"An old family recipe?"

"Yes, it goes back to a delightful camp on a granite ridge above the Wutach in 1915," Rachel said with a giggle. "It was created to make the best use of what we had."

"It's so delicious." He looked back and forth at the women as he nodded. "We need to continue with that theme. Examine what we have, discover what exists around us and sense how to make the best use of it all."

Chapter Thirty-Four

The sun was lighting the tree tops which poked over the slab when David woke on Sunday morning to the sound of church bells from below. He looked at his watch.

Seven o'clock. I slept long again.

Rachel was still asleep beside him, but Maria's spot was empty, though still slightly warm. He sat up and saw her at the stove, got up, walked over to her and kissed her good morning.

"Been up long?" he asked

"Only about five minutes. The tea water will be another seven or eight." She looked down, then up into his eyes with a smile and said, "I see you're up long."

"Just a morning pee hard. No emotion behind it." He looked at his stiffness and chuckled. "That's not to say I'm not excited to see you."

"Do you mind if I watch you pee? I'm curious about how it works."

He looked into her eyes.

She's so beautifully innocent. So beautiful. I'll miss her.

He shrugged then tilted his head toward the edge of the slab. "Come." She followed him across.

"Do you always peel it like that? Uncover your head to pee?"

"I guess that's automatic, I don't even think about it. But thinking now, it would be messier leaving it covered. Pee would run around inside, under the foreskin and I'd be quite wet."

As he peed, his stiffness slowly eased, and the flow increased in volume. By the time he had finished, his penis was no longer self-supporting. He shook it, then milked along the length of the underside to push the last of the pee to the end, shook again, slid the skin back over the head and then dropped it.

"That's quite the process."

"I take much longer to pee when I'm stiff. The tube is compressed from the swelling, and the pee comes out rather slowly until the stiffness eases."

"All the shaking and squeezing, I mean. Do you always do that?"

"That too is automatic. I learned early on that if I don't do it thoroughly, I end up with dribbles and wet trousers. There's a lot of draining to do before I tuck myself away." He caught her eyes and grinned. "Besides, it also feels good."

"Men are so different from women, and I sure do love the difference. You have such a nice difference." She giggled, then picked up his dangle and laid it along her hand and up her wrist. "I've heard this is larger than normal." She looked up with an impish grin.

"Completely normal for me." He grinned back and chuckled.

"For me also, I know no other size. I don't want to know any other. I don't want to know any other man. I love you, David. I don't even know the meaning of love, but I certainly know its feelings now. I know it has so little to do with this thing," she said looking down and hefting it. "This is certainly a lovely part of it, but the depth of my love is for your spirit, for your fresh mind, for your inventiveness, for your openness and honesty, for your steadiness, for your acceptance and for your constant optimism. You're a noble man, David. I love you."

She watched his limpness receding across her wrist to her hand, then she took it between her forefinger and thumb lightly, saying, "This is a nice leash. Come, you need to get dressed. The morning is still cool, and you'll catch a chill."

David remained speechless as he was led back across the granite terrace to the sleeping nook. His head was spinning, churning up so many random thoughts, confusing and conflicting thoughts. He was somewhere he had never been.

But I've spent much of my life exploring where I've never been. But that's been with mountains, with wilderness, with things, never with people. I truly don't know...

"Your eyes tell me you're confused," she said as she dropped the leash to allow him to pull on his trousers. "What's troubling your mind?"

He put on his shirt then his jacket before he said anything. "So many emotions, so many feelings, so many conflicting things. I'm not accustomed to these." He looked deeply into her eyes.

"That's the normal thing for women." She stroked his beard. "We so often have to juggle feelings and emotions which conflict with reality. Mama said that's a normal thing for us. Our strength is recognising what's real and acting on that, while allowing our emotions and our sensibilities to guide us."

She picked up his hand, put it on her shoulder, and they merged into a long hug. She felt him gently sobbing, and she tilted her head up to kiss his lips, tasted the salt of his tears, licked his bearded cheeks and kissed him again gently, saying, "I love you — you are such a magnificent man."

"But men don't cry. My father — everyone has always told me men don't cry. But I've cried at spectacular sunsets, I've cried for the sheer joy and the release of reaching the summit of an unclimbed peak. In the past weeks, I've cried so often at the loss of comrades in the fighting in Flanders. Now I cry because I love you and don't know what to do about it. I'm so very confused."

Maria held him more tightly and stroked the back of his head as they listened to Rachel saying from her bed, "Strong men cry, David. It's the weak ones who hide their feelings, who disguise them with pompous strutting, with anger, with rage."

"Good morning, Mama," Maria said, "Been awake for a while?"

"Long enough to confirm once again that David's a very special person, a very rare man and that we are so privileged to have him here with us. To have him in our lives."

"How's your foot this morning, Mama," David asked, as he bent to kiss her. "Pardon my wet face."

"So much better." She lifted her foot and slowly rotated it.

Maria bent to feel the ankle. "The heat's gone. Seems normal now. What should I get out for breakfast?".

"I was thinking of thinly slicing some of the Tannenhof Schinken and having it with sliced Appenzeller, knäckebrot and tea."

"What's Tannenhof Schinken?" David asked. "I know Schinken is ham."

"This is a special one," Rachel replied. "Cold smoked over fir and juniper twigs; subtle flavours. It's made a short distance north of here in the eastern slopes of the Schwarzwald. It's one of our favourites, and I always keep a piece on hand."

"The tea water is boiling away, I hadn't even noticed the rattling of the lid," David turned and looked. "I'll go tend to that."

"The rattle of the lid is what woke me," Rachel whispered to Maria after David had left. "I noticed you were leading him around on a leash," she added with a giggle. "I told you women control men."

As they were enjoying their breakfast, David discussed plans. "I think we should sit in the sun on the lookout slab and observe the activity below. Look for patterns of any kind, anything that would look like organised patrols or watch rotations. We need to find out if Fritz is down there, and if so, where. We can't make valid decisions until we know."

"There'll be a different activity in the valley today, a Sunday, than there'd be on a weekday," Rachel added. "Probably a good idea to watch again tomorrow. That will give me two more days to strengthen my ankle. Give us more time to think."

"We can finally put Herzog's telescope to good use." David pointed to the holster harness. "I had forgotten about it."

After breakfast, they packed snacking food, water canteens and a few other things into the small rucksack. David draped two folded bedrolls over his shoulder, and they headed around the rib and slightly down to the lookout rock only a few minutes away.

The rock was like the prow of a ship, jutting proudly out of the rib and sloping back slightly. Its tip was a good twenty feet above the surrounding terrain and from the prow was an unobstructed view into the valley. It was just coming on quarter to eight.

David looked back up the rib to determine whether they were visible from above, and he was pleased the line of trees and some large granite blocks screened the view from there. He and Maria took the two bedrolls and spread them out near the brink, and they all laid on their bellies and forearms to survey the scene below.

"The rail line was extended past here about a quarter century ago to link the Wutach with the Donau Valley," Rachel said.

"The Donau, that's the Danube in English, isn't it?" he asked for confirmation. "How far away is the Donau?"

"The Wutach and Danube at one point are only ten kilometres apart. They both rise in the Schwarzwald, to the north of Feldberg. Actually, Feldberg is the source of the Wutach. When we crossed the big cirque toward the saddle that first day, those little streams and gullies are its source. The Danube rises a short distance north."

"I saw on the map that the Wutach flows into the Rhein, so the continental watershed lies between the Wutach and the Danube, one flowing toward the North Sea, the other east across Europe to the Black Sea. The rail line appears to be an important link then, between the eastern and western parts of Germany."

"Yes, very important. The original route from the southern Rhein plains into south-central and eastern Germany passed through Schaffhausen, following the north side of the Rhein. But after the Germans seized Alsace and Lorraine in 1871, they need a strategic defensive connection entirely within Germany for transporting supplies and troops, in case the French counter-attacked."

She paused, shook her head, sighed and then continued. "Edom was fascinated with the line. It's an extremely twisting route with a full circle spiral tunnel and many full switchbacks. In the final rise to the pass, there are five tunnels, five major bridges and viaducts plus minor ones. It's so twisty and curly that locally it's called the Sauschwänzlebahn, the Pigtail Line. Edom was an overseer of labour on the rail beds for a while before we married. The new line was a huge undertaking and wasn't completed until the 1890s."

"The small road beside it doesn't seem as important."

"No, not important at all, at least back when I knew it. It only linked a few small communities up the Wutach and side valleys."

"And the road heading up the side valley from Eggingen? The one where we were accosted, does it lead anywhere?"

"Only to the tiny communities and farms up the valley. It doesn't go through to anywhere. At least that's how it was before we moved."

"So the rail line is the most important down there," he said. "Do you notice anything unusual? Take a close look, try to remember from all those years ago. Are there any significant changes?"

Rachel looked slowly from right to left, sweeping her eyes back and forth across the flat valley floor. "Over there in the field by the weir," she said, pointing to the left. "Those are new buildings. At least, I don't remember any being there. Hand me the telescope."

She extended the tubes and put it to her eye. "This is so blurry. I can't see a thing." She adjusted the eyepiece back and forth. "I can't see anything with this, and I can't seem to put it into focus." She handed it back to David.

David collapsed the tubes and extended them again, then he twisted. "There, the tubes twist to lock into place, try it now."

"Much better. They're not buildings, they're tents. Four long tents and one square one next to the weir. They appear to be military, and there are a lot of men milling about. Here, you look, you understand army better than I do."

He looked, then glanced at his watch. "It appears they're mustering into squads. There's the eight o'clock bell. I'll watch them, you continue to search for anything else that's strange."

David watched as the troops formed, and as they were inspected, he gave the girls a running commentary of his observations. He finished after a few minutes with, "Three squads are marching off now, across the field toward the road."

"I can see them plainly," Maria said, "looks like two rows of four and a leader in each."

"The other six squads were stood down, so it appears they have three watches," he said. "I wonder how long each shift is. I guess we'll find out; that's why we're here."

"They've split at the road," Rachel said. "One squad heading west, the other two east."

"You two continue watching the troops moving along the road, I'll examine the tent encampment and the activity there." He saw little movement, nothing that seemed organised as he tried to sort the arrangements in the five tents and figure out their meaning.

"I'm analysing the troop strength and their routine," he said. "I'll be thinking out loud as I do. Follow along and tell me if I'm not making sense. We saw nine squads, three have gone out, and six have remained in camp. The three that have gone out will relieve three other squads, so that's twelve squads. How long is each rotation? Are there other squads recently relieved still in bed?"

"The squad that headed this way has now stopped." Maria pointed.

"Beside the slough." Rachel nodded. "Seems they consider it a weakness."

David swung the telescope across to the slough and watched the activity as the squad milled at the side of the road. "I see only the nine fresh troops but not the squad they're relieving. You both watch the other two squads, I'll focus on this one."

He saw no other movement as he swept the telescope along both sides of the slough, examining the bushes, looking for movement, looking for Fritz. *Nothing.* He looked again at the fresh squad and saw them laying back against the slope of the dyke the road runs along. "They're lying on their backs. Guarding the sky, it seems. They don't appear to be motivated or well led."

"One of the other squads has stopped." Maria pointed to the left. "Over there at the end of the hedgerow that runs across the field from the river to the forest edge. The river is directly beside the road there, so the hedgerow looks to be in Switzerland."

"No, the hedgerow is in Germany." Rachel tapped the map. "Look here. The border jogs across the field halfway between the weir and the hedgerow, then runs along the base of the forested slope."

David looked at the map and at the terrain. "Another obviously vulnerable spot." He put the telescope to the start of the hedgerow a little over half a mile up the valley, and watched the troops lounging on the rocks at the edge of the river. No relieved squad was visible.

He swung his glass back to the slough to look for additional troops and still saw none. "I don't think the commander of this company takes his duty seriously. He has more than enough troops to maintain a twenty-four-hour guard, but from our observations so far, I'll wager he is doing daylight only. I'll bet he rotates again at noon then at sixteen hundred and that the third rotation finishes at twenty hundred. The troops appear totally uninspired."

"The third squad has stopped now," Maria said as she pointed. "A little farther along beside the river where the swath of trees zigzags across the fields. From at the map, it appears the swath of trees is also in Germany." She put her finger on the map to show David.

He lifted the telescope to the place and watched the squad as men sat or laid beside the river. "This doesn't speak well for their defences, but it sure improves our position. Let's not relax. Let's keep watching. Let's confirm we're right in our thinking."

Chapter Thirty-Five

"I'll watch the farthest one on the left. For ease, let's call it Zigzag. Maria, you take the next one — Hedgerow, and Mama, you do Slough," David said. "The best way to spot movement is with your eyes slightly out of focus. Don't look at anything, simply look. Any motion will jump out at you."

The sun was beginning to warm the day as they lay there sharing stories and looking out over the edge. The only movements from the troops were at Hedgerow and at Zigzag. Most of them appeared to be fishing. At Slough, the soldiers were too far from the river, so they did nothing but strip their shirts and lie in the sun.

Among the other movements were occasional waggons and automobiles passing along the road and many people out walking. Mid-morning a long freight train came slowly down the valley, pulled by three locomotives. "That looks to be a heavy load," he said. "Probably full of munitions from factories in the industrial heartland."

"It would save many lives if it could be destroyed," Maria said, "But how would you destroy it?"

"Destroy a bridge or viaduct as the train passes over. That would likely be the easiest way," he replied.

"But how would you do that? With what?"

"With dynamite or other explosives. The Army has engineers trained to do this. They examine the structure of a trestle or bridge and then determine where to place charges which will weaken the structure, not necessarily destroy it, but allow the weight of the train to finish the job and have the train plummet into the void, possibly destroying its entire load. If I were Fritz, I'd be guarding all the bridges, viaducts and tunnels along the vital rail lines. There must be saboteurs with thoughts similar to these."

They remained quiet in their thoughts and watching. Then they continued with their story telling until they heard the noon bell below them, when David said, "They appear to be getting ready for something. They're putting away their fishing poles over here."

"The Slough group is climbing up onto the road," Rachel said, "They're preparing to head back."

"Same over here," Maria said. "There's also activity in the camp, like the replacements are mustarding."

David chuckled loudly, "That's mustering, Maria, mus-ter-ing,"

"I knew it was something like that." She giggled. "Anyway, they're bunching together into little groups. Looks like six groups."

He handed her the telescope. "Here, take a closer look."

"Yes, six groups of eight and a leader, like the ones this morning, but six groups, not nine." She watched for a while longer, then said, "Three of the groups have unmustered, if that's a word. The other three are marching across the field toward the road."

They watched as each of the three pairs of squads met, paused for a minute or so and continued along. "I've been puzzling over this." David stroked his beard. "A German platoon is four sections, each with three squads of nine. They have four barrack tents down there. We've seen only nine squads, three sections. There's a missing section, three missing squads..." He paused to analyse.

"One section is probably on break for a day or two. Otherwise, they'd be working seven days a week. If my thoughts are right, we'll see some of the missing twenty-seven returning along the road later today. There may be some heading into town this afternoon..." He stopped again to reflect. "Did you see the men leaving the camp before the train went by?"

"Two small groups heading out," Maria said.

"One of the groups stopped to talk with the squad at the slough," Rachel added.

"So this explains the fourth tent, the missing section. We've learned some valuable information here this morning. We've done much more observing than Fritz has. Let's keep it this way. Let's continue to observe, try to confirm what we're thinking. Some landjäger will help me see more clearly. And some water, it's become rather warm here in the sun."

They sat and savoured the sausage, each looking down at all four posts two or three times a minute to watch for any change.

"The Platoon Lieutenant down there seems a weak leader," David mused as he nibbled. "He appears to be making it an easy job for his troops to keep them happy, perhaps to keep them from grumbling and complaining or he could be doing it so they'll like him. Whatever the reason, instead of having them perform the task properly and effectively, he's compromising their position, reducing the country's security and denying his troops the satisfaction they'd have from a duty well done."

After a few more bites he paused and mused aloud, "Leadership is an interesting thing. Some think it is bossing people around. But some who are placed in positions of authority are afraid to lead and they do nothing but watch the chaos happen around them as they blame everyone but themselves. Leaders should inspire people to work with them to find ways to best accomplish the task."

"That's you, David. That last one's exactly you." Maria said.

David smiled, then pointed. "Here comes another train, three locomotives again at its head. I'll count the cars as it goes by." They watched the train descend the low grade along the river.

"Forty-three cars, plus the three engines," he said, as the last car hove into view. "That's a lot of war supplies. I can't imagine the cost involved in this stupidity. People are starving, and instead of feeding them, they're spending fortunes throwing metal across a line to kill and maim others."

Maria put her fingers on David's scars and looked at them through his two-week beard. "I hadn't thought of your wounds until now. Guess we've been too busy with Mama's ankle."

"I've also forgotten about them, reminded only by the missing teeth when I eat."

"The jaw? Is it still sore?"

"It's background now. I don't notice the pain unless I think about it, so I choose to push it from my mind."

"That's the thing, isn't it? I've just finished four and a half days of abdominal cramping, pangs and discomfort. I chose to accept it and push it into the background..."

"Cramping? Pangs? Discomfort? What's going on with you? Are you alright?"

"Perfectly normal. Some women are near incapacitated with their monthly bleeding. Fortunately, Mama and I can work through ours. I push the pain and the strange emotions into the background. Now with my new school and book learning, I wonder if some of the pain might be our deeper nature suffering the loss of another egg which didn't make it."

"I hadn't thought of it that way, Maria, but that makes sense. There is a grieving — I often sense a loss when I bleed. I've been through it near three hundred times. Each time is strange."

"I'm a tyro at it." Maria paused to calculate. "Barely sixty times, but each time is so different. Sometimes I gush, sometimes I dribble. Sometimes I feel rather bland, other times I'm very low. I guess it has to do with what else is going on. This time, I was amazed at how high my spirit remained. I've never seen it like that through a bleeding."

"Emotions, feelings of security, feelings of being loved, a sense of being protected," Rachel said. "These all have a big impact on your level of comfort with the dramatic changes which are happening inside you. Inside you both physically and emotionally. There's a lot of change in such a short time. The end of one cycle of life, the start of the possibility of another."

"This is so enlightening for me. I've not before been this close to a woman — to women — to their inner beings. You two are so open, so sharing, such magnificent creatures. I love you both."

"There!" Maria said. "Four more men heading out from the camp, heading across the fields." She lifted the telescope and looked. "All in uniform, same as the ones this morning."

"We had no other clothes with us at the Front. When we fell back from the trenches for a break, we went into town in uniform. I'm sure this is the same with Fritz."

They watched the unarmed soldiers walk the remainder of the way across the field and up onto the road, then along toward Eggingen and disappear around the ridge. There was no other action in the scene below them.

"There is no need for three of us now. One can watch this scene," he said. "We know what is out there. At least we know what they're showing us. Now we need to confirm the incompetent display below us is not merely a ploy to give observers the impression the border is loosely guarded."

"That's another example of your careful thinking," Rachel said. "It hadn't occurred to me this might be a ruse. The incompetent leadership down there seems unbelievable, seems too good to be true."

"I'll keep watch here until the 1600 change, then we can all watch the new action. You girls go take a break, come back with tea when the clock strikes four. It's just about to strike one now."

After they had left, he lay again on his belly and began training the telescope slowly across the valley bottom, starting at his far left. He looked at each detail and identified it, then moved on to the next. There were a few things he couldn't identify, but there seemed to be nothing out of place or unusual.

He finished another sweep from left to right and was just starting back when he heard footsteps behind him, then a quiet voice saying, "I miss you. I've come to keep you company." He collapsed the telescope, rolled over and watched her drop her trousers and shuffle out of her shirt. He quickly telescoped.

As she knelt to begin undoing his trouser front, he caught her hands and squeezed them gently. "We have other things to do at the moment. We need to concentrate on activities below."

"I can sit on you and watch the valley while we play. I've missed you, David."

"I've missed you also, Maria. We've been a bit busy with details. We still need to be."

"I can see the whole valley kneeling here. I'll have the same view sitting up on you. Can we just for a while? I need a long deep massage after those days of cramps and pangs." She giggled.

A few minutes later he felt her tightening on him and then more tightly in a long series of pulses. She threw her head back and roared from deep in her throat, her whole body quaking, her chest heaving. She pressed her mound into him and ground it around, let out a few whoops and collapsed again onto him, kissing his face randomly.

"Need I ask if that was pleasing to you?"

"It keeps getting better," she said, still panting and involuntarily twitching. "I can't imagine anything better, but each time it is."

He rolled over with her and raised to his elbows to take a look below, tilting his hips slowly back and forth as he scanned up and down the valley. He began again to scan the three posts and the tent camp without pausing his slow thrusts.

After a while, he sat up and pulled her up onto his lap facing him and they sat gently churning and caressing each other between looks into the valley. They were the only action around until a train headed past, up the tracks.

"I wonder what they carry on the return trip," he mused. "Can't be much, only one locomotive appears to have steam up."

They continued with occasional churns, soft caresses and talk as they looked out over the valley. "Mama asked me how I could last so long doing this. She told me she used to get so sore from all the friction. I told her there's no friction, that you move within your own skin, and she immediately understood. She cursed the rabbis and the religion for destroying such a marvellous thing."

"I can't imagine how awful it would be to not have this skin. When Mama pulled it all the way back hard to show us how your father's was, it was painful. It was like a broomstick, and I understand how it would soon get sore for both. They must have started the mutilations to keep people from enjoying using them. What a horrible tradition."

"More horrible that it's done in the name of God." She shook her head. "I had heard of circumcision when I was growing up but never understood how horrible it is. We were told it's a simple ceremony, a simple cut to honour God. I don't think many do understand how much is butchered away. They blindly follow the old tradition. They follow the rabbis telling them the Torah says they must make the cut. To remove the foreskin seems to say God's design was wrong."

She tilted her pelvis to stroke his shaft against her button, lightly shuddering as she did. "This certainly feels like an excellent design to me. I could keep on doing this forever with you."

Chapter Thirty-Six

Rachel found them still cuddling, Maria sitting on David's lap with her back along his chest, gently rocking her hips as his hands did a slow exploration of her peaks and valleys and their eyes studied the valley floor below them, watching another changing of the guard.

"I'm delighted at how passionately you maintain your watch," she giggled as she walked up behind them and kissed them both on the cheek.

"I heard the four bells a minute ago as I was hobbling down here with tea."

"We almost missed the bells," Maria said, "disguised in our own noise-making. We've been watching the same squad rotation ceremonies in the valley. The last of the relieved squads is almost back at the camp."

"There have been several more soldiers coming and going between the camp and the town," David added, "and again none of them with their rifles."

"You two are so comfortable with each other, so comfortable with your own selves." Rachel smiled at them. "You're so beautiful to watch. When you've finished, there's tea, crispbread and cheese."

"We've finished several times, Mama, we're just sitting here and enjoying each other. I so wish you had someone like David to love you."

"Don't you worry about that, Sweetheart. It will happen. I'll make it happen."

"You'll have to find a non-Kosher man, Mama, someone outside the synagogue. You need a non-mutilated man. I couldn't imagine doing this with a broomstick."

"Maybe I'll have to borrow David." She smiled and giggled.

"Do you want to do that, Mama?" Maria looked at her and then at David. They all looked at each other and laughed. Then they looked again quietly from face to face with expressions a little more serious.

"Would you want to share?" Rachel tilted her head and bit her lip. "It's certainly not a normal thing to share."

Maria looked into David's eyes. "What's normal? Seems like we're back to that again, and back to my curiosity. I'm intrigued — I've never watched." She licked her lips and tilted her head.

David shrugged his shoulders and looked back and forth between the women a few times. "If it's what you both want... Truly want."

Maria lifted herself slowly off David. "He's a bit messy, Mama, let me wipe him off for you." She picked up a towel, tucked one end of it between her lips and closed her legs, and with the other end, she went gently to work on David.

"Let's start with the basics first," Rachel said. "Foreplay is an important part of this entire process. It sets the mood, confirms mutual desire, gets the blood flowing to the right places and prepares the lubrication. It often involves light caresses, gentle massage, kissing, nibbling and licking in non-intimate places."

She ran her eyes over David's body. "Foreplay can be entirely non-physical, softly spoken words, suggestive or erotic body moves. That eye massage you did on Maria at the spa last week was a magnificent example of non-physical. It turns me on to think about that performance. I would love you to do that to me."

She did a slow, sensuous strip, dropped her trousers, and teasingly undid her shirt buttons, leaving a tail to cover her blond patch, then undraped a breast, shuffled her arm out of one sleeve and let the shirt fall to the granite, all the while watching for him to start thickening.

He took her hand and kissed it, kissed her fingertips, then gently her lips as he led her down onto the cushion of the folded bedrolls.

Rachel lay back, pulled up her knees and let them fall out to the sides, exposing her folds. David knelt at her feet and set his eyes on a slow exploration of her body. He watched her mouth open and her jaw relax, saw the brown rings around her nipples wrinkle even further, watched the nipples extending longer, ran his eyes slowly over the ripples across her lower abdomen and down through the short blond hair. He saw her button sitting proudly out in the complexity of folds.

Brown fringed folds, not pink like Maria's.

He looked up at Maria and saw her smiling as she gazed into his eyes and nodded.

She truly does want me to do this. I know Mama does. That's certain. Come on, David. Need to get it up.

He continued down the inside of Rachel's left thigh, turned at her knee and started up. As he arrived again at her open lips, he saw the glistening moisture there and bent forward to smell its exotic scent, causing him to quickly rise. Her abdomen was pulsing as his eyes passed up across it, the skin on her upper chest had deepened in colour, the expression on her face was sublime.

She reached up, took his hand and pulled him toward her. "Fuck me, David. Fuck me, please. Fuck me now before I burst."

David looked at Maria, saw her nodding, then he slipped inside and did a few slow long strokes before he played his head a much shorter distance in. A few minutes later she was overcome with twitching, then with convulsions. Her hips thrust wildly, she let out a deep-throated howl as her chest heaved heavily and she stared wide-eyed at him.

After she had regained her composure, she said through her panting, "I can't believe I've missed it so much. Do you two mind if I continue playing? I've fantasised about this since my first spying look at you by the pool. I would dearly love to explore some more."

David looked at Maria's smiling face, wet with tears as she nodded. He gave a gentle thrust "I'm still up for it. Let me lie on my back, that way you can use me as it pleases you best."

Maria ran her fingers through Rachel's hair. "Mama, this is the best I can offer you for all the wonderful things you've done for me. I've had so little to give back to you over the years. I've never had anything to give that you needed except my love and appreciation. I love you, Mama. I love you, David."

Maria sat alternating her gaze between the action on the valley floor and the action on the slab beside her. The closer one was dramatically more interesting to her, but she managed to divert her eyes occasionally to check for movement much farther below.

"There are places in here I didn't know existed," Rachel said as she tried a variety of postures. "You're right, Maria. This is a much better tool for the job, so much more comfortable than the peeled version. I now know why you spend so much time with this inside — no friction — only pleasure — such intense pleasure — pardon me a moment..."

Rachel crested again, this time, a little less loudly, but with the same intensity of tremor and convulsions, the same pelvic pulsations. She was on all fours, knees spread apart as she hung her head and tried to catch her breath again. Bending her elbows, she lowered to graze her nipples across his chest as she swung her breasts side to side, exciting them both.

She looked down her body between her breasts at his thickness barely half into her, and began another slow gyration, tilting and thrusting her hips as she watched almost hypnotised by the sight of their juncture. She sped the pace of her short strokes as a growl rose in her throat, "Again — my God — again..." She collapsed in heaving convulsions and lay deeply impaled on him, twitching and panting.

As she slowly recovered, she said, "This is very addicting, David. I can see why Maria is so eager for you."

"Maybe the addiction is why they mutilate them," he said. "They mutilate them to prevent addiction to pleasure. I saw a few bare heads in the showers, but I didn't understand what they were. I've never looked at one closely."

"What a waste that is, ruining such a marvellous tool." Rachel shook her head. "But Edom used what he was left with very well. It depends so much on the man it's attached to. Most men won't have the patience, the skill or the control to make such fine use of their equipment. I remember before I met Edom, most of the men just wanted to pop quickly with no concern at all for me, other than as their popper, something to pop into."

She looked across at Maria, then back to David. "Speaking of being a popper, I'd love to have you pop inside me, so I can stop hogging you. That was the five o'clock bell a few minutes ago. The tea has gone cold, and I've been rather selfish here."

"You crouch on top, play yourself." David nodded. "I'll know when to follow. I'm ready anytime you are."

In less than five minutes they exploded together, she collapsed onto him, and they lay entangled and gasping. "That was a quick one, Mama," he said. "A superb cap to an amazing hour. You certainly haven't lost your passion or your skill. There's a very fortunate man over there in Switzerland looking for you."

Maria watched as their breathing became more regular and as Rachel began to stir, she said, "I have a clean towel here, Mama, when you're ready. Don't rush. He is so amazingly comfortable, and I love the sensations of him shrinking inside. Stay a while and enjoy that. It's a delightful feeling."

She looked at David. "Thank you so much for giving Mama a gift I couldn't give her. I'm astonished at your endurance, at your continued passion, at your loving tenderness. You're an amazingly special person. I love you so deeply."

She knelt beside him, bent and kissed his lips, ran her tongue across them and then through them into his mouth as they merged in a deep, passionate kiss.

"Stop that, you two, he's expanding again inside me," Rachel giggled. "That feels so delightful."

"An extra little gift we wanted to give you, Mama."

David throbbed out a Morse message and Rachel giggled as she read it aloud as the words came into form, "We — love — you — Mama."

Rachel let out a loud sigh. "You're such wondrous people. So full of life, so giving. I love you both. Both of you as my children. David, you are as fine a person as I had hoped my sons would become. I had such high hopes for them, but now all I have left are some papers, a few photographs and many wonderful memories."

She looked down, and a huge smile spread across her face, then she let go a deep laugh. "My children have all come out of my birth canal. David still hasn't but when I bear him shortly, I can honestly say he came out of there. Are you ready to be reborn?"

"Whenever you're ready, Mama." He laughed with her continuing mirth.

She slowly rose from her kneeling crouch, pulling away from him until his limpness flopped out and fell against his belly. "That was, without doubt, the most pleasurable of my childbirths," she said with a giggle.

She leaned and kissed his forehead, the tip of his nose and his lips. "Welcome to the world." She giggled more loudly. "May I introduce you to your sister, Maria?"

Chapter Thirty-Seven

David and Rachel cleaned and dressed, then they all sat drinking their cool tea, nibbling on the Gruyère and knäckebrot and watching the valley. "It's a good thing I took the tea ball out before I came over," Rachel said, "otherwise this would be terribly tannic."

Maria told them about the activities she had seen in the valley while they were occupied with other things. Two more trains had gone by, one down and one up. All the soldier movement had been back to camp, mostly shortly past five.

"Something must have closed or finished in town at five," she said. "There were two groups; one ten the other eight. After them, there was only a single. None had rifles. The three guard posts are still casually manned in the same disinterested way."

Maria pointed across to the horizon. "Over the top of that ridge, there to the left end of it, there's been steady movement on the road, a regular foot traffic and many automobiles." She passed the telescope to David.

He studied it for a while, then looked at the map. "That appears to be a little beyond Erzingen, this road leading out of town into Switzerland." He passed the scope to Rachel. "What do you think, Mama?"

"That's the border post. I recognise it. It looks like people are crossing. It appears as if they've reopened the border." She looked at the map then back through the scope. "Yes, that's it."

They remained quiet for another long while, watching for activity in the valley. There was none. The six o'clock bell rang, then the seven. A short while later he told the girls to go start dinner.

As the daylight faded, he watched the three guard squads muster and slowly march... *No, saunter is a better way to describe their movement.* David corrected himself and looked at his watch. *Not quite seven fifteen.*

He continued to watch the squads as they moved along the road. There was a random lighting of lamps in both the town and the encampment.

The eight o'clock bell sounded, and he watched the steady lights in the valley for movement, but saw none. Then there was a growing loom of light on the rock slab around him and he turned to watch a candle lantern moving toward him with a shadowy yellow figure faintly behind it.

"The chef has advised dinner will be served in ten minutes," Maria said with a giggle as she bent to kiss him.

"Have you brought matches to relight the candle?"

"No, I didn't think of it."

"Then let's put the light far behind us, lie at the lip, readjust our eyes and look into the valley for a few minutes. One last check for any movement, for any moving light."

Satisfied, he rolled to kiss her again, and they lay in a long, warm embrace. "I love your thoroughness," she said. "Your extreme care and attention to detail. Your mind sees such a broader picture than I ever imagine exists."

"The more we know about the enemy, the stronger we are." He took her hand and assisted her up. "Move back a good distance from the rim before you lift the lamp. Don't let it be seen from below. I'll roll up the bedroll. It's beginning to dampen from the dew. What else is there here?"

"We took the other bedroll and everything else a while ago when we left. That's all there is."

She led him back across the ridge to their camp, deftly swinging the lamp to light his steps and hers. "You use the lantern well," he said as they arrived.

"Six nights a week since early October, walking home after eleven, after the gasthaus closed. It became second nature."

They sat around the granite table enjoying the stew. "Rice and barley with diced ham, salami, half an onion, half a carrot, the last of the pleurottes and lots of garlic," Rachel said. "It isn't elegant, but it's nutritious and filling."

"And also delicious." David smacked his lips. "This is amazingly flavourful, Mama, much better than the Army food, better than any of the camp stews I've ever had in the mountains."

Rachel smiled at him. "We've enough for a few more meals. While we were preparing dinner, we did an inventory. We've eight cloves of garlic, an onion, a carrot left and a few morels left; that's the end of our fresh. There's still a few days of rice, lentils, barley and split peas, we have five pair of landjäger and the last of the Tanenhof schinken. We've cheese for another two days, maybe three and we're down our last package of knäckebrot. There's still lots of tea left in the tin."

"So we can continue to eat well for two or three days with what we have," Maria said. "Do we need to begin rationing?"

David shook his head. "No, with the border now appearing to be open, you two can walk across. You have Swiss papers so it should be no problem. Besides, they'd be suspicious of men, not women."

"But what about you?" Maria asked.

"Don't worry about me, I'll gather more information, bide my time and find a way to cross. There's a week of food here for one person. Let's analyse the situation down there in the valley, think quietly for a few minutes, let our minds wander through possibilities, reasonable ones, strange ones, totally weird ones. Don't chase them too far, simply think about them lightly and move on to other possibilities. From what we've seen below today, what do you see as my best way to cross?"

They ate as they thought. After several minutes he said, "The obvious one is to head down to the woods at the bottom of the rib and wait until dark before I go through the trees by the slough and cross the river into Switzerland. I'm sure we all thought of that."

Both Maria and Rachel nodded. "That seems so simple," Maria said, "Almost as if they are inviting it to happen."

Rachel nodded. "That's also my sense."

"I tried with the telescope to see if they had barbed wire, but it isn't a sufficiently powerful lens. We use coils of barbed wire at our trenches and string trip wires to trigger bells. I told you about almost stumbling into one of their traps near Weil am Rhein."

"What about farther along the valley, beyond Hedgerow and Zigzag?" Maria asked. "Away from the town. Maybe they're not watching up there. That seems like a lot of soldiers to be watching such a short stretch of the border. Could they be set up only at the easy places?"

"That's one of the things I was thinking of investigating." They sat silently eating for a while as he looked back and forth between their faces which were yellowed and shadowed by the candlelight. "It seems we don't know enough yet for me to safely move. I'll need to take my time to observe more, to look at other —"

"What's that?" Rachel said, pointing up out over the valley in front of her. "The bright clouds over the —"

They heard gunshots. Two in near unison. David and Maria turned their heads and looked up to where Rachel was pointing. A long patch of light on the bottoms of the clouds.

"A nice little trap they have down there," David said. "They must have trip wires which turn on electrical lights in the trees by the river. That was one of the things my mind played with a while ago. That's the duty of the other platoon. They're snipers sitting at night, like spiders waiting for flies in their webs."

He blew out a deep breath. "Don't worry about me. I'll find a way across and meet you in Unterhallau, in Küsnacht, wherever. You can walk through the border crossing with your Swiss papers."

"Swiss papers! How stupid of me." Rachel slapped her leg, sat straight up and stared at David. "How incredibly stupid of me. How absolutely and utterly dumb. Sometimes I'm an idiot."

"What is it, Mama?" Maria asked, "What's stupid? What's dumb?"

"Here we've been forging papers for David, making him a German, all the while in my little leather sheaf I've had his Swiss birth certificate. He's my son, we need only to decide which one."

"When were they born?" David asked, his eyes widening.

"Jacob was September 1894, Nathan was September 1895, and Maria was September 1896." She laughed. "I was very regular."

"I was born the thirteenth of September 1894. Can I be Jacob?"

"Jacob's birthday was the twenty-second, Nathan's was on the eighteenth and Maria's was on the twelfth. September was one long series of birthday celebrations for us, I was born on the fifth." Rachel smiled. "Edom almost made it, he was born the last day of August, but we forgave him that shortcoming."

"Does it give eye or hair colour on the paper?" he asked.

"No, only his name, Jacob David Meier, the date, the place of birth and the parents' names, plus the official stamps."

"Do you mind if I use David, my middle name?" He looked at her and laughed. "I'm rather accustomed to that name."

"Funny, we had actually debated whether to call him by David or by Jacob."

After a long pause, David chuckled, "Mama, I've been wondering, now I'm a Jewish boy, do I have to get circumcised?"

"Over my dead body will any rabbi take a knife to you." She shook her head as she giggled. "If anybody questions, we can tell them the rabbi couldn't find a knife big enough."

She was quiet for a while before she spoke again. "Seriously, when we get out of here, I'm going to start a campaign to try to stop this barbaric practice of mutilating our baby boys."

"So, brother David," Maria said with a wide smile, "if the border is open, we can all walk along the roads in broad daylight without our packs. We can cross the bridge at Eggingen and head innocently toward Erzingen, to the border crossing."

"We'd look strange in our trousers," Rachel glanced down. "Out of place in men's clothing and cause questions. We don't want the German soldiers or border guards asking questions with David's suspicious accent."

"I could go into town and buy working dresses for us." Maria shook her head. "No, it would be much easier to modify these trousers." She looked at her lap. "We can split the inside seams of the legs and add wide darts in the front and the back using the cloth from the legs of our second pairs. Trim will be easy to add to our shirts, and we can make bodices with the flannel from a bedroll. We have a needle and a bit of thread in the biscuit box."

"I have a card of needles and plenty of thread." He paused and looked at each of them "Alright, we've now chased this idea along to a reasonable possibility. Have we any other ideas which make as much sense as this?"

They sat quietly for several minutes. Finally, Rachel said, "I really like the daylight approach." She leaned over and kissed David's cheek as she continued, "Thank you for being so careful."

"How long will it take to convert the trousers?"

"With all of us working on it, I can't see more than three or four hours," Rachel said. "We can start after breakfast over at the lookout as we watch what else is happening below us."

"I'll look suspicious down there as a healthy, fit young man. Most of those have been swept into the war. I'm glad now I strapped the crutches to my pack in case Mama needed them. They'll allow me to play invalid."

"We can be a little family group out for a walk." Rachel looked at him and smiled. "My son is recovering from an injury."

Maria pulled the lantern closer as David unfolded the map. "We can head across through here." He ran his finger across the forested slope from the rib to the road leading down into Eggingen. "It appears to be a more gentle slope back to the meadow than the route we followed in." Tapping his finger, he continued, "This road will lead us innocently into town to begin our own ruse."

Chapter Thirty-Eight

They were all up, dressed and partway through breakfast when the seven o'clock bell sounded below in Eggingen. "Looks like we'll have a beautiful sunny day for our family stroll." Rachel smiled at David and Maria. "The more I think about it, the more it makes sense to do it this way. Simply be down there as part of the scene."

"We need to sort out what to carry with us," David said. "We don't need much... In Freiburg, in Gottenheim, did the German soldiers or other officials stop to question people? Ask for identification like those two soldiers did the other day? Did they search?"

"Never happened to me." Maria shook her head. "I spent a lot of time walking into town to school, exploring at lunch break, walking through town to the gasthaus. The soldiers looked at me a lot, but I was never stopped. But it's not close to the border like here."

"They looked at you because you are so spectacularly beautiful," he said. "No healthy man could keep from looking at you, at the graceful way you move, the confidence you exude."

"He's right, Maria, even if you weren't my daughter, I'd still say you're the most beautiful woman I've ever seen, even more beautiful than I was at your age and I'm told I turned a lot of men's eyes and hearts in those days."

"You two are making me blush."

"The colour looks so good on you," Rachel said. "Come, let's finish breakfast and go set-up a dressmaking shop."

In addition to the seamstress supplies and the other bedrolls to sit on, David took the crutches and began practising on a circuit of the lookout slab, pausing each time he passed the prow to take a thorough look down on the valley floor. He watched the Erzingen border, the eight o'clock mustering of the troops and the three squads as they headed out to the same posts as they had on the previous day.

New activity was a squad heading along the line of trees beside the river downstream of the camp. They stopped a short distance beyond the slough, then four of the soldiers headed back with a body slung by ankles and wrists, head dragging on the ground.

The other five members of the squad remained and moved in a seemingly random fashion. After confirming their activity, he said to the girls, "They're hauling back the corpse. Others are resetting the trap. How are the dresses coming? Do you need any help?"

"No, we're moving along well. An extra hand at the moment would only complicate it," Rachel said. "We've ripped the leg seams, have the darts cut, and we're just now beginning to stitch the skirts together. These will be surprisingly fashionable. We'll do a modelling session within the hour."

He bent and kissed each of them before he returned to his crutch practice and watch routine. He was lying on his belly at the prow, scoping the valley when he heard Maria behind him.

"Introducing the latest in ladies' summer fashion."

He rolled over and sat up as mother and daughter strutted arm-in-arm back and forth across the granite, swishing their full woollen skirts which swept about three inches above the slab.

"Those drape wonderfully, nicely rounded folds, they move well and have a high-quality look to them. You could go into business."

"We're not finished yet," Rachel said. "I'm going to work on completing Maria's outfit, make a simple laced bodice, modify her shirt sleeves and add some shoulder puffs and details. We have lots of material from our spare shirts, the flannel and the clean white cottons. When I've finished with hers, she'll do mine."

He admired the way Rachel lifted a piece of cloth, placed it on Maria's shirt, moved it around and tried another piece, tilting her head. "I'll go back to watching valley. I want you to surprise me with the finished outfit."

He listened to the nine o'clock bells and saw much more traffic on the little road than there had been on Sunday. Horse carriages, waggons, motorcars and a few small trucks passed and a train descended. There were no further activities around the camp at the weir. People were working in the fields, a horse was pulling a plough back and forth in a plot across the river in Switzerland. There was a sparse but regular traffic at the border crossing.

He listened as the bells pealed ten, and was tempted to turn around and look at the progress on the dress, but he resisted as he continued his slow sweeps with the telescope, looking for activity between Eggingen and Zigzag. His telescope sweep had reached the edge of town and was starting back along the road and rail line when he heard a soft swish behind him.

"What do you think, David?" Maria asked.

He rolled over, sat up and stared. "Absolutely gorgeous. The outfit is also." He stood, then slowly walked around her, trying to take in all the detail. "I'm stunned. Amazed you could do all that so quickly, Mama."

"Quickly is the thing. It won't hold together long. Most of the long seams are simply basted. Closer stitching where needed, but more just tacked together. From a metre away, even a seamstress wouldn't know at a glance. It will hold well for a few days."

"Mama's going to keep playing seamstress with me as her dress form," Maria said as she unbuttoned the front of her skirt and let it drop to the granite as she rotated her hips provocatively.

David began swelling.

Maria undid the laces down the front of her bodice, and he swelled further as the bulge of her breasts moved down beneath her shirt. *Blouse,* he corrected himself in his mind. *So cleverly modified,* he thought as she undid its buttons and shook her bared breasts at him.

"Mama said I could take a break from modelling." She stepped out of the skirt toward him. "Care to join me?"

"You've trapped me down my trousers again," he said as he lifted his left thigh above horizontal, unclasped his belt, unbuttoned his front, popped out and dropped the trousers. She had his shirt unbuttoned and off his shoulders by this time, and he dropped it behind. She pushed his stiffness down a bit, got up on her toes and straddled its top as they merged in a hug, deeply kissing.

Maria grabbed his butt cheeks and pulled closer as she ground down on the top of his shaft with her lips and tickler. It was a long embrace, intensely passionate, tears rolling down into their mouths as they kissed. They held tighter, ground their bodies together more forcefully. She started twitching, then heaving. She let go the kiss, growled a moan from deep inside and stood in a tremor, squeezing him tighter still as she quaked.

He gently held the sides of her head, licked the tears from her cheeks and softly said, "You were crying too, I thought it was only me, crying for the joy of you."

"I thought they were only mine. Crying because I'm so happy to know you. You stir me so deeply in so many ways, you inspire me, you caress my soul." She lifted onto her toes and began licking his beard. "This has really grown."

"It's half a month old, beyond the itchy stage. Was that hug good for you?"

"I would never have imagined such a thing was possible," she said, "I'm still in recovery." She looked around and asked, "Mama, have you ever had an orgasm from a hug?"

"I still can't believe what I just saw. I am in awe at the passion you two have." Rachel giggled and added, "Next, you'll be popping just holding hands."

"Whatever it takes, Mama," she giggled back. "Whatever it takes."

"I see David still has his battering ram, Sweetheart. It's poking proudly out beyond your cheeks. Something needs to be done with it, otherwise, he'll have aching balls."

"What would you suggest, Mama?"

"Why not ask him, Sweetheart? He knows best what he wants."

"David?"

"Kneel and straddle me, take me in, gyrate and caress your nipples across my chest. That will pop me rather quickly. Do you want to come again?"

"Yes! — oh God, yes."

"You lead, I'll follow. We'll do it together."

And they did. They did rather noisily. She collapsed, and they writhed together in a tangle on the flannel for a long while after.

"Don't worry about the valley, David," Rachel said. "I'm watching it for us now I've managed to stop watching you. How wonderful you two are together. There's a damp towel beside you when you're ready. It hasn't quite dried yet from its washing."

The day had warmed appreciably, and it was just after half past ten as Maria unplugged and began using the towel on David. "It's like you have two different pieces here. One soft and floppy, the other an oak shaft in a chamois sleeve. Each so different. Both of them so wondrous."

David kissed Rachel's cheek as he relieved her from the lookout task. "Thank you, Mama. Thank you for being so attentive."

"I'm still thinking about that hug." She shook her head. "It would be completely unbelievable if I were told about it. It was incredible to see it evolve."

"Tell me if you ever need a hug, Mama." David winked at her and chuckled. "I have an unlimited supply of them in many different styles and intensities." He took a step forward and wrapped his arms around her. "You're a very special person, Mama. We both love you dearly."

They went back to their tasks, Rachel slipping out of her shirt and handing it to Maria to put on so she could begin converting it into something much more feminine.

David was monitoring the same routine changing of the guard at noon, when Maria said close behind him, "It's time for another fashion show."

He rolled over and sat as two elegantly-dressed ladies paraded across the slab then stopped in front of him to strike a few poses, similar to ones he had seen in newspaper advertisements. He was speechless.

"Well?" Maria asked.

"I'm struck dumb," he said. "I'm amazed at the transformation, amazed by the difference made by moving around a few pieces of cloth."

He got up, slowly walked around them, looking them up and down, looking at every detail, feeling much like the Regimental Sergeant-Major doing a pre-inspection before the officers came. "You ladies pass inspection. Where did you get those handbags?"

"This is my little clutch bag in which I keep documents. Your birth certificate and Swiss papers are in here among them."

"And your lovely little purse, Maria?"

"I put this together while Mama was stitching. It's made from the sleeve of a pullover. I decorated it with buttons from the fronts of the other trousers and the matching macramé strap is from yarns unravelled from the pullover."

"Very inventive." He bowed. "Would you two beautiful ladies care to join me and take a stroll into town, maybe find a nice little café or gasthaus to pause for some lunch?"

"What a splendid idea," Rachel looked at him with a broad smile as she curtsied.

"Mama and I decided it's best if we take our skirts off to get through the first bit of rough blocks and the tangle of bushes." Maria giggled, "I hope you don't mind seeing our bare bottoms."

Chapter Thirty-Nine

David brought the bedrolls over to their work area, laid one of them out, and they placed all the dressmaking goods and remnants in its centre. He pulled the corners together into a large bag and slung it over his shoulder as Rachel and Maria stepped out of their skirts and folded them neatly on the slab. They all took a last long look down at the valley, searching for any changes, then they headed back across to their camp.

He laid out his good wool trousers, best shirt and clean socks, all freshly laundered a few days previously at the hot pool. He cleaned their shoes and boots with the boiled linseed oil and polished them using a beeswax candle.

They quickly sorted and packed the small rucksack with the things they wanted to take with them. The remainder was packed into the three large rucksacks, which were then placed at the back of the small grotto. He dressed, hanging his jacket over his shoulders as a cape in the fashion he had seen in Freiburg.

After he had slung the rucksack over his left shoulder and put on his loden jägerhut, he said, "A quick look around, ladies. Check to see if we've missed anything."

"One thing," Maria said. "Let me adjust the feather in your hat. For you, it has to be much more jaunty. How's this, Mama?"

"He looks like he belongs here, between the Black Forest and the Alps." She picked up her cane and pointed it across the ridge. "Let's go have lunch."

They regained the lookout slab, David walked over to the prow and did one more check of the valley, and after half a minute he said, "I see nothing different down there."

The ladies picked up their skirts and draped them over their arms, David picked up the crutches and led the way across the rugged ridge. He turned frequently to watch the ladies, to confirm their safe progress, but more fascinated by the play of their lips as they stretched long steps between some blocks and down off others.

Within five minutes he had reached the edge of the granitic intrusion, and he looked back to watch in wonder at the beauty of the ladies manoeuvring toward him.

"You're an attentive guide," Maria said as she approached. "Very concerned at our safe steps."

"That, certainly." He looked down. "But my attention is also with the movements here." Running his fingers through her folds, he leaned forward to kiss her. "I'm fascinated with it."

"Fascinated with what?" Rachel asked as she arrived beside them.

"Folds, lips, beautiful moving flesh. You both are so fascinating to watch. I've not before had the opportunity to study the action, the interaction of your legs and lips, the interaction between your lips and your flaps. It's so beautiful to me, so different from anything I know."

"It's probably like my having you swing and pendulum so close in front of my face back there at the hot pools." Rachel shuddered lightly. "So wonderfully different."

"That's the thing, isn't it? Difference." He nodded. "We're built so differently, inside and out, emotionally, mentally, physically. The biggest differences, the physical ones are kept hidden. Why? Our culture seems to bury the wonder of, the reality of our differences."

"Buried somewhere in ancient religious tradition is most likely the answer." Rachel shrugged.

"Let's press on." He pointed. "There's the beginning of a more gentle slope ahead with less tangled undergrowth. Let's head there and see if it's a good place to dress. How's the ankle, Mama?"

"It's so much stronger today. I'm pleased with how it's healed — not quite a week yet. The cane is still welcome, but I can now place much more weight on my foot."

They crossed a more even forest floor, though it was still tangled with dead-falls and low bushes which would be awkward to negotiate in long skirts. After about two hundred yards they came to the edge of the wild forest floor and looked into a narrow, sloping meadow with the road running down its centre.

"Time to dress for the performance, ladies," he said. "Remember, this isn't a dress rehearsal; this is the real performance. Our lives could depend on our acting. Remember, you are who you are, except you've never left Unterhallau but to go shopping in Erzingen and Eggingen. Same with me, I've never left there either, which is the truth." He chuckled. "Actually true, since I've never been there."

"Play dumb again for me, David." Maria laughed. "I loved the way you do that."

He played a mute again for them, with his tongue flopping and chewed as he moaned and mumbled near incomprehensibly. "Remember, this is mainly if we're challenged and I'm required to speak. Hint at brain damage at birth."

He watched the ladies finish fastening their skirts and then turn to check and adjust each other. "Ready for Act One?"

"Let's do it, as you say." Maria giggled.

They took a few steps toward the meadow, paused to check up and down the slope, then sauntered across the to the road and started down the hill, David acting a maimed left foot with the crutches.

The one o'clock bell rang as they strolled through the streets to the centre of town, Rachel returning greetings of *guten tag* and *guten mittag* to those they met as Maria and David nodded.

"I've been looking at the women," Maria said. "We need hats, all the women are wearing hats. The shops are closed now for lunch."

Rachel looked around and nodded. "Let's find a place to have our own lunch. We can ask the frau there if there is a good *Modistin* in town. There must be, everyone is wearing hats."

"There's a delightful patio over there, across the corner." Maria pointed to the other side of the street.

As they examined it, four people rose from a table in a sunny back corner. Rachel led them across the street and pointed to the table when they were greeted. The fraülein looked back at it, then down at her book, nodded, ordered it cleared and set, then a short while later led them back to it.

"This is an ideal table," he said. "From here we can see everybody and everything around us, but we're rather hidden."

Maria engaged the serving fraülein in conversation, and among other things, asked her who was the best Modistin in town, she and her mother needed new hats.

"The best one is two blocks along and just around the corner, in Brückestraße, the street which heads toward the bridge. She usually opens at half past two on Mondays." Maria explained to David after the fraülein had left.

"Amazingly, I got most of that." David smiled and nodded. "I could probably polish my German quite quickly around here."

"It would be better to do it a few kilometres from here, across the line in Switzerland," Rachel said. "It's nearly the same dialect. We're not much more than half a kilometre from Switzerland right now, but the safest way is longer, probably six or seven."

The trio shared a half litre carafe of wine and a huge jägerschnitzel mit knöpfl, and they enjoyed the sun until twenty past two, by which time the patio had nearly cleared.

They slowly walked along the streets, enjoying the sun as they headed to the millinery shop. It was still closed when they arrived, so they looked at the displays in the windows.

"This must be where all those strange red pompom hats come from," David said. "The windows are full of them."

"Those are *bollenhuten*; we don't want them." Rachel shook her head. "They're the tradition here on this side, but unseen across the border. We want something more neutral, ideally the little lace-trimmed caps Swiss women wear. I should have thought earlier."

"There's a linen shop across there, Mama," Maria said. "Let's get two lace-edged table napkins and fold them cleverly. I have several spare hair pins."

"Splendid idea, Sweetheart. We can create something which will fit better with these outfits than a bollenhut would."

Rachel told the woman in the linen shop what they wanted to do, and she showed them a selection she had culled for small snags or weaving imperfections. *"Das wäre perfekt für Sie."* The shopkeeper laid out a variety of pieces, explaining they would be perfect since the flaws can be folded out of sight.

Rachel picked up a bright white piece with a wide lace border, folded it and put it to her hair, then turned to Maria. *"Was denken Sie?"*

Maria shook her head and held up a piece. *"Ich dachte, diese"*

David admired Maria's taste, also thinking the warm cream colour complements the tone of Rachel's outfit and that the white one was a bit stark.

The frau brought out a mirror and propped it against a pile of fluffy towels on the next table. *"Hier, schauen Sie, ich glaube, Ihre Tochter ist richtig."*

Rachel looked at her image and nodded. *"Das ist ideal. Jetzt eine für dich, Schatz."*

David picked up a pale pink piece with an undulating lace frill in a deeper pink and held it to Maria's hair. He looked around at Rachel and the frau with a big smile on his face and mumbled a few sounds ending with something resembling, "... laps, Mama."

"Das ist perfekt, David. Du hast Recht. Es deutet auf ihre errötende Delikatesse."

David chuckled inwardly that Rachel had picked up on his hint of a similarity to Maria's blushing delicacy.

The shopkeeper nodded toward David as she told Rachel, *"Eine solche hübschen Sohn haben Sie."*

David smiled at the compliment on his handsomeness.

Rachel nodded and replied, *"Er war sehr groß, ein langer, langsamer Prozess."*

David put a hand to his mouth to stifled a laugh as he reflected on his size and the long, slow process.

Rachel paused and looked him up and down. *"Er hat ein Problem mit der Rede."*

David smiled as he nodded and mumbled, "yamama."

Rachel and Maria returned their attention to their hats, trying various folds, fitting and looking in the mirror. David saw the price sign, reached into his pocket, pulled out some change and handed the frau a Two Mark piece. She came back with the change and a shallow dish of pins for the girls.

The shop frau was assisting with Rachel's fitting, when she quietly asked with a nod toward David, *"Die Krücken?"*

"Für einen verstauchten Knöchel letzte Woche" Rachel replied, then she paused for a few moments before she lifted her ankle and moved it around, then added, *"Meine — es ist jetzt viel besser."* She explained the cane works well, but her son brought the crutches along in case they were needed.

The frau asked where they were from.

Rachel thought a moment, and then replied, *"Gegenüber in der Nähe von Unterhallau."* She added that they had come shopping, and since it was such a nice day, they decided to continue along to Eggingen to exercise and strengthen her ankle.

"Wir bekommen nicht so viele Schweizer mehr" The frau talked about missing the Swiss shoppers while the border was closed, and how pleased she was it had reopened. Then she asked if they any trouble coming across the border?

"Nein, gar keine."

"Gut. Ich bin, dass so lange gesagt, wie Sie Papiere."

David was relieved to hear that with proper papers, they should have no problem crossing now. He thought, *Why punish innocent business people?*

Rachel looked again at her image in the mirror, and after adjusting her hair, she thanked the frau for her wonderful assistance. Then adding they have a long walk ahead, she led David and Maria to the door.

Chapter Forty

David walked with Maria and Rachel on his arms, following the road which led out of town toward the bridge over the Wutach. As they neared the river, a train slowly passed down the valley. This one was pulled by four locomotives, only two of them with steam up now on the gentle downhill run. The ground quaked noticeably as they turned to walk the road beside the tracks.

"That's a heavy one." David sighed. "I'd love to destroy one of the bridges up the valley and stop these trains for a long while."

"I'm sure the vulnerable spots are all heavily guarded," Rachel said. "This is too important a line for them to ignore."

After the last cars had passed, Rachel turned her head. "Back there where we turned is the bridge across the Wutach. The border angles away from the river here. That road leads to small farms and ends at the top of the ridge near the border. It's better for us in our current garb and roles to continue down the valley another two kilometres or so to the next bridge near Wutöschingen. From there, a small road leads up over the pass and down into Erzingen."

"How high is the rise to the pass?" David asked.

"It goes up rather steeply about a hundred metres, maybe one twenty, and is level for a while before it descends toward town and the border post. That's the way we used early on, before we started taking the short-cut and sneaking across the border. We saved over ten kilometres from home to the rocky rib doing the straight line."

Half an hour later they were across the bridge and well along the narrow road which wound up the shallow valley.

"How's the ankle, Mama?" David asked.

"The boot is supporting it well. The cane helps with steadying and takes a bit of the weight, but much less weight than before. I'm delighted how quickly it has mended."

"Let me know when you need to take a break."

"A pee break would be nice in a while — actually, now because I'm thinking about it. Strange how it often does that." She giggled.

"There's a little grove at the end of this switchback." He pointed up the slope a hundred yards. "Can you last to there?"

"Yes, I can easily do that."

"Good, we can sit in the trees, enjoy the shade, take a break and refresh. We'll pause to take stock of our situation."

They moved in past a few trees and paused at a large fallen trunk. "This is a delightful little spot," Maria said, as she put her handbag on the log and sat.

Rachel turned her back to them as she bent and lifted the front hem of her skirt. She straightened up with the material and held it across her waist, then arching her back and spreading her knees, she let go a big arching stream.

"I've never done it standing, Mama," Maria said. "I've always sat or squatted, but I've seen you do it a few times the past while."

"It's a good alternative." Rachel dropped her skirt and turned. "The secret is to always clear your flaps. You know how they want to stick together, and if you don't separate them, you'll squirt and dribble all over yourself. It's similar to what I taught you to do when you sit or squat. Otherwise, it becomes messy."

Maria unbuttoned her skirt, let it fall, stepped out of it and walked a few steps. She spread her legs, arched her back, ran a finger up between her lips and left it resting against her button to keep the flaps apart as she smiled down at the graceful arc of pale yellow. Moving her finger side to side, and turning her head toward them, she chuckled and said, "Look, Mama, I can steer this. It's the same as the tiller action as on Grandada's sailboats; push it one way and it goes the other."

"I'm fascinated with these demonstrations." David tilted his head. "These are not things usually seen or spoken. Until last week I'd never thought of women standing to pee."

"Edom suggested I try it. He couldn't see any reason it wouldn't work. Now in the wilds, in places such as this or in those awful French WCs, it's my favourite."

Maria stepped back into her skirt, lifted and buttoned it, and they all sat on the log passing one of the water canteens to rinse fingers and then quench thirsts. After a quiet minute or so, David asked, "How was our act back there. Were we convincing? Did you notice any hint of suspicion that something was odd?"

"She was a warm, genuine person, I thought." Rachel shrugged. "I sense she was completely unaware of anything odd. I don't think we gave her any reason to suspect there was anything out of place about us."

Maria added, "My feeling is we came across as a friendly Swiss family. Mama's mix of Unterhallau and Zürich dialect is so convincing because it's so genuine. It's what she grew up with. Mine is more purely Unterhallau, and David, I loved your comparison and your pronunciation of Mama."

"I was choking back a laugh, Mama, when you said I was big when I came out and that it took a long time." He chuckled.

"But it's true, though you were considerably bigger when you went in." She closed her eyes and smiled. "And you did take a long time to come out, such a delightfully long time."

Maria pointed toward the road. "We saw many out walking in town, and several along the road to Wutöschingen. But once we started up this road, we've seen only the farmer with the barrow and that young couple a while ago. Them, and a few automobiles."

"I think we're still a part of the scene. We simply have to remain as such." He glanced at his watch, "It's almost three thirty, and it looks as if we're a little over halfway to the pass. Shall we press on again, my dear ladies?"

"Let's do it," the girls said in harmony, then giggled.

The steepness of the road eased, and they followed a more gradual bending climb. It continued to ease, and shortly after four, they began slowly descending. Ten minutes later they rounded a bend and saw Erzingen emerging from behind the slope's shoulder.

As they continued down the hill, Rachel pointed to the soldiers patrolling the field beside them. "Guards make sense; the border is about two hundred metres away; it's that fence. We used to save three kilometres climbing over it. Our first short-cut." She pointed ahead. "The border post is about a kilometre and a half from here, through Erzingen. Those white buildings on the road to the left of town. One German and one Swiss."

The trio continued along toward town, seeing soldiers ranged out all along the border, but none on the road. As they passed the first houses, they met people walking, and in a field, there was a small group of children playing an unidentifiable game with a ball. Life was happening around them.

They continued into town, meeting increasing numbers of people as they went. Rachel returned greetings, and David, now carrying the crutches, tipped his hat to the ladies, as he had seen being done by some other men. They felt as part of the scene as they arrived in the Hauptstraße and turned left to walk along it.

David looked at his watch. "Twenty past four. That was a lovely day of shopping. Shall we head home?"

"We need a few small parcels to carry with us," Maria said. "Otherwise, we'll look strange returning from shopping with nothing."

"Now who's the careful thinker?" David asked. "That is the kind of detail we need to continue with. What should we get?"

"I'd love a Schwarzwälder Kirschtorte." Maria sighed. "I haven't had any since my last day at the gasthaus. The staff always shared the remains of older ones before they became stale."

"What else is typically bought here?" David asked.

"Cuckoo clocks, bland cheese, wood carvings, kirsch, kitsch, things we don't want... Wait!" Rachel blurted, "Tante Bethia's Schinken, we used to come over to buy it. I wonder if Tante Bethia still has the little Metzgerei. We can easily find out — follow me, it was just along and then a few doors in, to the left."

Chapter Forty-One

Rachel looked up the side streets as they passed them, searching for familiar things. Three blocks along they turned and were soon standing in front of Klettgau Metzgerei. She led Maria and David into the shop, hearing the familiar bell as the door moved it. An elderly woman came through the curtained doorway from the back, wiping her hands on a towel in her apron strings.

"Tante, you're still here!" Rachel's face was beaming.

The woman looked questioningly at her. She adjusted her glasses and beckoned Rachel forward. "Come closer dear, my eyes have faded. You look familiar."

"Tante, it's Rachel, Rachel Meier from over in Unterhallau."

"*Gott im Himmel* — I haven't seen you in years. You're still as beautiful as ever. That can't be little Maria. I last remember her when her eyes didn't make it over the counter. Which of your sons is this? My God, he's a handsome one."

"This is David."

"You've hurt yourself? You're using a cane."

"A silly sprained ankle getting out of a hot bath last week. It's so much better now. We're out walking and exercising it today... But, enough of this, let me hug you; you're still my favourite aunt."

Part way through the long embrace, Rachel asked, "How is Onkel Aaron?"

"God took him last summer, I've been trying to find a way to move back to Küsnacht, but it has been difficult with the war."

She squeezed Bethia a bit more firmly and said, "Very difficult with the war. Edom was killed fighting in Elsass in September, then Jacob and Nathan in October. Only Maria and me left."

The hug continued. Then Bethia looked up and across to David. "So who's this handsome young lad then?"

"David's a Canadian soldier escaping from capture after he was severely wounded at the front in Belgium. We've adopted each other, all three of us. He's led us over the hills from Gottenheim to here, starting eleven days ago. I had almost forgotten about you."

"What are we doing standing around out here?" Bethia motioned to the curtains. "Come, let's go into the back, sit and relax. What can I get you?"

She led them into the back, through the kitchen, paused to put on a kettle of water, then continued leading them into the parlour. "The crutches? What are they for? David's just carrying them."

"Part of our disguise," David said. "To keep the soldiers from wondering what a healthy young man is doing not in uniform and so close to the border."

"Ingenious. Sit! Sit! You all must be tired. Will you stay here with me for a while? I have two spare rooms. You wouldn't mind sharing a bed with your mother, would you, Maria? My God, but you're beautiful. Just like your mother. The tea water should be boiling soon, what can I bring you? You must be starving."

Maria followed Bethia into the kitchen and started telling her the story of their trip, skimming over the emotional parts, but describing in detail the layout of the spa and the sequence of events there as Bethia scurried around assembling large platters.

She interrupted Maria "You haven't gone back to Kosher, have you?"

"Certainly not. The world is too delicious and exciting to restrict living to old traditions."

"Good, I didn't think so. I'll keep adding the hams. We have a fine variety of them here. Please, go on with your story. What did you do with the venison?"

Maria was part way into the description of the hot pools as she carried two trays into the parlour, following Bethia, who carried the tea and a third tray.

"From what Maria has been telling me, it sounds as though you had a rather comfortable time, even with the Germans killing themselves all around you. So tell me more of the hot pool... Eat! Eat! That's why it's there."

Bethia interrupted Maria again when she was telling about soaking in the hot pool. "Like Adam and Eve?"

"No, Tante, more like Eve and Adam and Eve. We surrounded him. We had only one soaking pool and one bed to share."

"That sounds a cosy arrangement." She looked at David, slowly eyed him up and down, pausing for a long while at his thigh. "Such a handsome young man, he looks very well built — Rachel, I remember you were a wild one when you were young. That was so refreshing for some of us older folk to see. It was so different from the old traditions... So was he a good boy?"

"Very very good," Maria said as she bit her lower lip and shivered.

"Are you catching a chill? Do we want a fire?"

"No, not that at all. I was just reliving how good he was." She was also recalling stories her mother had told her about her Tante Bethia and how she had encouraged her and instructed her when she entered her teens. Maria was now seeing the deeper meaning of the stories.

"So he was that kind of good." Bethia pursed her lips and nodded. "I am so pleased for you." Then she smiled broadly as she looked again more closely at David. "I can see he would be very good. I'm so pleased to see Rachel is passing on the new tradition. Tell me more of the adventures which brought you here."

Maria continued with the story, and she was describing treating Mama's sprained ankle when the shop door bell tinkled.

"I'll be back shortly," Bethia said as she headed off toward the shop front. "Business is calling."

Rachel looked at David after Bethia had left and said, "She was my early mentor. She's the one who encouraged me to explore and to enjoy. She's such a dear person, so loving."

"I sensed that." He nodded. "She still exudes a wonderful passion. How old is she? She's your mother's sister or your father's?"

"She's my mother's older sister. Mama was born in 1854 and Bethia is five years older, so she's now sixty-six. She moved to Switzerland after visiting Mama and Papa a few years after they had settled. I was just beginning to walk then. She taught me how to swim, and later how to soar."

"I think we should stay the night." He looked around. "There's a lot we can offer each other."

"Yes, I agree." Rachel nodded. "We're safe here, and less than a hundred metres from the border. We can monitor the procedure, see what the foot traffic is like, plan the safest way to cross. Also, we can help Bethia to organise her own return to Switzerland."

"Why is she living here in Germany?" David looked at Rachel with a puzzled expression.

"She met Aaron, whose family lived here and owned and ran a slaughter house. They moved to assist and take over as his parents aged. She opened the delicatessen and joked that she sold Kosher ham. She's a real character."

"Tante's taking quite a while out front." Maria stood. "I'll go see if she needs assistance."

She quietly moved across the kitchen, parted the curtains a crack and peeked out through. Bethia was sitting at one of the two tables in a deep conversation with a young couple, probably in their mid-thirties. She listened and heard friendly, but forceful negotiation with large sums of money being mentioned. She backed away and returned to the parlour.

"I'm not sure," Maria said as she sat on the settee. "But it sounds as if she's negotiating the sale of her business. There's a prosperous-looking couple out there at the table with her, and they were talking large sums of money, June, July, August, I couldn't quite follow them, some of the words were unfamiliar to me."

Chapter Forty-Two

A few minutes later, David stood as Bethia rejoined them in the parlour. She was quiet and appeared to be deep in thought as she sat. After a minute, she looked up. "Pardon my distraction. I'm forgetting I have guests — no, not guests — family. I have family to enfold and to welcome, and here I am, off somewhere in my mind doing business."

"Tante, business is important," Rachel said.

"Never more important than family."

"I was concerned, Tante Bethia," Maria said. "I peeked through the curtains to check on you. Who was that elegant couple?"

"They want to buy the *Schlachthof*, the slaughterhouse. This was their third visit. I've tried to convince them to also take the Metzgerei, but they say they know nothing of this end of the business."

"So where do the negotiations sit?" David asked.

"Their lawyer is coming on Wednesday. I need to find out who our lawyer is. Aaron always did such things. Unimportant things to me. People are so much more important. Will you stay?"

"Of course, we'll stay, Tante." Maria nodded. "How can we not support family? David was studying business and accounting before the war. He's wonderfully inventive and creative with everything I've seen. He's wise far beyond his age, so I'm sure he can poke holes in any strange offers and give their lawyer every good reason to be reasonable. How could we not stay?"

"I've locked and shuttered the front and tomorrow is our closed day. Now we can relax and enjoy each other without interruption. I'm excited by your adventure getting here. Please, Maria, continue the story. More tea?"

Maria continued to unfold their adventure, often pausing in amazement it had happened, or pausing at memories so deeply intense in her nethers and in her soul. She led the story to the door of Tante's Delicatessen.

She looked up into her great aunt's eyes and said, "And that's how we've arrived here, ragged, exposed and vulnerable. Far out on a limb whose strength we're unsure of, but wrapped in the confidence the power we share will pull us through."

"I'm in awe. What strong people you are. I'm honoured and privileged to have you under my roof."

They sat and caught up on family since Edom had moved Rachel and the children to the Kaiserstühl in 1905. Bethia told stories of people Rachel had long since forgotten about, but she kept going back to the relationship among the three of them. She sensed there was more than just David and Maria involved after such a close, intense encounter.

Rachel finally said, "Tante, this may seem strange, but bear with me as I unfold it. I'm not sure where this is going, but there is a strong force inside me pushing. Please don't be taken aback by this question. I need to know. Have you ever experienced an uncircumcised penis?"

Bethia looked her in the eyes, paused only a second or two and said, "The only non-Kosher men's meat I've seen were a week or less old, before their circumcision. They were the size of the tip of my little finger, impossible to see any detail. I have no idea what a grown one looks like."

"Tante, they are so completely different. The rabbis have been cheating us. Robbing us of God's design. I discovered what the actual design is during the past week and a half. We must stop the horrid mutilation of our boys."

"Am I correct in assuming David isn't circumcised?"

"Yes, you are. That tiny skin snip the book and the rabbis talk about, Tante, that snip is a major mutilation. I don't think many are aware how much is destroyed. Tradition doesn't allow us to venture outside the faith to experience."

"You experienced?"

"Oh, my God! Yes!"

"And you, Maria?"

"So many times."

"What have I missed?"

"Reality. God's design. Bliss."

"I must see this." Bethia looked at David. "Would you mind?"

David had sat wide-eyed through the entire conversation, part of him questioning whether he was dreaming, part of him in awe of the openness and freedom shared by the three women. *Three women from three generations, but each so wonderfully open and adventurous.*

He watched his hands unbuttoning his trouser front, seeing them not as his own. He seemed to have no control of it as his right hand reached in and pulled out his penis and laid it onto the settee cushion.

Bethia stared at it, speechless. After the shock had subsided, she asked, "The cutting impairs its growth?"

Maria picked it up and slowly rolled the skin back, gradually exposing the head and continuing to peel the foreskin back, having to take another grip to get it all the way off.

"That's how much the rabbis remove." Rachel sighed. "Look at this now, peeled to resemble a broomstick. God designed it to slide smoothly within its own glove. Remember you talked of pain from friction? That's not a part of the design. The rabbis design the friction and add the pain."

"May I?" Bethia looked back and forth between Maria and David. "I don't know which of you to ask. You seem to both own this."

"Please." David nodded, still completely awestruck.

She ran her fingers along it, pulled at the loose skin covering, moved it along farther over the head, pulled it back to begin exposing the head. She shook her head and stared up at Rachel. "What the fuck have the rabbis done? This is a superb tool. I can see how beautifully this fits with our design. I can imagine how wonderful this must be inside."

As Bethia moved the skin gently on and off the head, Maria nudged David, caught his eye and nodded her head up. He began expanding as Bethia continued to slowly stroke. "What a magnificent man you have, Maria. I'm so delighted his sausage is non-Kosher. And it grows still bigger? What are the rabbis doing?"

"Tante, I had both Jacob and Nathan mutilated. I was unaware of what I was doing. I was following tradition, following the rabbi's instruction, following expectation."

"We have all done that since Abraham, for two hundred and more generations we have blindly done that, Rachel. We now need to work to stop it. The more women become aware this is horrid mutilation, the more quickly it will stop. But how do we make them aware? We can't haul David around as a demonstration of the cruelty of circumcision. How will we do this?"

As she spoke, Bethia continued to hold and slowly stroke David, who was now fully erect. "How does the cutting away of skin impair the growth?"

"Look here." Maria pointed at wrinkles and folds under the head. "David says these are his most sensitive parts. Mama told us Dada had none. The rabbis had cut them away."

Bethia looked to where Maria was pointing, ran her fingers across the frenulum gently a few times, seeing and feeling him pulse with the touch. "I can sense he likes that. Aaron's was flat, nothing but scarred skin. The rabbis had removed all the frills, had removed all the thrills. What the fuck are they thinking?"

"Not thinking," Rachel said. "They're blindly following tradition."

Bethia continued to gently stroke, staring at the action as if hypnotised. "This must be so delightful inside."

"So, Tante, will you work with me? Will you help educate? It will be difficult for us because we've slipped outside the faith, but I'm sure some will listen. We need only a few to start expanding the awareness."

Bethia resumed her slow stroking as she moved her face closer to minutely study the action of the folding skin. "They don't simply snip a piece off the end, as we're told. They cut out a huge section from the middle, wrap-up the remains and hope the ends heal. That's why Aaron had those strange scars and a flap of loose skin. What a horrid tradition. We need to stop it."

"Look at this, Tante." Rachel knelt and took over the stroking. She pulled the skin all the way up and let it relax in a spout beyond the end. Then she circled his head with her fingers and started rolling the skin slowly down his shaft until she got to its root at his pubes. "After his entire length, there's still more skin. Watch again as I pull the rest down."

She moved her other hand to circle his shaft midway along and pulled down almost to the root until the skin was taut and shiny. Does this resemble Aaron's erection?

"The same tightness he used to be, though so much larger."

"I've peeled nearly one and a half lengths of skin off his shaft to get here. That's how much our tradition has stolen from our men, how much has been stolen from our enjoyment. With an unmutilated man, there's no harsh friction, no pain, just soft velvety motion and changing pressure. This makes it easy for multiple orgasms for us, he can continue for hours at a time if we want."

"I had no idea." Bethia shook her head and stared as Rachel let go of the skin and they all watched it move up and stop short of the head, retained there by the ridge. "Why would anyone want to destroy such a practical and beautiful design?"

"In my mind," Rachel said, "it's because the tradition goes back so far, goes back to Abraham in Genesis and Moses in Exodus. For thousands of years, our people have forgotten what a real penis looks like beyond a few days old, forgotten the beauty and workings of its intended design."

"I've never seen a mutilated one except at a distance in the Army showers. Those were soft, so I can only imagine what they're like when hard."

"I would think this is the same for the mutilated boys and men," Bethia said. "There would be little opportunity to see others and much less opportunity to see the real design or to understand how wonderfully it is meant to work. This is not the sort of thing men share. Men don't seem to share much of themselves, much of their real being, even with women."

"In the Army camps, I saw that any of the men who took more than casual interest were labelled 'queer', and they were then poorly treated by the others. Word was quickly passed around to be careful with *that one* or don't drop your soap near *him*. Curiosity had to be satisfied with quick, fleeting glances. Men don't discuss these things, except in crude jokes and bravado stories."

"Women share much more about such things with each other than men do," Rachel shrugged and nodded.

"You're right, Mama," he said. "I could never talk like this with men. I'd be labelled a queer... Thinking now further, the biggest difference between using a mutilated one and a whole one would be the friction. My method is to keep my head covered while inside. To glide there within my own skin. There I can keep myself excited and wonderfully on the edge, and I can stay that way for as long as my energy lasts. When I want to finish, I need only to lower a hand and peel the double layer of skin back to bare my head. Quickly, with the increased friction, I pop."

"That seems the secret." Rachel sighed. "So many times, in the beginning, Edom couldn't last long enough inside to satisfy me. We had to do other things to excite me. We thought the problem was me, and I visited the doctor. He said it was normal."

David had allowed his penis to gradually deflate as they talked, and it slowly tilted and fell across his thigh as it contracted. The skin puckered into a longer spout out beyond the head.

"So, that's what a real one looks like," Bethia said after she had watched it change. "All these years and I never suspected it was supposed to have two layers of sensitivity protection. Aaron had so much trouble lasting long enough to please me."

She continued to stare at it, then said, "Peel it back again for me, David. Your head looked and felt so smooth when it was hard. I'm curious to know how it is when soft?" She looked at the exposed glans closely, then ran her fingers across it. "So soft and smooth. That cover serves many fine purposes — Aaron's head was wrinkled, and he had so much trouble with dryness, sometimes with cracking. We often had to use olive oil on it. What a sin we remove this beautiful protection and stunt the growth."

David picked up his penis and looked at it, slid its skin back over its head, tucked it into his trousers, adjusted it down his leg and buttoned up his front. He looked up and shrugged. "This is perfectly normal to me, and from what I've been hearing, I'm so delighted it is."

Chapter Forty-Three

After they had refreshed, Bethia remained quiet as she sat sipping tea with David, Rachel and Maria, who were also deep in thought as they nibbled from the tray. David was the first to speak. "This is delicious ham, Tante. I've not had any as fine. Such a variety. The sausages are all amazing. Are these all produced in this region?"

"They're all made rather close to here," Bethia replied with a big smile. "The smokehouse is out through the kitchen. Some of them I age up in the dry warmth of the attic, others down in the cool moistness of the cellar. I can show you later."

"You make these?" he asked with wide eyes.

"Not as much anymore. We once sold to many of the shops up and down the Wutach, but now I make only enough for the shop out front and for here." She looked down and patted her belly.

"Do you get many Swiss people coming across?"

"They slowed in September, not long after Aaron died. The war made it much more difficult to cross, then stopped when the border closed later in the year. People are just beginning again to visit. It must be hard for some of the shop-keepers who depend on Swiss business."

"So tell me about the slaughter house. I'd like to know more about it for Wednesday. Has it been affected by the war?"

"Yes, it certainly has been. In August we received a large standing order for beef and pork from the *Deutsches Heer*, the German Army, their Badisches Infanterie-Regiment."

"That sounds very good."

"That was a very difficult time. Aaron had negotiated the contract, brought in new workers, bought a new delivery lorry. He worked himself to death. Three weeks into the contract, his sixty-seven-year-old heart gave out. I had told him he was working too hard. It's been difficult for me running both that business and this... too much for me, that's why I'm trying to sell."

"Your slaughter business is worth more now you're supplying the Army. How long is the contract?"

"The first one was for three months. They renewed for another three in November, and in February we signed for another six months. They seem pleased."

"How much do they purchase?"

"We started with one tonne of beef and two tonnes of pork delivered to Donaueschingen every three days. Simple split carcasses, easy to prepare. Now we're also delivering similar quantities to their kasernen in Lahr and Freiburg. We have to process three tonnes a day just for the Army. It's now half our business, the easy half."

"How many sides are there in a tonne?"

"With beef, it varies between seven and eight, depending on the size of the animal. With pork, about twenty-five per tonne. We do nearly sixty sides a day just for the Army."

"You still have only one delivery truck?"

"No, two. The new one and the old one, but we use the new one only for the Army and keep the old one in case of a breakdown."

"I know Freiburg, and I saw the name Lahr north of there when the train stopped on my way south, but I'm not familiar with Donaueschingen. Sounds like it's in the Danube Valley, how far is it from here?"

"Forty kilometres by road, at the source of the Danube, up a narrow, winding road, thankfully not as crooked as the Sauschwänzlebahn. I've gone twice now to sign new contracts."

"Sauschwänzlebahn. That's the twisting railway with all the bridges and tunnels, isn't it?"

"Yes, an amazing line. Aaron and I travelled across it a few years ago on a trip to Munich. I came back with another gold medal for my Klettgauschinken — this one," she said as she prepared to pop a slice into her mouth. "Have you tried it?"

"I've had several slices; it's one of my favourites. To be fair, though, they are all my favourites."

"You are a true sweetheart, you certainly are." She beamed a proud smile.

"So, your truck is out every day delivering beef and hog sides to the Army. A day to Donaueschingen, a day to Lahr and a day to Freiburg, then repeat."

"No, we do the Freiburg and Lahr deliveries in one trip, a hundred and twenty kilometres to Freiburg and another forty beyond there to Lahr. It's a long day for the driver. The lorry is out two days and in one for any needed repairs or maintenance. Gives the driver a break too, only local deliveries to do."

"I'd like to look at your books, your accounts tomorrow to gain a proper perspective of the businesses. Would you mind?"

"I'd be delighted to show them to you; I'm proud of the ledgers I keep, that was my part of the administration... But enough with business. Let's get back to being family, that's so much more enjoyable for me. Let me make more tea... No, let me bring up some wine from the cellar, that's a better idea. Come, let me show you the curing hams and we can bring up some wine for the evening and for dinner."

She led them through the kitchen, through the doorway in its rear and down five broad stone steps into the large courtyard. Standing in one corner, against the kitchen was a tall, circular brick tower with two inset rectangular iron doors, one above the other. "This is the smoker. The fire is set in here, the wood chips and other aromatics are placed in here if I want them, and ashes are hauled out through that opening in the bottom."

"I don't see a place for the hams and sausages. Where do they go?" David asked, looking around and adding, "From the kitchen?"

"Yes, there are doors in the kitchen, I'll show you that later." She led them across to a set of stone steps descending beside a ramp to a landing in front of a pair of doors under the centre of the house. She keyed the lock and swung one heavy oak door in. "Come in. This is the brining room, and over through that door, is the wine cellar."

She pointed to a small shaft running floor to ceiling, explaining, "This is the elevator I use to move the meats between here and the kitchen. That crank winds it up and down. There's another crank in the kitchen and a third one in the attic. Aaron built this many years ago to his own design."

"I remember Dada scolding Jacob and Nathan for playing on this," Maria said with a vacant stare, her eyes beginning to water. "That's so long ago..."

David put a hand on her shoulder, and she turned to place her head against his chest as she began quietly sobbing. They merged into a hug.

They all stood silent for a long while before Bethia spoke, "Come, help me get the wine, we can look at the ham and sausage operation tomorrow."

She unlocked the cellar door and asked David to push it open, "It's getting a bit heavy for me now."

"This is large," Rachel said as they entered. "I don't remember you making wine."

"We started the year you left for the Kaiserstühl. Aaron thought if you could start a vineyard, so could we. He found a sloping piece of land a short distance north of town, along the border. Across the line from it and along a bit was a vineyard producing wonderful Blauburgunder and Weißburgunder, so that's what we planted."

"How big is the vineyard?"

"Quite small, a little under a half hectare, this was just a hobby for us, we had fun and the wine is good. We decided to make it in the Burgundy style. Last year there were four barrels of each, about 2500 bottles. I sell some upstairs and to two restaurants in town."

She looked around at the twelve barrels. "I need to bottle last year's Weißburgunder and the 1913 Blauburgunder. I need to find someone to replace Franz."

"We can bottle for you, Tante," Rachel said. "Marie and I do ours and we've become rather good. Do the vineyards need work?"

"I'm sure they do. They've been neglected since Franz was taken by the Army last month — nearly two months ago now, that was before Passover.

We have a new plot next to it which we planted last spring. I'm sure it needs attention. At least Franz finished with the pruning before he left. We can talk about that later, now we need some wine." She searched among the masonry bins.

"Here, the 1911s one of each. Careful with the red, David." She handed him the bottle. "Keep this on its side, move it gently; there's a lot of sediment we don't want to disturb."

She handed the other bottle to Maria, and motioning to the door, said, "Let's go back upstairs and enjoy."

Bethia took the red as they arrived in the parlour and placed it in a wicker cradle. "We'll let that rest a while and start with the white. We ferment this in the barrel and stir the lees regularly through the winter," she said as she pulled the cork. "That's one of the tricks we learned on our visit to the Burgundy as we were trying to figure out how to make wine."

She poured four glasses, and Maria passed them around. "These are interesting glasses, Tante," she said. "Much bigger bowls and thinner, more elegant stems than ours."

"These are Burgundy glasses, Dear. They're much more suited to enjoying this style of wine. Hold the stem and swirl the wine in the glass like this, then stick your nose in and inhale gently."

They all followed her instructions and demonstration. Rachel was the first to comment, "This is so like the Meursault and the Montrachet we had a few years ago at a conference in Dijon." She nosed her glass again and took a sip, moved the wine around in her mouth, pulled some air over it through pursed lips. "This is closer to the complexity of the Montrachet."

She looked up at Bethia's beaming face and continued, "This is superb wine."

"I told you it was good."

"Tante Bethia, this is so far beyond good. This is superb wine. Have you entered it in any competitions?"

"We can't, we didn't make enough to qualify."

"I've never had a taste like this," David said, looking back and forth between his glass and Bethia. "Tell me about it. I'm amazed by the smell and the taste."

"You tell me what you smell and taste, Dear."

"I don't know how to describe... so complicated, buttery, rich, like papayas and ripe peaches, like cinnamon and vanilla and deliciousness. I'm astounded with the complexity of aromas and flavours." He swirled the glass again and put his nose back in. "There's a hint of the smell of bread rising mixed with ripe fruits, so many fruits. This is made from only grapes?"

"Yes, Dear. Made from the Weißburgunder, the Burgundians call this grape Chardonnay. Small berries, tightly clustered and our south-facing slope allows them to ripen to a very high Oechsle."

"What's Oechsle?"

"That's the measure of sugar in the juice. The riper the grape, the more sugar, but we also have to watch the acid. As the grapes ripen, the acidity declines. Too little acid and the wine is flaccid and rather lifeless. Good for pissing, not for making love to the palate."

"That's always the thing, isn't it," Rachel said, looking at Bethia. "Finding the exact moment to harvest. Too early gives green, acidic wine; too late gives lacklustre flabby wine. You can correct a bit with added sugar or citric acid, but you end up with an uninteresting, unnatural wine. Wine is nature speaking through the hands and the souls of the winemakers."

"Spoken like a passionate winemaker," Bethia said. "We can do nothing to improve the quality. Once the grapes are picked, all we can do is work to maintain as much of the quality as possible. We cannot make good wine from bad grapes, but it's easily possible to make poor wine from great grapes."

"Is the Blauburgunder superb like this?" Marie asked.

"No, Dear, I think it is much better." Bethia smiled as she looked around at each of the three faces in turn. "It's so good to have family again. It's been so quiet here these last months. What shall we do for dinner?"

"Why don't we continue with these platters?" Rachel said. "We have a small piece of Appenzeller and some Gruyère in the pack that need finishing. Let's enjoy each other and the wine."

"Let me get more bread," Bethia said.

"Stay where you are, Tante." Maria stood. "Tell me where it is and I'll get it. You stay here and open the red, I'm curious to taste that after your comments. Mama and David must also be."

The red had been opened and carefully poured off its sediment when Maria returned with bread and cheese. Bethia handed her a glass, saying, "Alright, now we can begin." She swirled her wine and smiled.

"The French call this grape Pinot Noir, one of the most difficult wines to make. Most often it's good, but it can be magnificent. Once you've had a great Blauburgunder, you'll chase another forever. This is a great one; the growing conditions were near perfect."

The four sat swirling and nosing their glasses, looking up and smiling and going back at it. "This bouquet is nearly orgasmic," Rachel said to finally break the long silence.

David flipped a hand to his trousers, shifted in his seat and said, "This has certainly stirred something in me. The aroma moves me in the same manner as does Maria's bouquet."

Maria looked down at his lap and smiled at the sight of the bulge. "I have tingles down the back of my head, my neck. My nipples have tightened. My God! Tante Bethia, this is beyond superb."

"I've always thought so. That's why we haven't sold any, we kept it all for ourselves. We made only five hundred and sixty bottles. It was a small, concentrated crop that year."

They all took sips from their glasses and tasted. Rachel looked up and around at the others, then stopped at Bethia. "This reminds me of the Chambertin from our Burgundy trip. Incredibly complex with so many layers of flavour. Sensuous and soft on the one hand, so firmly structured on the other. Earthy and fruity and alive."

"I'm so pleased you like it. Last year with some other winemakers, we tasted this with a Clos de Bèze and a Musigny. None of the group could tell which was which."

"What's klo de bez and moosingyee?" Maria asked.

"Clos de Bèze is one of the two finest vineyards in Chambertin, which is one of the greatest wine areas of the Burgundy, and Musigny is as fine or finer. Great Burgundy is one of the finest red wines in the world."

"I thought it had to be something like that," Maria said. "I am speechless to describe this. It's so far beyond my experience."

"We were delighted with its quality. The vines were only six years old when we harvested this, and we knew as it was fermenting that it would be extraordinary. Aaron tried to buy the neighbouring plots to expand the vineyard, but the owners wouldn't sell. We finally had to settle on buying the small plot which abuts it across the border."

"You own a piece of the Swiss border?" David asked, his mind spinning up rapidly.

"Yes, I suppose in a way, we do. The vineyard now runs across the border, 43 ares on this side and 61 in Switzerland. A little over a hectare in total now, all in the same streak of chalky marl."

"Your train trip on the Sauschwänzlebahn. I haven't been able to push that very far back in my mind since you mentioned it. Do you have any maps or drawings of the route?"

"Aaron has a dossier of papers and drawings on it. He was fascinated with the engineering. That was his profession. He shot many photographs of the bridges both coming and going on that trip and on many other trips. I love the spiral tunnel and the upside-down arches on the bridges. Aaron worked..."

"Upside-down arches?"

"Yes, instead of arching up like that," she said, pointing to the arch over the doorway, "they hang down underneath the bridges."

"How close to the railway does your truck go on its delivery?"

"It follows closely for a good distance, crosses under it several times. You seem very interested in the Sauschwänzlebahn."

"I'm just thinking of ways I can help with the war."

Chapter Forty-Four

David paused, nosed his wine, looked from face to face and said, "But let's get back to here, back to us, back to these superb wines and to these delicious meats. I'm so delighted to have met you, Tante Bethia."

They enjoyed a long rambling conversation through the evening, sharing stories and reminiscences as they slowly cleared the platters and savoured the wines to depletion. Shortly after the clock had cuckooed ten, Bethia stood. "I must go prepare your rooms, make your beds, get towels..."

"I'll come with you." Maria rose to join her. "Four hands will make it much easier."

As they reached the top of the stairs, Bethia paused for a breath and looked back down, then into Maria's eyes. "What a magnificent man you have found. We mustn't let him get away. Come, let's prepare a love nest for you in the corner room."

She led Maria along the cross hall to the doorway at the end, pushed the door the rest of the way open and stepped in. "This was our room, but a few months ago I decided the stairs were too much every night, so I now use the side parlour downstairs."

"What a delightful room. So many windows."

"Look out here." Bethia took her hand and lead her to a pair of doors and opened them. "My little Juliet balcony. It looks over the courtyard a hundred metres into Switzerland."

"This is so beautiful." Maria stepped out. "It must be a marvellous view in daylight."

"The summer sunsets are over there." Bethia pointed toward the right. "And over there, over the other corner are our vineyards, half a kilometre away. In daylight, we can see them clearly. But come, Sweetheart, let's make you a love nest."

"Sweetheart," Maria said with a warm smile, "that's what Mama calls me."

"That's what I used to call her. You're both such sweethearts. I'm so delighted that she has kept her free spirit and is passing it along."

As they pulled satin sheets and pillowcases out of drawers, fluffed pillows, stuffed a duvet into a cover and slowly arranged the room, Bethia asked many questions about David. They paused often as Maria freely shared her experiences.

"He is such a magnificent man, but I've said that so many times already, Sweetheart. I haven't had warm loins like this, not been wet this way for such a long while."

"He did that to me the first time I saw him. I don't know what it was. His face was bandaged, I couldn't see how handsome he was, only hints of it. But it was the way he looked at me. It was as if he was looking deep into my soul. I tingled all over each time I approached his table. I quickly became wet. He must have smelled it. He loves my aroma."

"That aroma is part of God's design," Bethia paused and shook her head, then continued, "Like the beautiful cover he has on his huge sausage. That is huge, Sweetheart. Huge. I had never imagined that's how they're supposed to be. Oh, to be young again and exploring."

"I don't know if you've ever done this, but on the second evening in the gasthaus, after he started me flowing again, I went to the back and dipped my fingers under my skirts to relieve the buzz. I dabbed some of my wetness between my breasts and behind my ears. When I returned to his table, he became much more interested."

"That's nature's original perfume, Sweetheart, and still the most successful one. I'm so pleased Rachel passed that on to you."

"She didn't. I love the aroma, and I thought it must be there for a purpose. I thought it made sense and did it."

"You are a natural, you truly are. Come let's do fresh towels in your bath-room," Bethia said as she led Maria into the attached room. "After that we'll make up your mother's rooms."

They finished half an hour later and rejoined Rachel and David, who were in a deep discussion. "We'll continue this later," Rachel said as David rose when the ladies entered the room.

"You come from a formal background," Bethia said. "Obviously from a very polite one. We rarely see that here anymore."

"Mamère is French, from Castelnaudary, east of Toulouse. Her father was a baron, but the hereditary peerage system had changed so much with the Revolution, with Napoleon, Louis Eighteen... He did nothing with the title, he had no sons, so the title died with him. In an equal world, my mother would be a baroness, and she raised us strictly, properly and politely."

"I sensed a nobility about you the moment Maria introduced us," Rachel said. "It's even more obvious now with our discussions."

"Your father, where is he from?" Maria asked.

"His family was from Galway, Ireland. They had fled the potato famine in the 1840s for Canada and continued moving west, finally stopping on the banks of the Columbia River, surrounded by mountains. They were the first settlers in the area."

"So how did he meet your mother, a French woman out there?"

"On a train in the Rockies. I've never dug into the story, and they've never shared much of it. I know they became friends when they were snowbound in a blizzard west of Banff. They spent four days on the train over Christmas waiting to be dug-out."

His eyes widened, he looked around and smiled. "Now I understand what he meant when he told me they found creative ways to stay warm. That's where I started; I was born nine months later."

"So you're part restless Irishman, part French baroness and part mountain blizzard. What a wonderfully wild and noble combination." Maria looked at him, then at her mother with a wide grin. "He followed me home, Mama. Can I keep him?" She added with a giggle, "You let me keep the cat."

"He's the one who has to decide that, Sweetheart," Rachel said in a serious tone. "You simply have to make him want to come back."

"Come back?" She shook her head. "What do you mean, come back?"

"Sweetheart, he has responsibilities. Responsibilities that reach far beyond here. He's a soldier sworn to the King to defend against the Germanic aggression. He has to continue the fight. As easy and pleasant as it would be for him to do so, and as much as he wants to, he cannot stop here. His integrity, his character won't allow him to. He's deeply in love with you, but he's honour-bound. We've just spent much of an hour discussing it."

Maria began to sag like a rag doll gradually losing its stuffing as she listened to this. David moved up behind her wilting form and wrapped his arms around her, gently kissing her neck and shoulder, whispering 'I love you' into her ear.

Tears were streaming down her face as she trembled, trying to hold her composure. She twisted in David's arms, buried her face into his chest and let the sobs deepen, allowed the convulsions to pummel her body, did nothing to muffle the sounds of her crying, she just let it go. She tightened her grip around him. Then tighter.

This story has not ended; it is just beginning.
It continues in:

MISSING

by

Michael Walsh

ISBN: 978-0-9940936-3-9

* 9 7 8 0 9 9 9 4 0 9 3 6 2 2 *